VOLUME 2

THE TIGER TERROR

Story by **Terrance Griep**

Art by **Zack Turner** & **Write Height Media**

Bonus Story
FOUR'S A CROWD

Story by **Mike Raicht**

Art by **Zack Turner**

REDAKAI™

REDAKAI
Volume 2
The Tiger Terror

The Tiger Terror
Story by Terrance Griep
Art by Zack Turner & Write Height Media

Four's a Crowd
Story by Mike Raicht
Art by Zack Turner

Design/Sam Elzway
Editor/Joel Enos

Printed in China

Published by VIZ Media, LLC
P.O. Box 77010
San Francisco, CA 94107

10 9 8 7 6 5 4 3 2 1
First printing, February 2013

vizkids
www.vizkids.com

RATED A FOR ALL AGES
PARENTAL ADVISORY
REDAKAI is rated A and is suitable for readers of all ages.
ratings.viz.com

VIZ MEDIA
www.viz.com

VOLUME 2
THE TIGER TERROR

TABLE OF CONTENTS

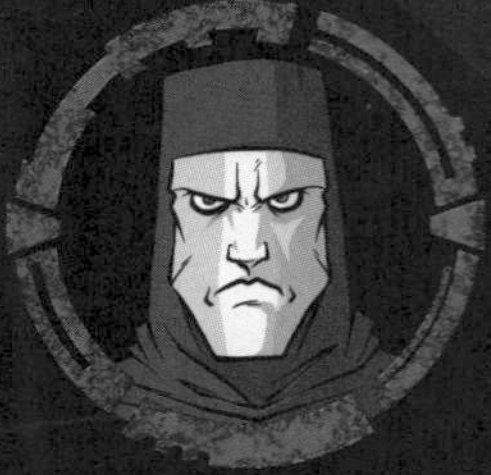

LOKAR

Lokar is the enemy of all Redakai and especially Team Stax. He and Boaddai were friends when they were young warriors, but while Master Boaddai uses his powers for good, Lokar is all evil.

E-TEENS

Lokar has gathered bullies and bad guys from all over the universe to do his bidding and search for more kairu. Though some have been tricked into helping Lokar, most E-Teens strive to be just as evil as Lokar himself. Team Stax has encountered many, and as long as Lokar wants to rule the universe, they'll be meeting even more!

TEAM HIVERAX

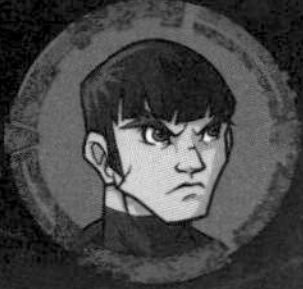

NEXUS

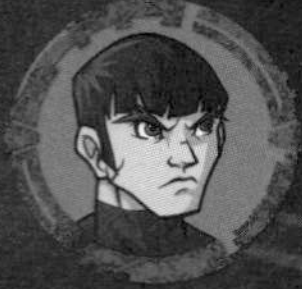

VEXUS

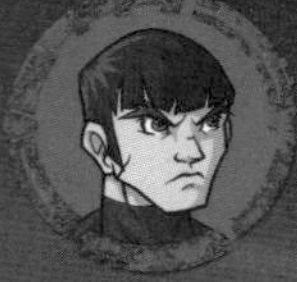

HEXUS

The Story of Redakai

In the hands of good, the energy known as kairu is a living force that guides the universe. But in the hands of evil, kairu is the most dangerous power you could imagine. Those who learn to wield kairu become kairu warriors.

They can control kairu and harness elemental energies to use them to attack, defend, and even transform into monstrous physical manifestations of unimaginable power.

Using an X-Drive to store their kairu energy and an X-Reader to activate it, both good and bad kairu warriors and masters travel the world in search of more kairu to become powerful enough to join the ranks of the most esteemed of all kairu masters: the Redakai.

CHARACTERS

TEAM STAX

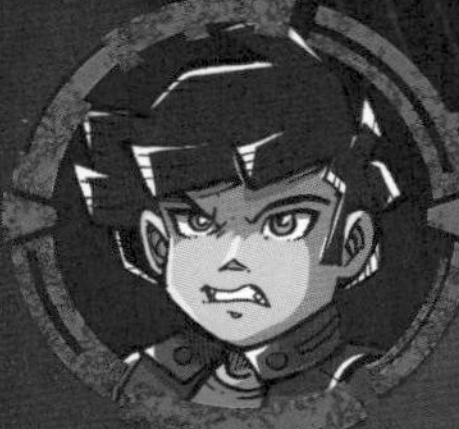

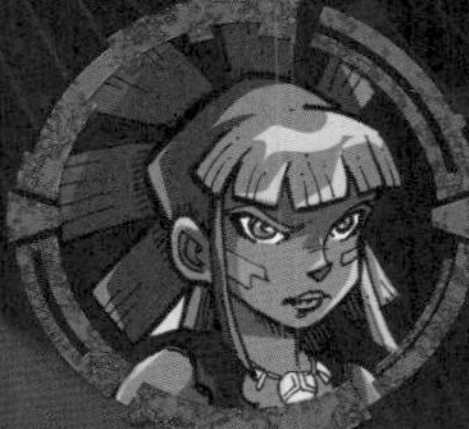

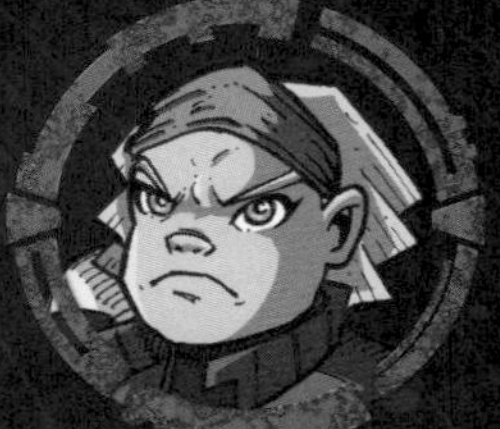

KY

Ky's father, Connor, was also a kairu warrior. Ky trained with Master Boaddai to become the best warrior he can be. He is now the leader of Team Stax. His signature monster is the plasma-powered Metanoid.

MAYA

Maya is the voice of reason and the most levelheaded member of Team Stax. She can sense when Kairu is nearby. She's an orphan who was raised like a grand-daughter by Master Boaddai. Her signature monster is Harrier.

BOOMER

Boomer is the brawns and funny-bone of Team Stax. Ky's best friend since they were kids, Boomer left his parents' farm to travel the world with Ky and Maya to find more kairu. His signature monster is Froztok.

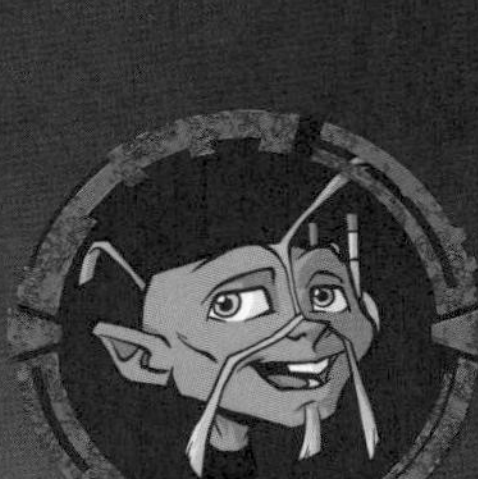

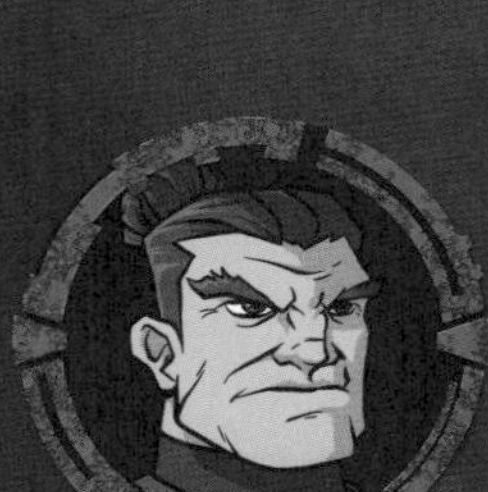

MOOKEE

Mookee's planet was destroyed by the evil Lokar during the Great Cataclysm. He's the mechanic and cook for Master Boaddai, though not all his dishes are edible! He's become an important honorary member of Team Stax!

MASTER BOADDAI

Master Boaddai is a wise and powerful Redakai and works hard to train Team Stax in the way of the kairu warrior. He'll stop at nothing to keep Lokar from getting his hands on more kairu.

THE TIGER TERROR
CHAPTER 1
The Tiger Relic

Story by **Terrance Griep**
Art by **Zack Turner**

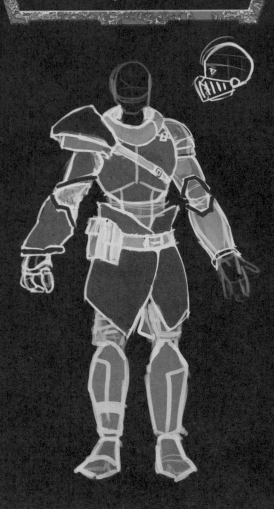

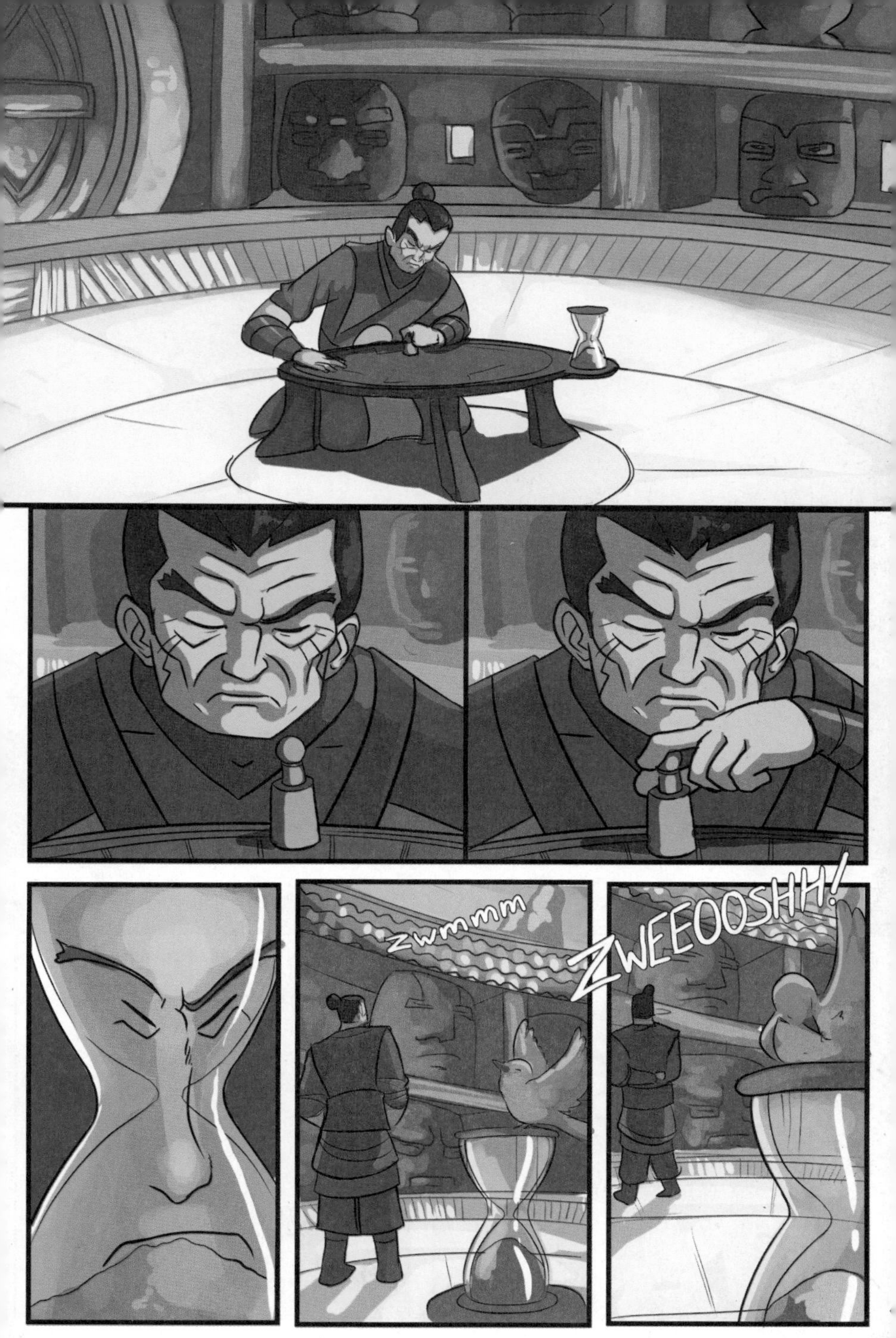

zwmmm
ZWEEOOSHH!

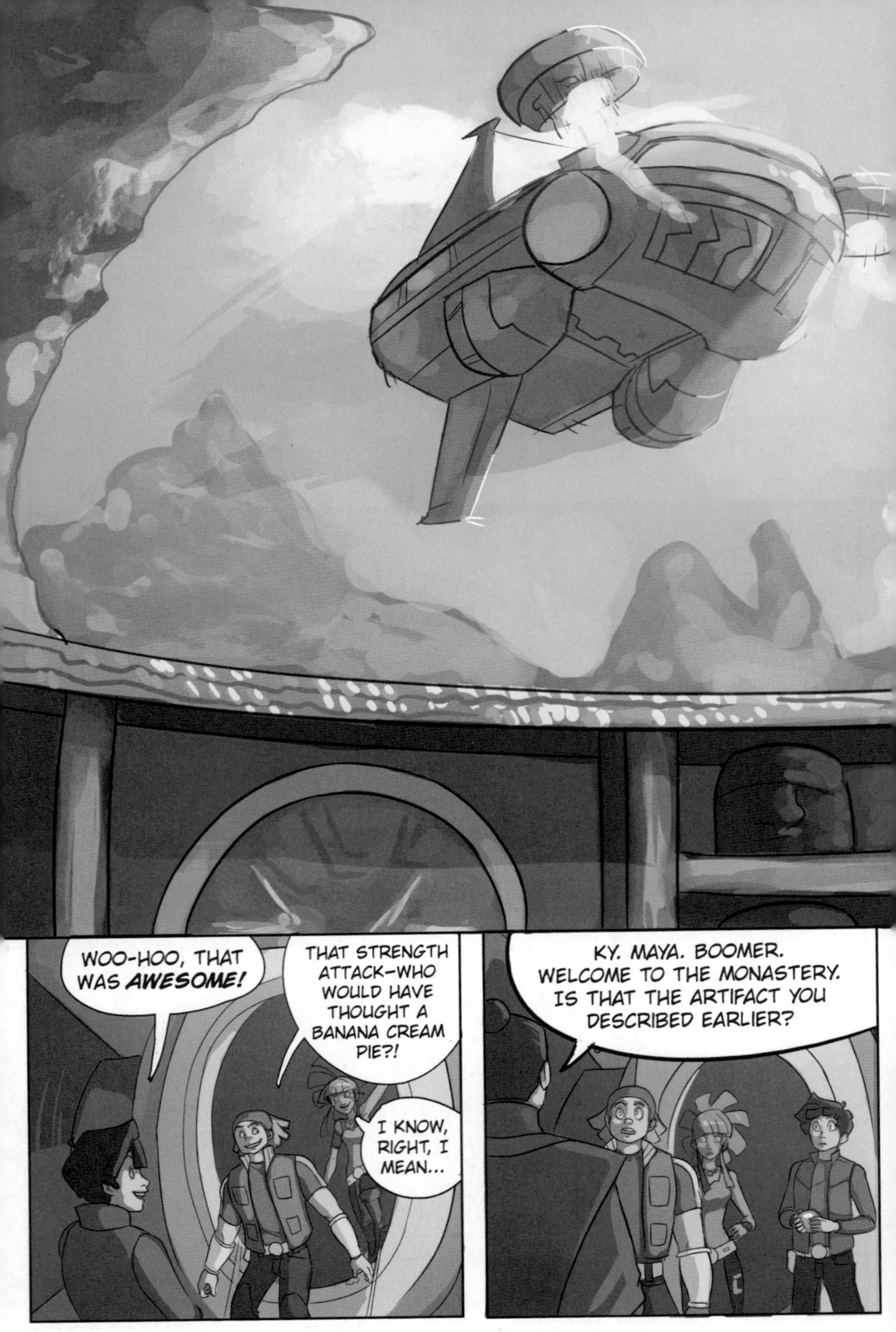

WOO-HOO, THAT WAS **AWESOME!**
THAT STRENGTH ATTACK–WHO WOULD HAVE THOUGHT A BANANA CREAM PIE?!
I KNOW, RIGHT, I MEAN...
KY. MAYA. BOOMER. WELCOME TO THE MONASTERY. IS THAT THE ARTIFACT YOU DESCRIBED EARLIER?

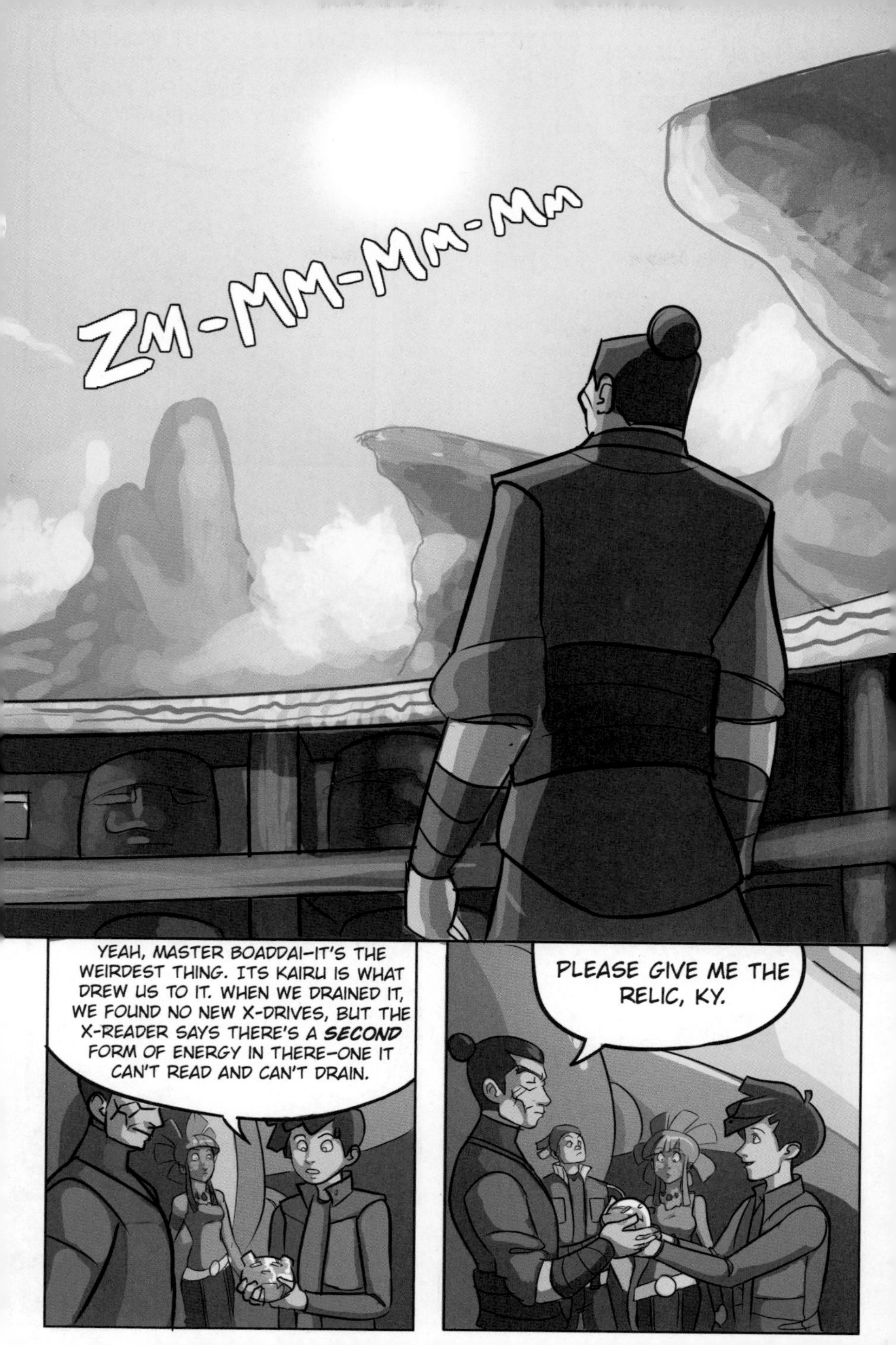
ZM-MM-MM-MM
YEAH, MASTER BOADDAI–IT'S THE WEIRDEST THING. ITS KAIRU IS WHAT DREW US TO IT. WHEN WE DRAINED IT, WE FOUND NO NEW X-DRIVES, BUT THE X-READER SAYS THERE'S A *SECOND* FORM OF ENERGY IN THERE–ONE IT CAN'T READ AND CAN'T DRAIN.
PLEASE GIVE ME THE RELIC, KY.

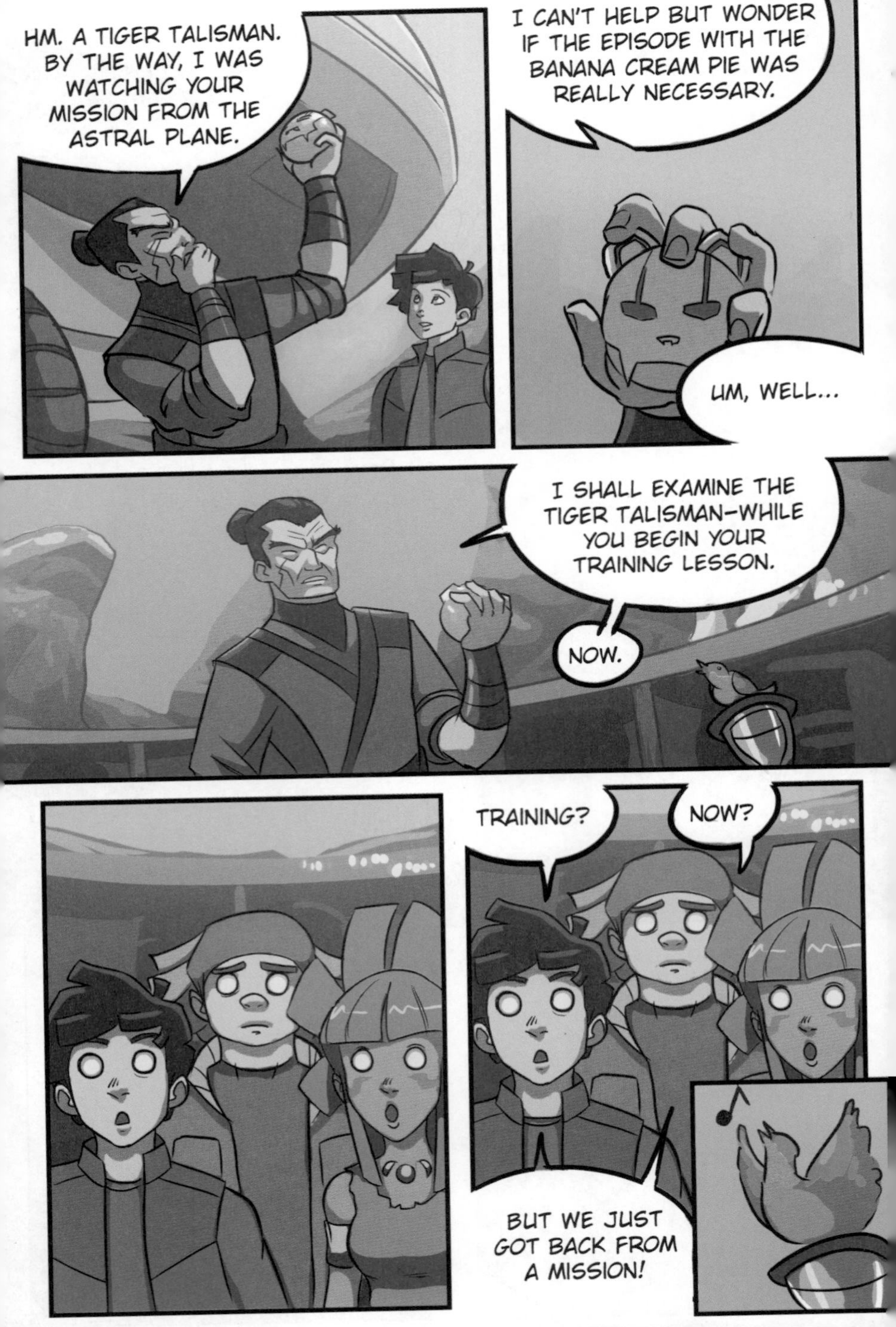
HM. A TIGER TALISMAN. BY THE WAY, I WAS WATCHING YOUR MISSION FROM THE ASTRAL PLANE.
I CAN'T HELP BUT WONDER IF THE EPISODE WITH THE BANANA CREAM PIE WAS REALLY NECESSARY.
UM, WELL...
I SHALL EXAMINE THE TIGER TALISMAN—WHILE YOU BEGIN YOUR TRAINING LESSON.
NOW.
TRAINING?
NOW?
BUT WE JUST GOT BACK FROM A MISSION!

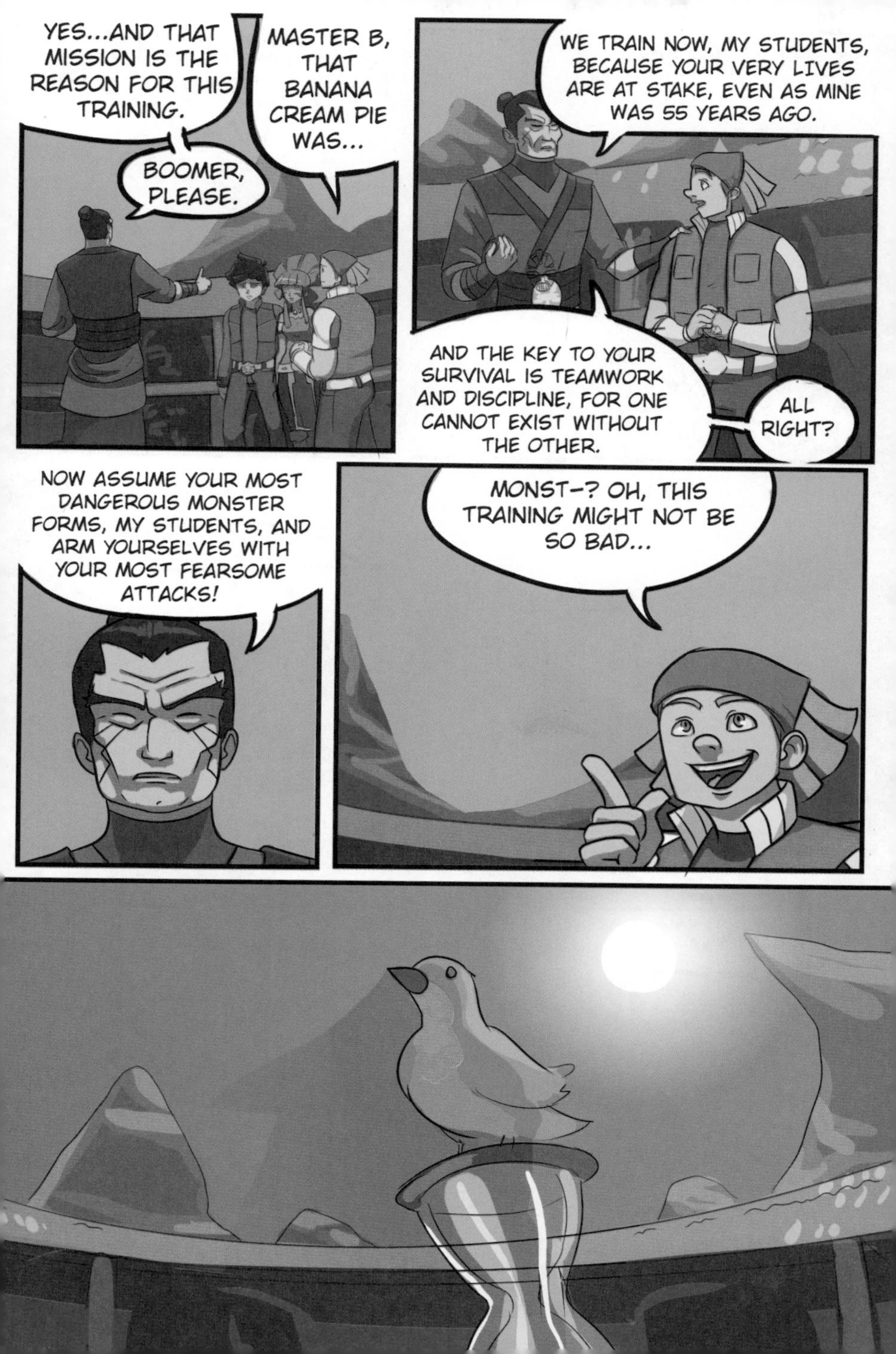
YES...AND THAT MISSION IS THE REASON FOR THIS TRAINING.
MASTER B, THAT BANANA CREAM PIE WAS...
BOOMER, PLEASE.
WE TRAIN NOW, MY STUDENTS, BECAUSE YOUR VERY LIVES ARE AT STAKE, EVEN AS MINE WAS 55 YEARS AGO.
AND THE KEY TO YOUR SURVIVAL IS TEAMWORK AND DISCIPLINE, FOR ONE CANNOT EXIST WITHOUT THE OTHER.
ALL RIGHT?
NOW ASSUME YOUR MOST DANGEROUS MONSTER FORMS, MY STUDENTS, AND ARM YOURSELVES WITH YOUR MOST FEARSOME ATTACKS!
MONST-? OH, THIS TRAINING MIGHT NOT BE SO BAD...

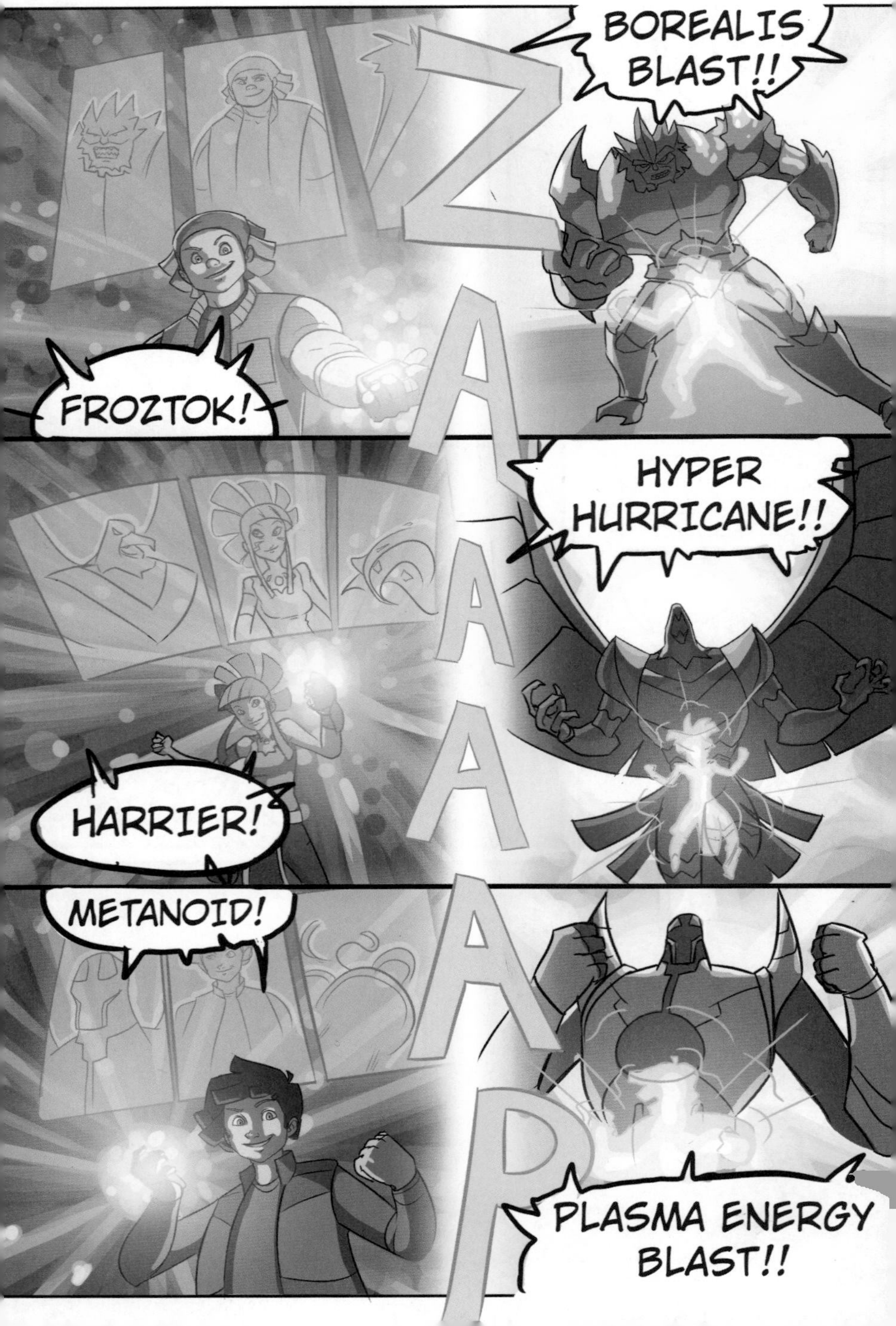
FROZTOK!
BOREALIS BLAST!!
HARRIER!
HYPER HURRICANE!!
METANOID!
PLASMA ENERGY BLAST!!
ZAAAAP

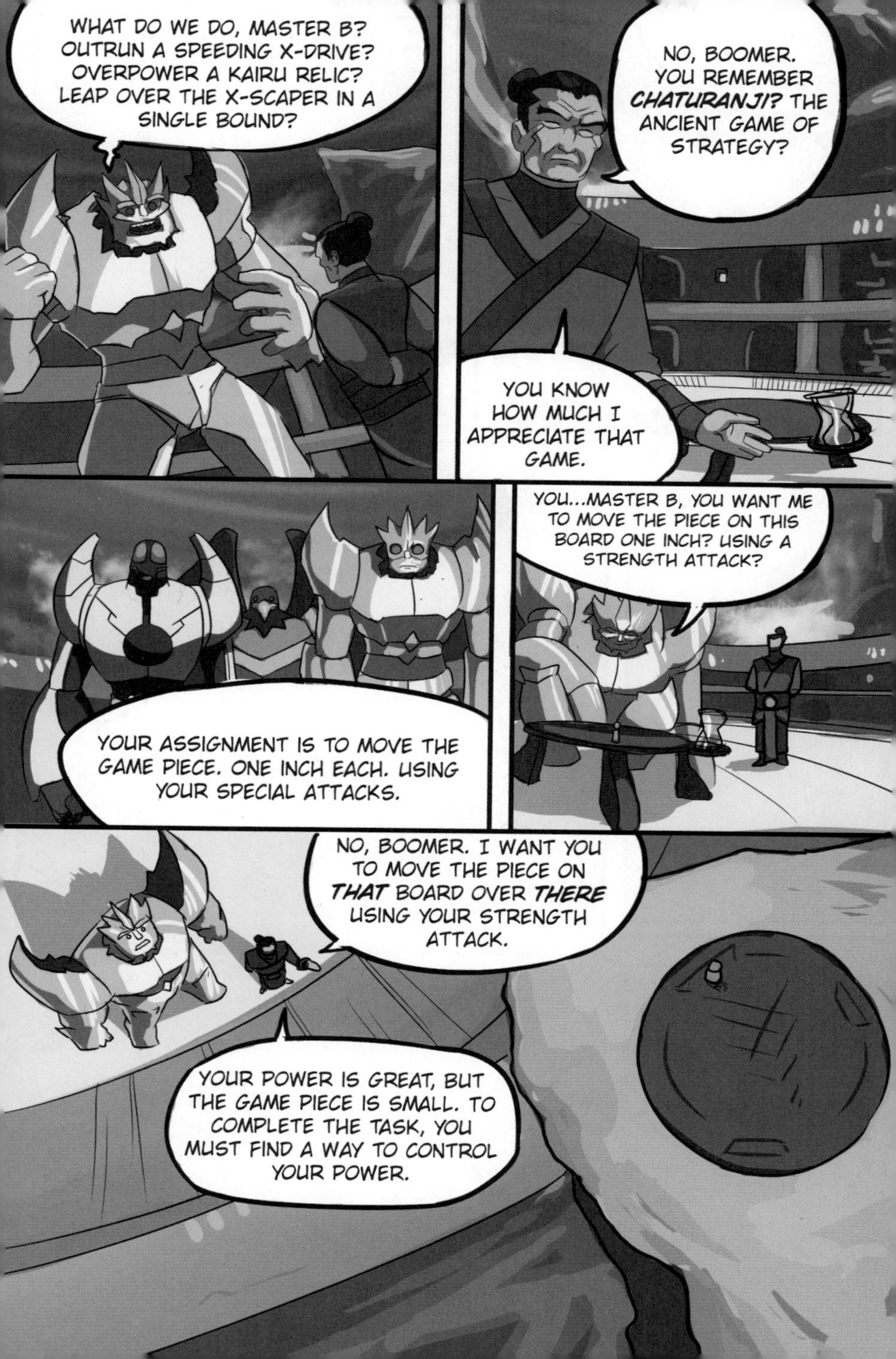
WHAT DO WE DO, MASTER B? OUTRUN A SPEEDING X-DRIVE? OVERPOWER A KAIRU RELIC? LEAP OVER THE X-SCAPER IN A SINGLE BOUND?
NO, BOOMER. YOU REMEMBER *CHATURANJI?* THE ANCIENT GAME OF STRATEGY?
YOU KNOW HOW MUCH I APPRECIATE THAT GAME.
YOUR ASSIGNMENT IS TO MOVE THE GAME PIECE. ONE INCH EACH. USING YOUR SPECIAL ATTACKS.
YOU...MASTER B, YOU WANT ME TO MOVE THE PIECE ON THIS BOARD ONE INCH? USING A STRENGTH ATTACK?
NO, BOOMER. I WANT YOU TO MOVE THE PIECE ON *THAT* BOARD OVER *THERE* USING YOUR STRENGTH ATTACK.
YOUR POWER IS GREAT, BUT THE GAME PIECE IS SMALL. TO COMPLETE THE TASK, YOU MUST FIND A WAY TO CONTROL YOUR POWER.

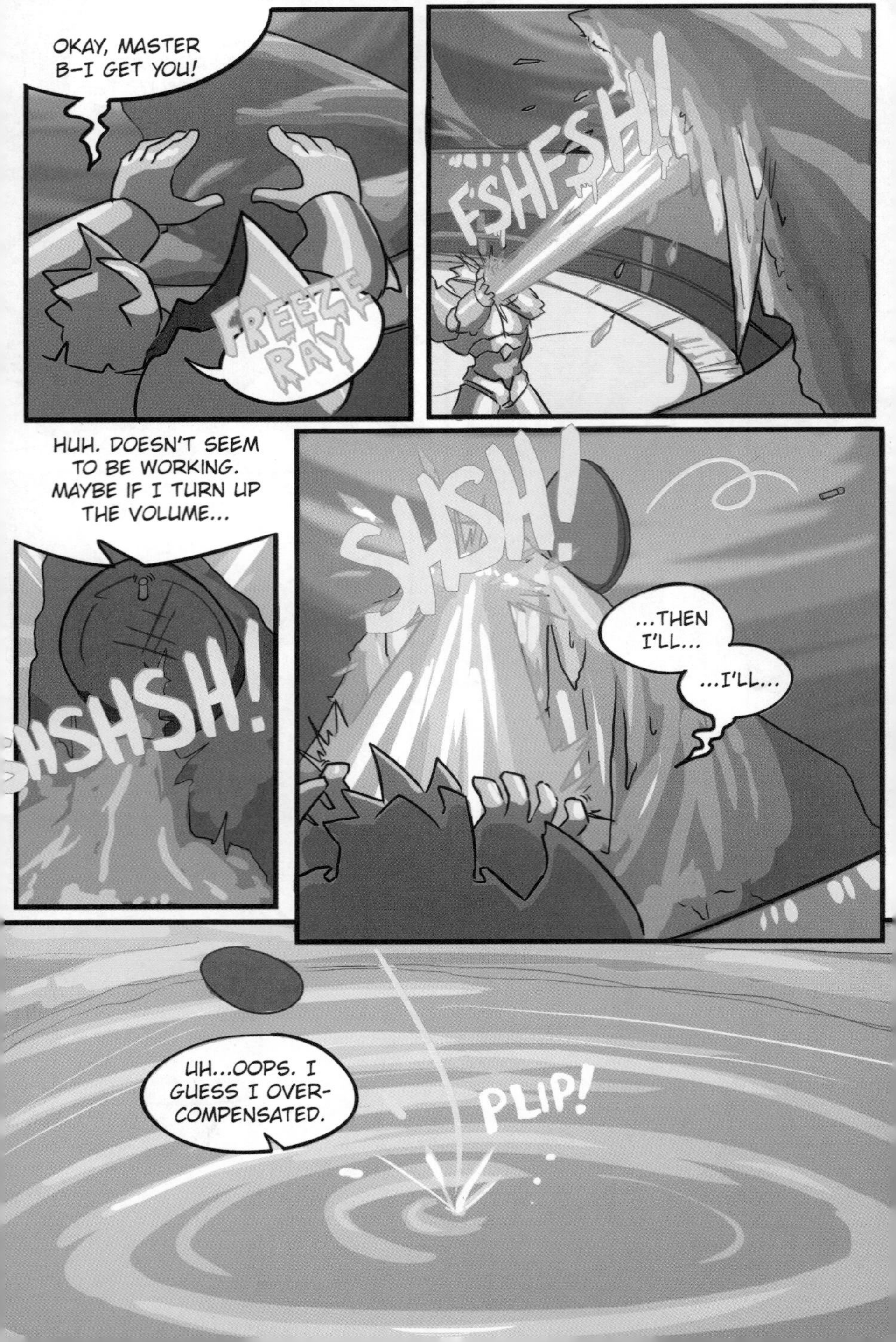
OKAY, MASTER B–I GET YOU!
FREEZE RAY
FSHFSH!
HUH. DOESN'T SEEM TO BE WORKING. MAYBE IF I TURN UP THE VOLUME...
SHSHSH!
SHSH!
...THEN I'LL...
...I'LL...
UH...OOPS. I GUESS I OVER-COMPENSATED.
PLIP!

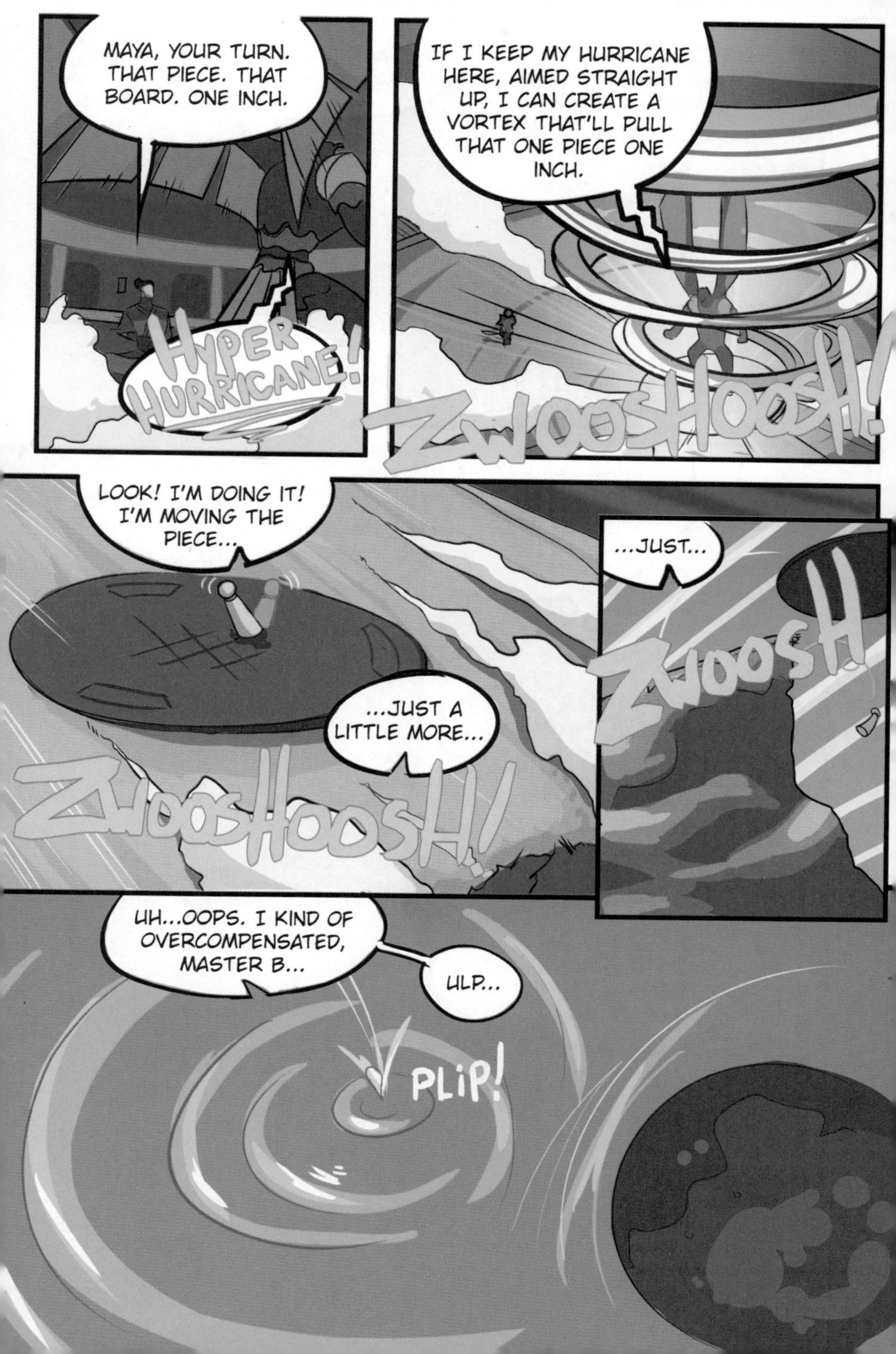
MAYA, YOUR TURN. THAT PIECE. THAT BOARD. ONE INCH.
HYPER HURRICANE!
IF I KEEP MY HURRICANE HERE, AIMED STRAIGHT UP, I CAN CREATE A VORTEX THAT'LL PULL THAT ONE PIECE ONE INCH.
ZWOOSHOOSH!
LOOK! I'M DOING IT! I'M MOVING THE PIECE...
...JUST A LITTLE MORE...
ZWOOSHOOSH!
...JUST...
ZWOOSH
UH...OOPS. I KIND OF OVERCOMPENSATED, MASTER B...
ULP...
PLIP!

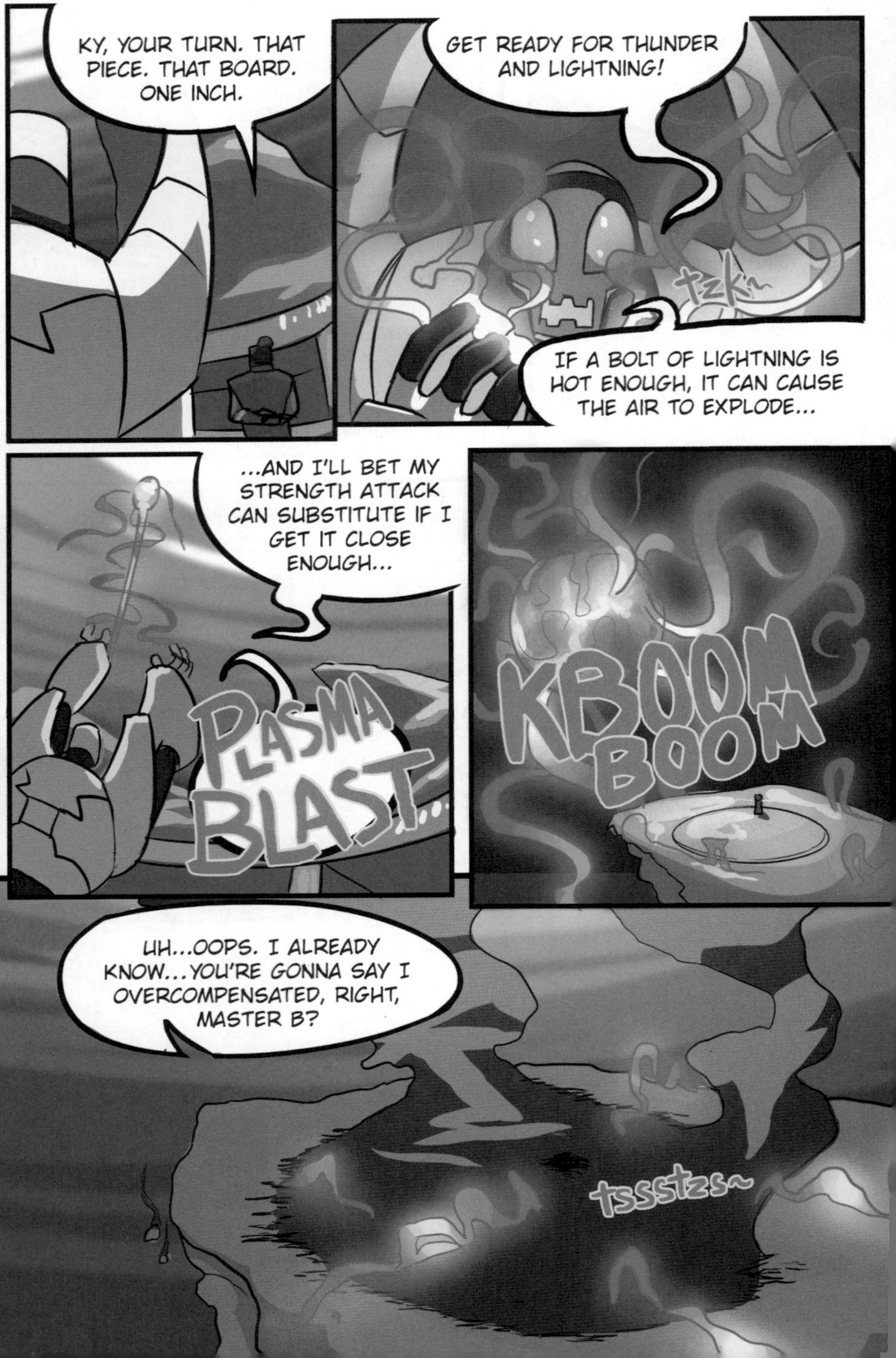
KY, YOUR TURN. THAT PIECE. THAT BOARD. ONE INCH.
GET READY FOR THUNDER AND LIGHTNING!
tzk~
IF A BOLT OF LIGHTNING IS HOT ENOUGH, IT CAN CAUSE THE AIR TO EXPLODE...
...AND I'LL BET MY STRENGTH ATTACK CAN SUBSTITUTE IF I GET IT CLOSE ENOUGH...
PLASMA BLAST...
KBOOM BOOM
UH...OOPS. I ALREADY KNOW...YOU'RE GONNA SAY I OVERCOMPENSATED, RIGHT, MASTER B?
tssstzs~

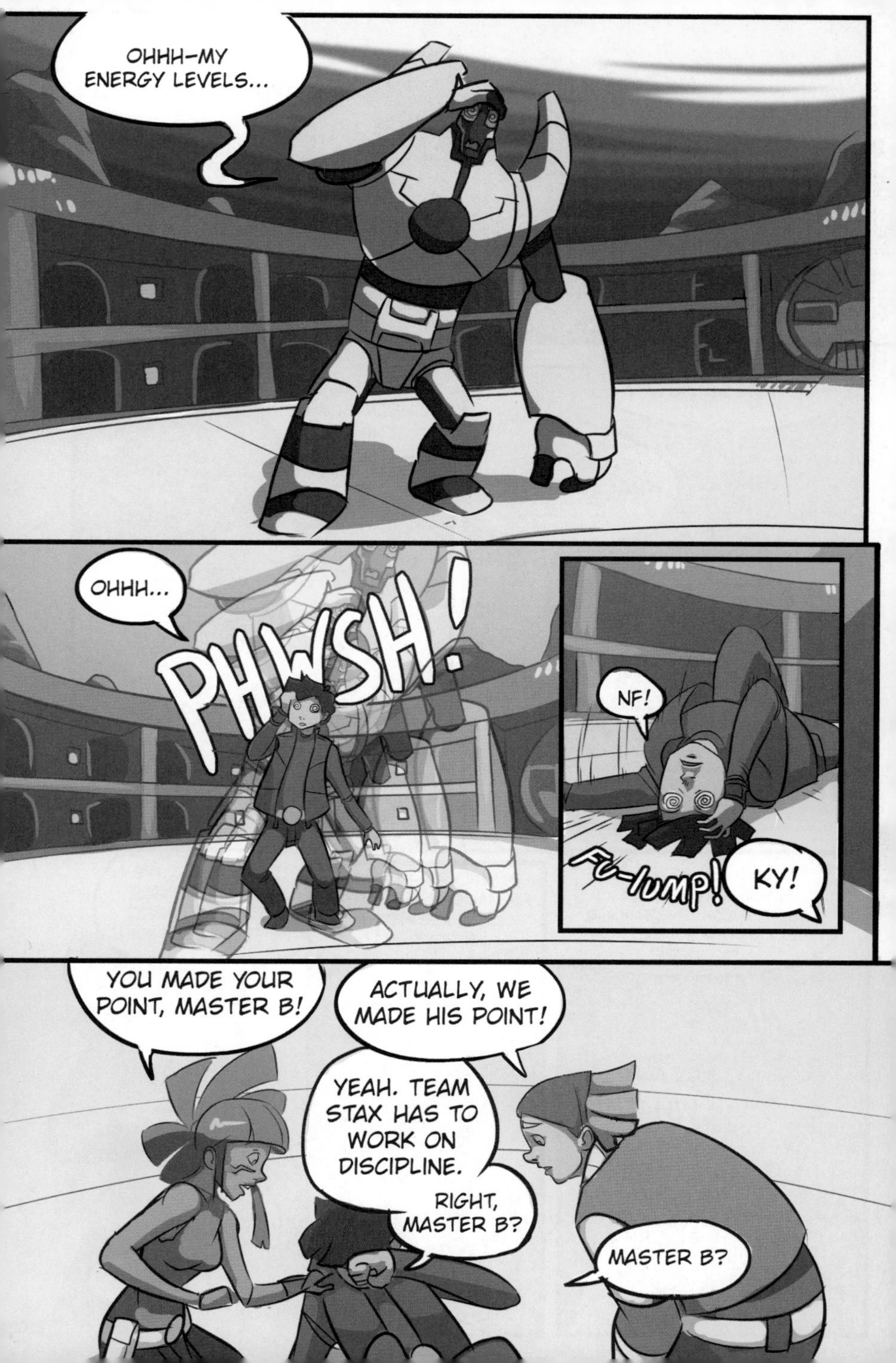
OHHH–MY ENERGY LEVELS...
OHHH...
PHWSH!
NF!
FU-LUMP!
KY!
YOU MADE YOUR POINT, MASTER B!
ACTUALLY, WE MADE HIS POINT!
YEAH. TEAM STAX HAS TO WORK ON DISCIPLINE.
RIGHT, MASTER B?
MASTER B?

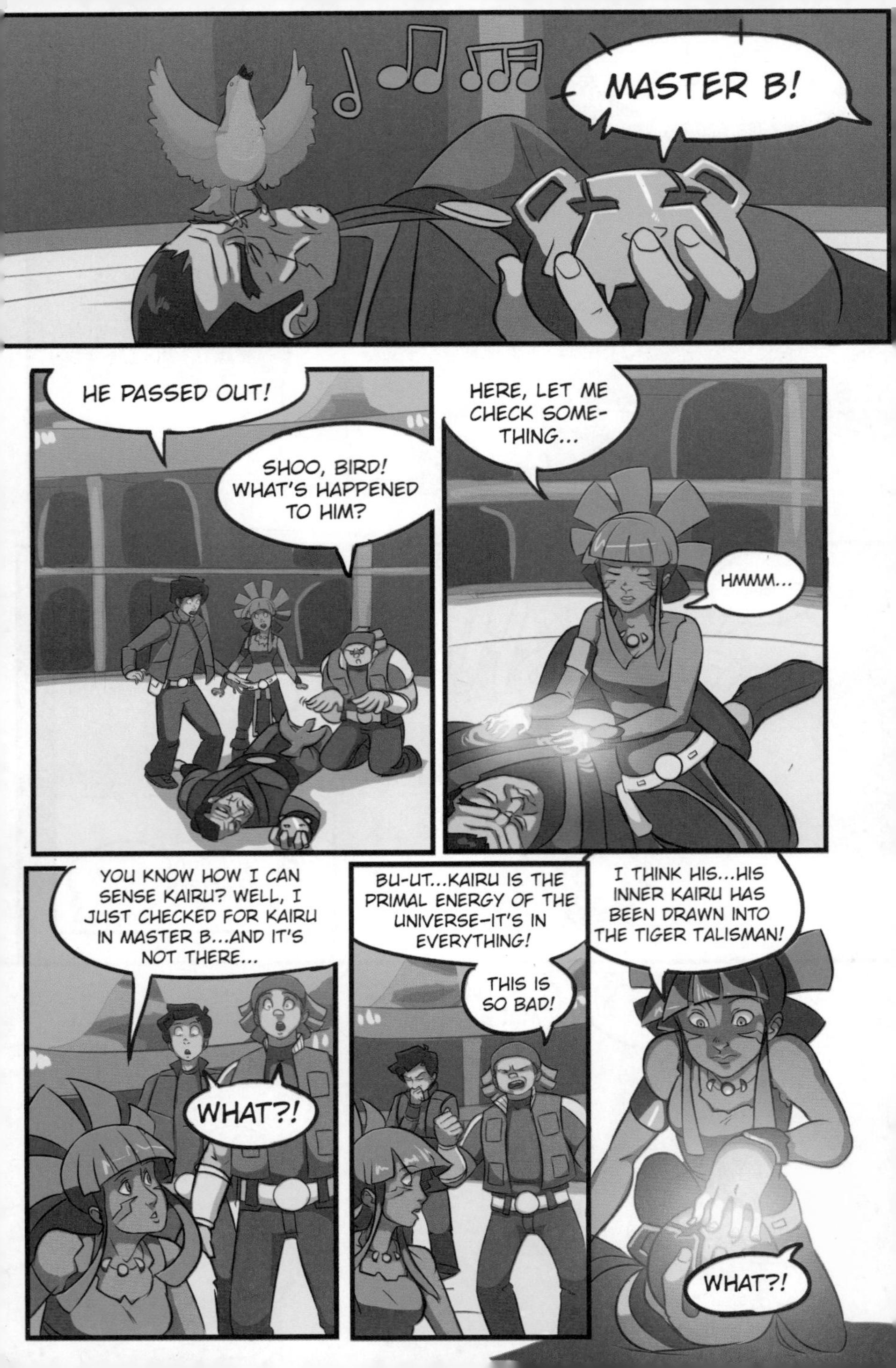
MASTER B!
HE PASSED OUT!
SHOO, BIRD! WHAT'S HAPPENED TO HIM?
HERE, LET ME CHECK SOME-THING...
HMMM...
YOU KNOW HOW I CAN SENSE KAIRU? WELL, I JUST CHECKED FOR KAIRU IN MASTER B...AND IT'S NOT THERE...
WHAT?!
BU-UT...KAIRU IS THE PRIMAL ENERGY OF THE UNIVERSE—IT'S IN EVERYTHING!
THIS IS SO BAD!
I THINK HIS...HIS INNER KAIRU HAS BEEN DRAWN INTO THE TIGER TALISMAN!
WHAT?!

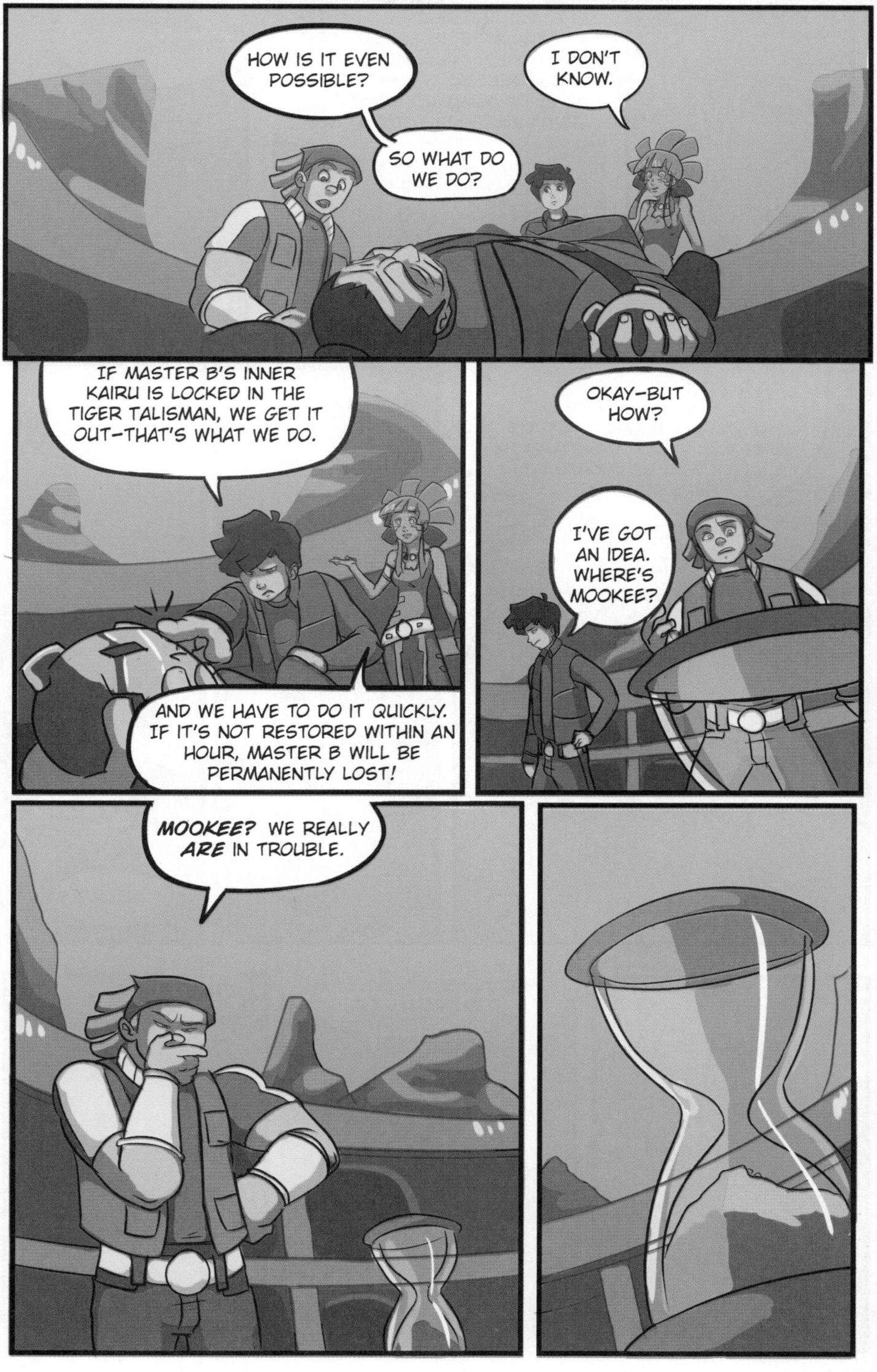
HOW IS IT EVEN POSSIBLE?
I DON'T KNOW.
SO WHAT DO WE DO?
IF MASTER B'S INNER KAIRU IS LOCKED IN THE TIGER TALISMAN, WE GET IT OUT–THAT'S WHAT WE DO.
AND WE HAVE TO DO IT QUICKLY. IF IT'S NOT RESTORED WITHIN AN HOUR, MASTER B WILL BE PERMANENTLY LOST!
OKAY–BUT HOW?
I'VE GOT AN IDEA. WHERE'S MOOKEE?
MOOKEE? WE REALLY *ARE* IN TROUBLE.

IT'S ALL SET. MOOKEE HAS RE-PROGRAMMED OUR X-READERS: RATHER THAN DRAW KAIRU OUT OF RELICS AND INTO THE X-READERS, THEY'RE GOING TO DRAW OUR OWN INNER KAIRU OUT OF OUR BODIES...

...AND INTO THE TIGER TALISMAN.

>ULP!< THAT SOUNDS DANGEROUS. EVEN FOR US.

YES, BOOM, IT IS. BUT IF WE DON'T MAKE THE TRIP AND RESTORE MASTER BOADDAI'S PERSONAL KAIRU, THEN MASTER BOADDAI WILL BE LOCKED UP IN THERE FOREVER...

COME ON, GOTTA DO THIS!

OKAY. JUST ACTIVATE YOUR X-READERS, AND...

SHING

BLOOP

...RELAAAX.

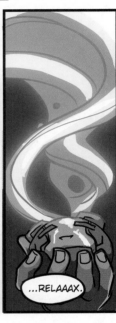

OKAY, GUYS—YOU HAVE 45 MINUTES LEFT.

GUYS?

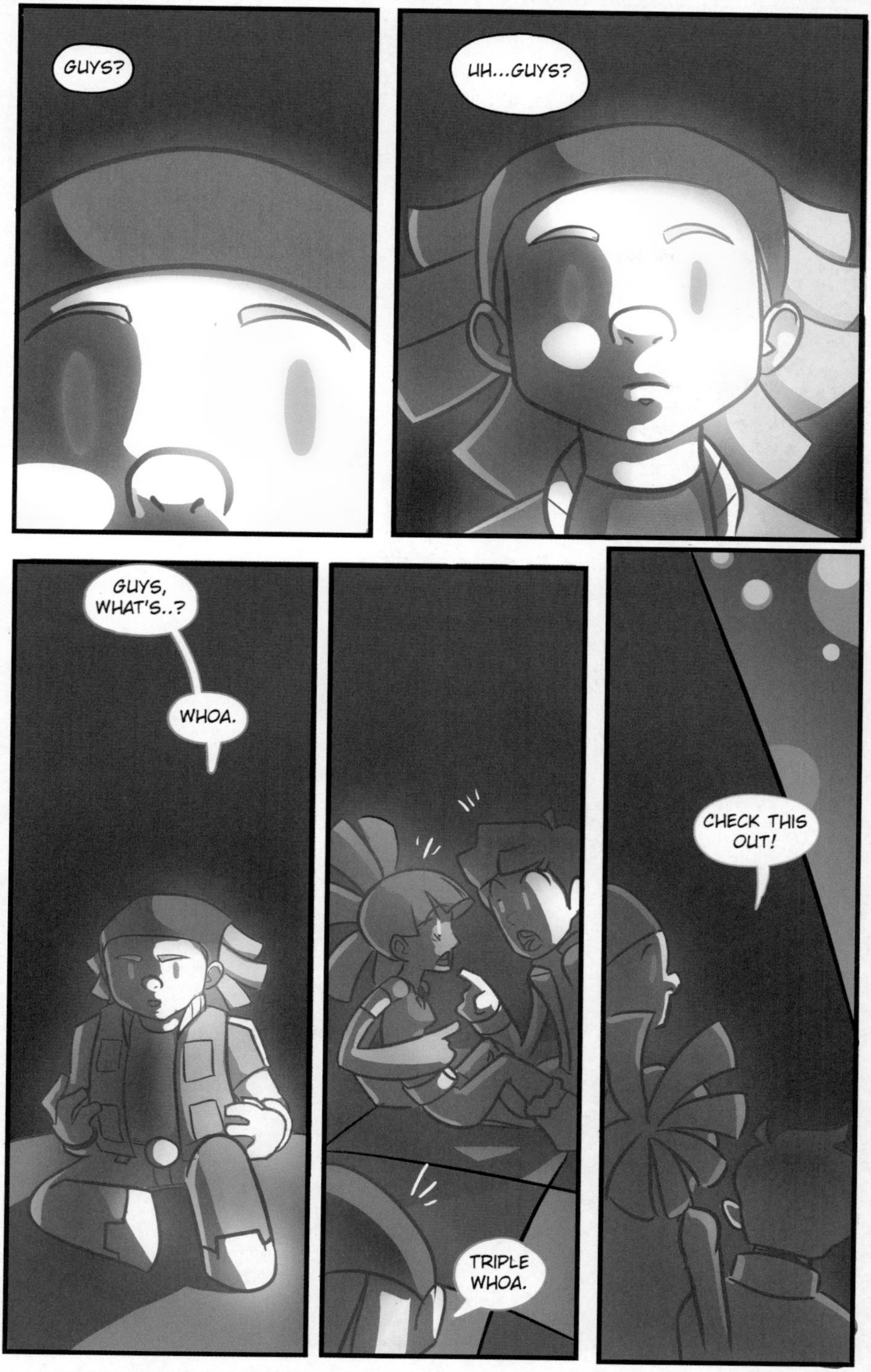
GUYS?
UH...GUYS?
GUYS, WHAT'S..?
WHOA.
TRIPLE WHOA.
CHECK THIS OUT!

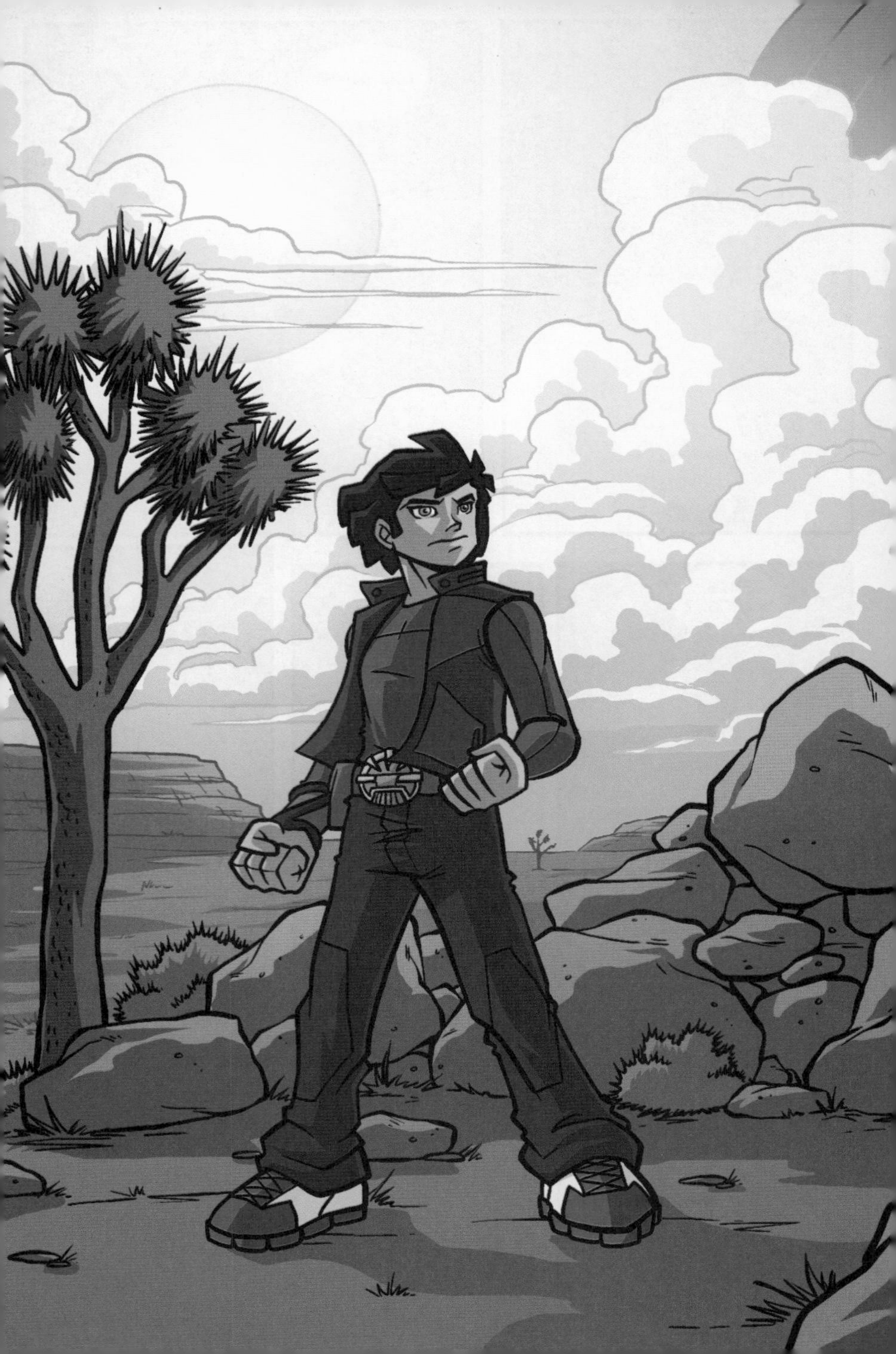

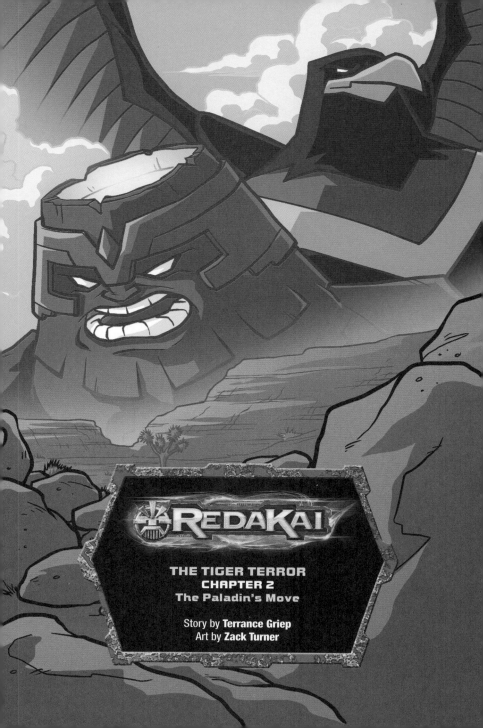

REDAKAI

THE TIGER TERROR
CHAPTER 2
The Paladin's Move

Story by **Terrance Griep**
Art by **Zack Turner**

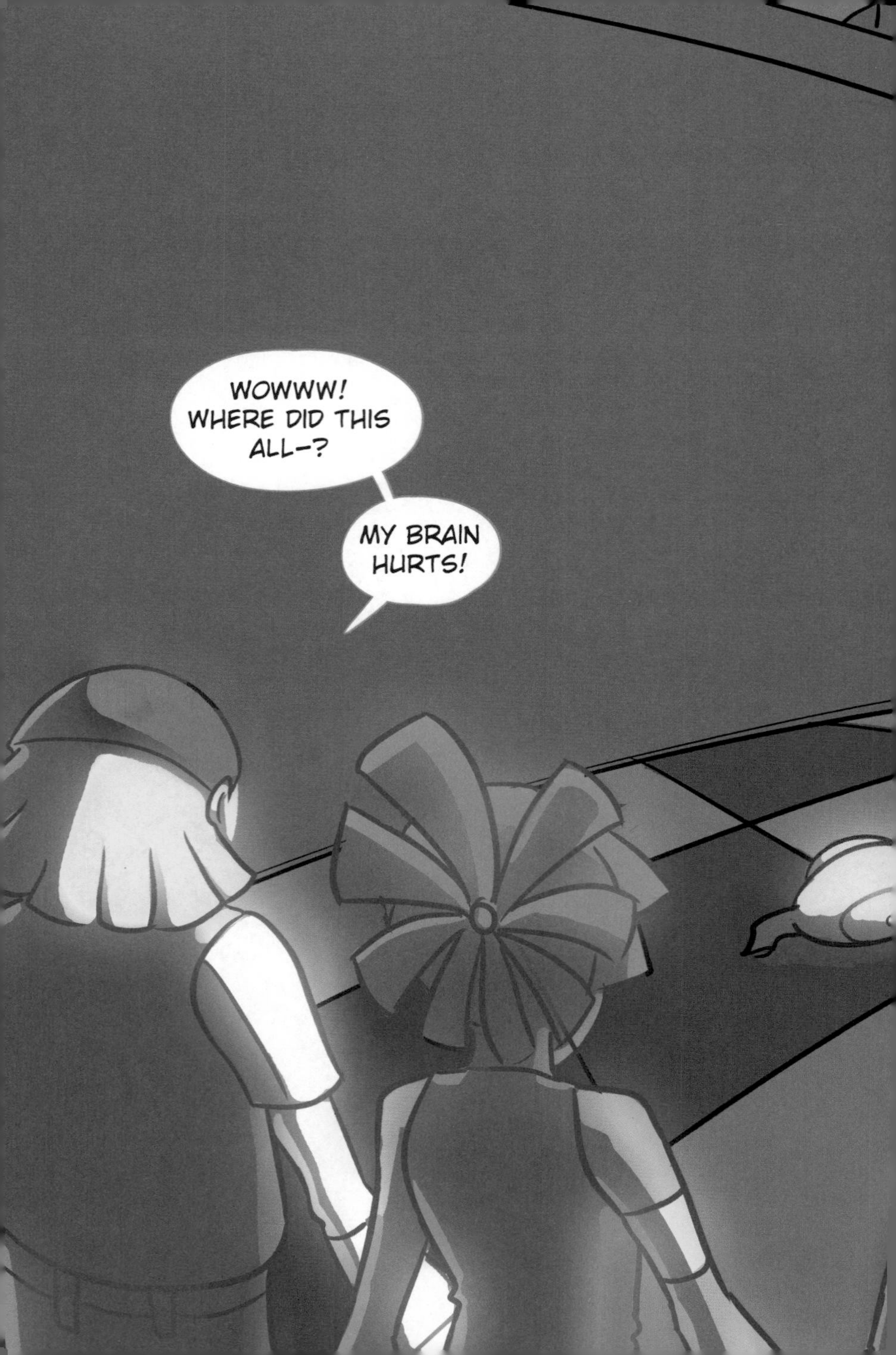
WOWWW! WHERE DID THIS ALL-?
MY BRAIN HURTS!

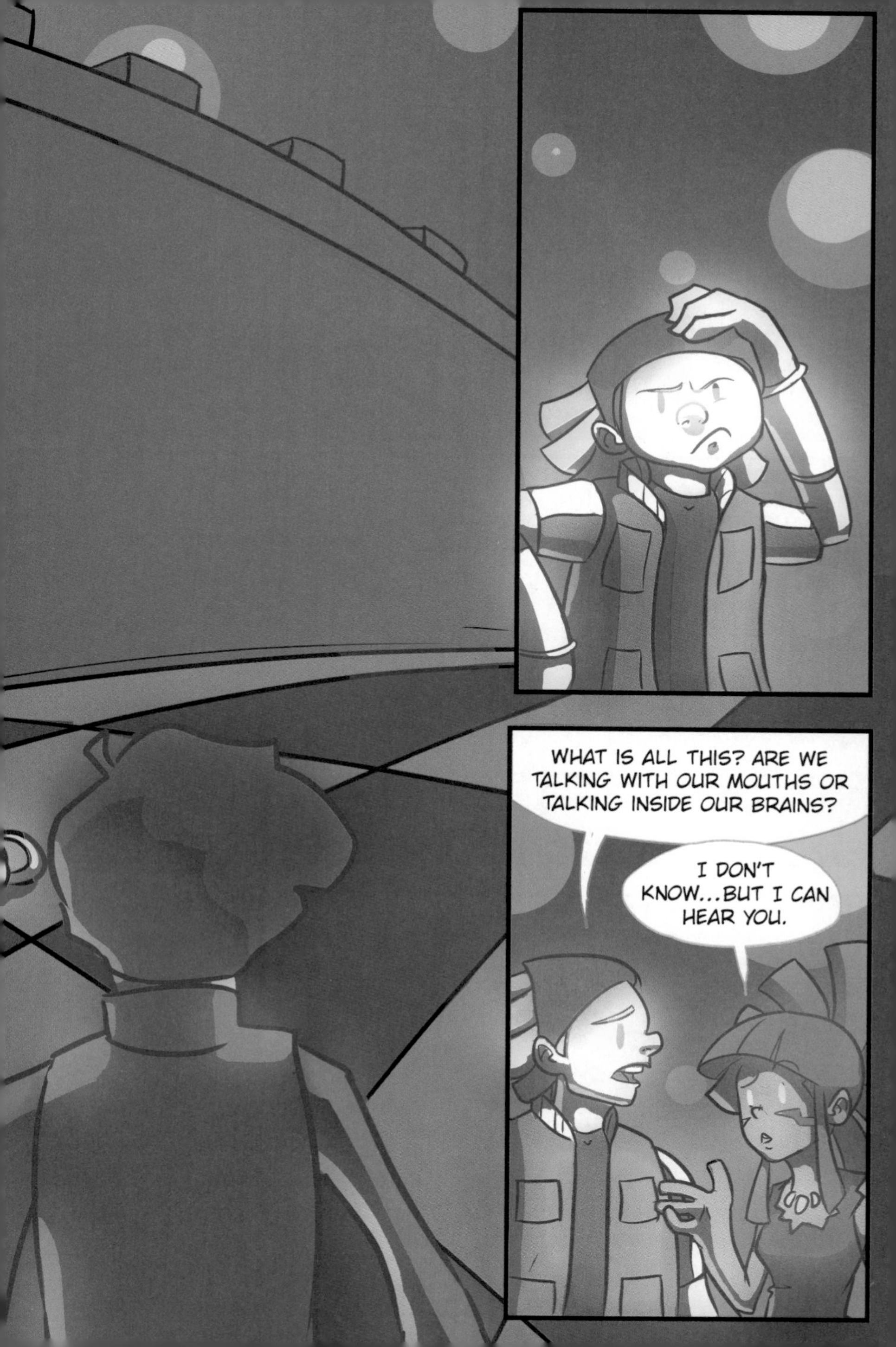
WHAT IS ALL THIS? ARE WE TALKING WITH OUR MOUTHS OR TALKING INSIDE OUR BRAINS?
I DON'T KNOW...BUT I CAN HEAR YOU.

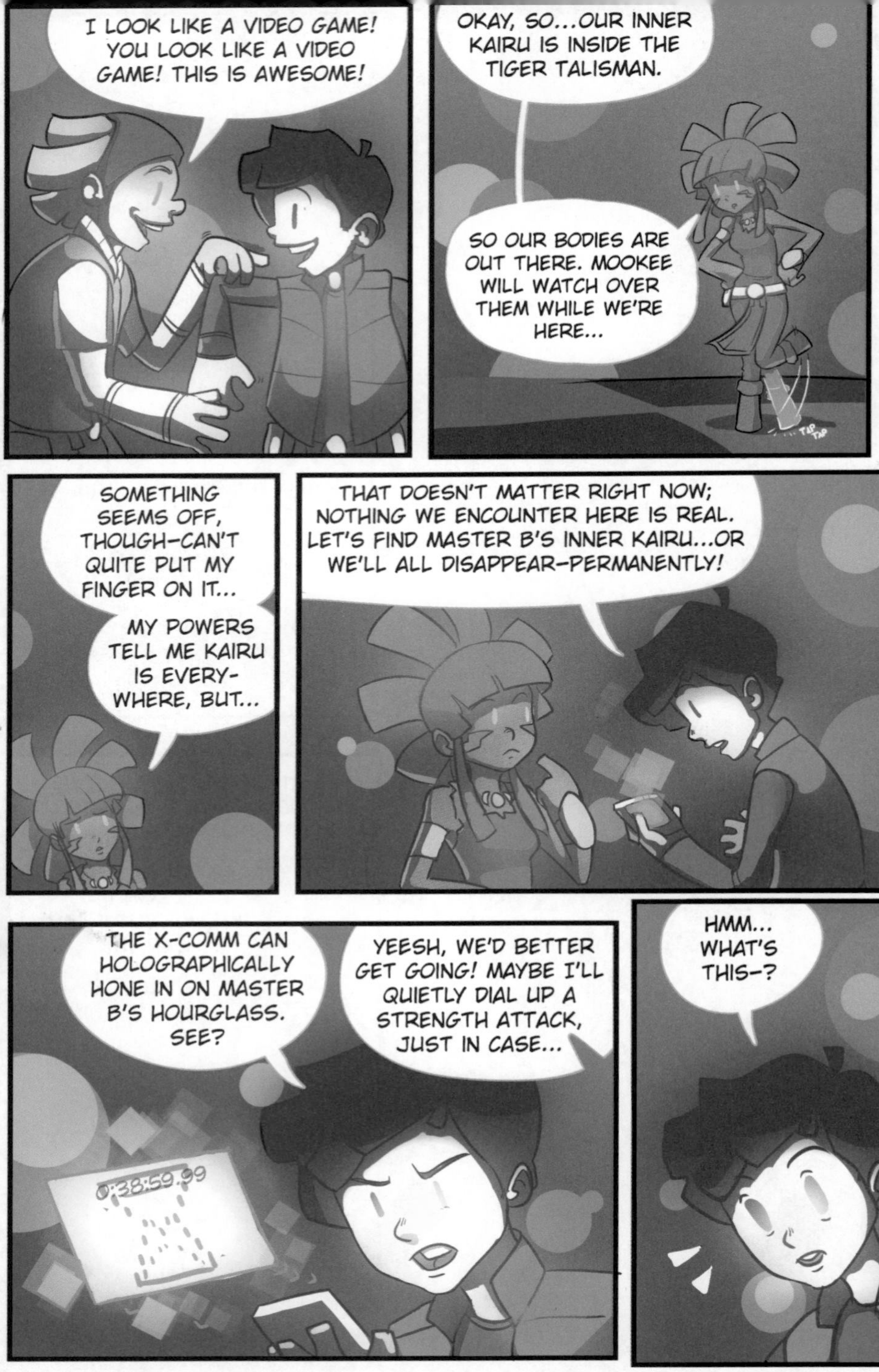
I LOOK LIKE A VIDEO GAME! YOU LOOK LIKE A VIDEO GAME! THIS IS AWESOME!
OKAY, SO...OUR INNER KAIRU IS INSIDE THE TIGER TALISMAN.
SO OUR BODIES ARE OUT THERE. MOOKEE WILL WATCH OVER THEM WHILE WE'RE HERE...
TAP TAP
SOMETHING SEEMS OFF, THOUGH–CAN'T QUITE PUT MY FINGER ON IT...
MY POWERS TELL ME KAIRU IS EVERY-WHERE, BUT...
THAT DOESN'T MATTER RIGHT NOW; NOTHING WE ENCOUNTER HERE IS REAL. LET'S FIND MASTER B'S INNER KAIRU...OR WE'LL ALL DISAPPEAR–PERMANENTLY!
THE X-COMM CAN HOLOGRAPHICALLY HONE IN ON MASTER B'S HOURGLASS. SEE?
YEESH, WE'D BETTER GET GOING! MAYBE I'LL QUIETLY DIAL UP A STRENGTH ATTACK, JUST IN CASE...
0:38:59.99
HMM... WHAT'S THIS–?

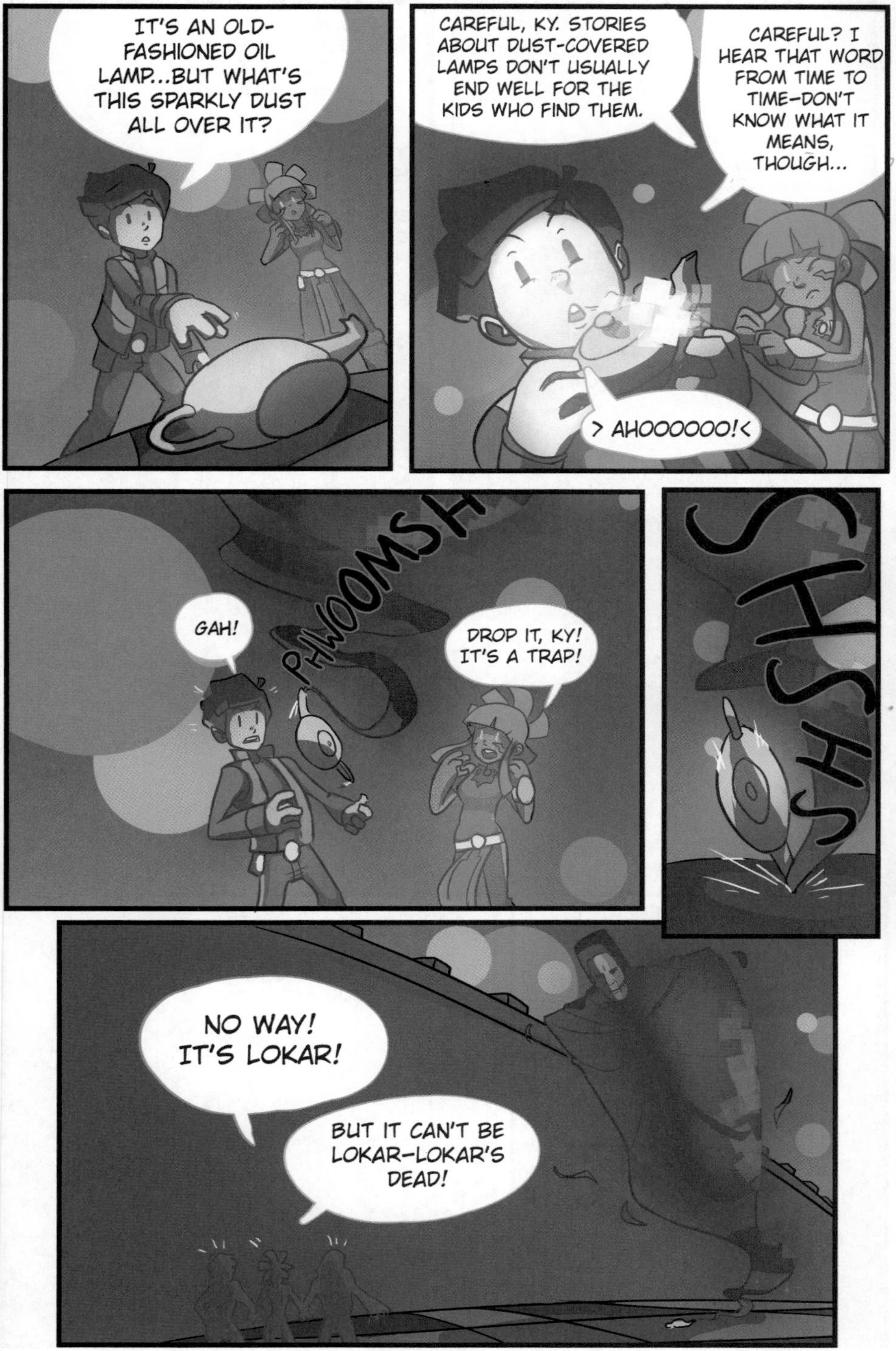
IT'S AN OLD-FASHIONED OIL LAMP...BUT WHAT'S THIS SPARKLY DUST ALL OVER IT?
CAREFUL, KY. STORIES ABOUT DUST-COVERED LAMPS DON'T USUALLY END WELL FOR THE KIDS WHO FIND THEM.
CAREFUL? I HEAR THAT WORD FROM TIME TO TIME—DON'T KNOW WHAT IT MEANS, THOUGH...
> AHOOOOOO!<
PHWOOMSH
GAH!
DROP IT, KY! IT'S A TRAP!
SHSHSH
NO WAY! IT'S LOKAR!
BUT IT CAN'T BE LOKAR—LOKAR'S DEAD!

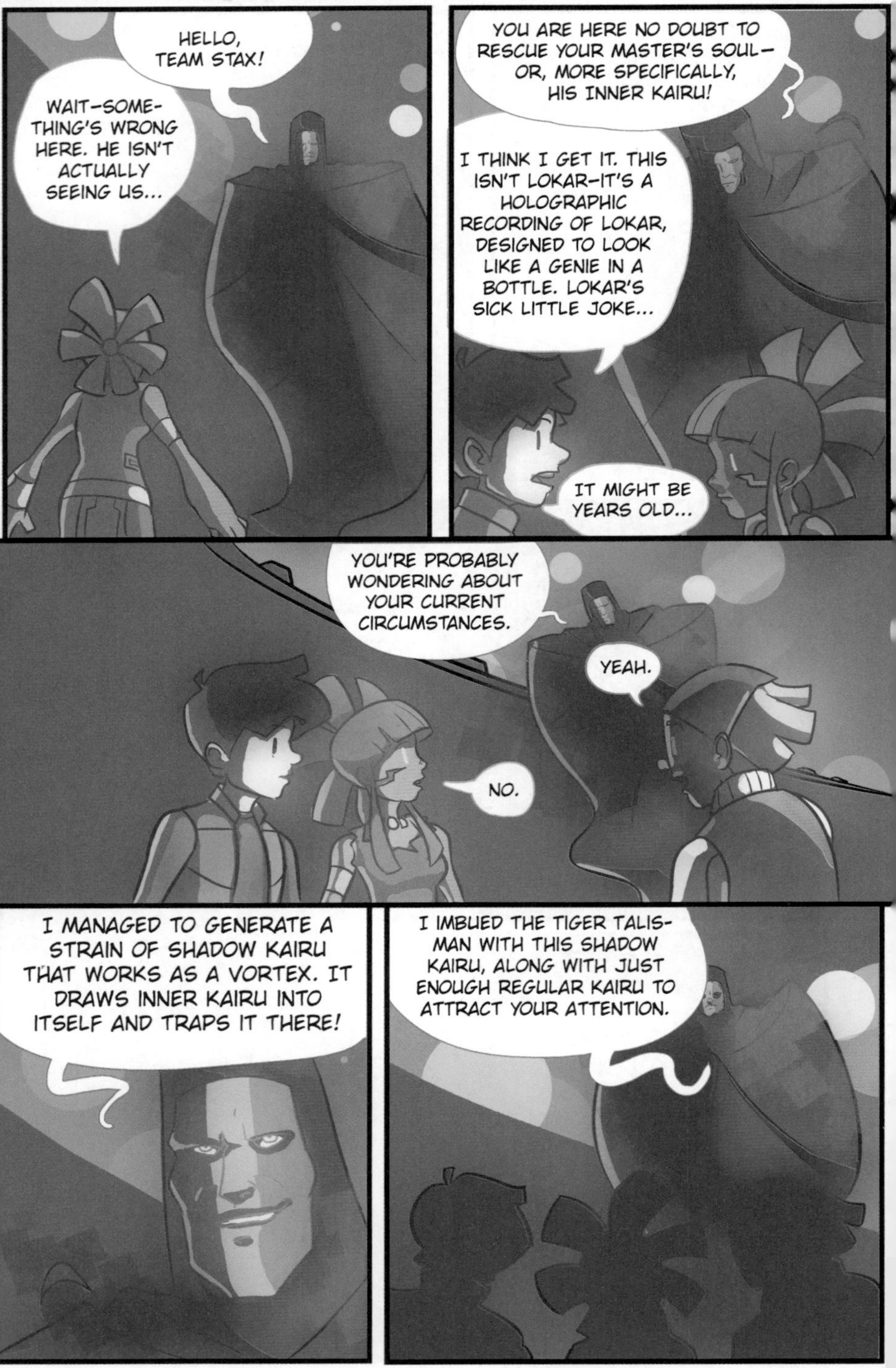
HELLO, TEAM STAX!
WAIT—SOME-THING'S WRONG HERE. HE ISN'T ACTUALLY SEEING US...
YOU ARE HERE NO DOUBT TO RESCUE YOUR MASTER'S SOUL—OR, MORE SPECIFICALLY, HIS INNER KAIRU!
I THINK I GET IT. THIS ISN'T LOKAR—IT'S A HOLOGRAPHIC RECORDING OF LOKAR, DESIGNED TO LOOK LIKE A GENIE IN A BOTTLE. LOKAR'S SICK LITTLE JOKE...
IT MIGHT BE YEARS OLD...
YOU'RE PROBABLY WONDERING ABOUT YOUR CURRENT CIRCUMSTANCES.
YEAH.
NO.
I MANAGED TO GENERATE A STRAIN OF SHADOW KAIRU THAT WORKS AS A VORTEX. IT DRAWS INNER KAIRU INTO ITSELF AND TRAPS IT THERE!
I IMBUED THE TIGER TALIS-MAN WITH THIS SHADOW KAIRU, ALONG WITH JUST ENOUGH REGULAR KAIRU TO ATTRACT YOUR ATTENTION.

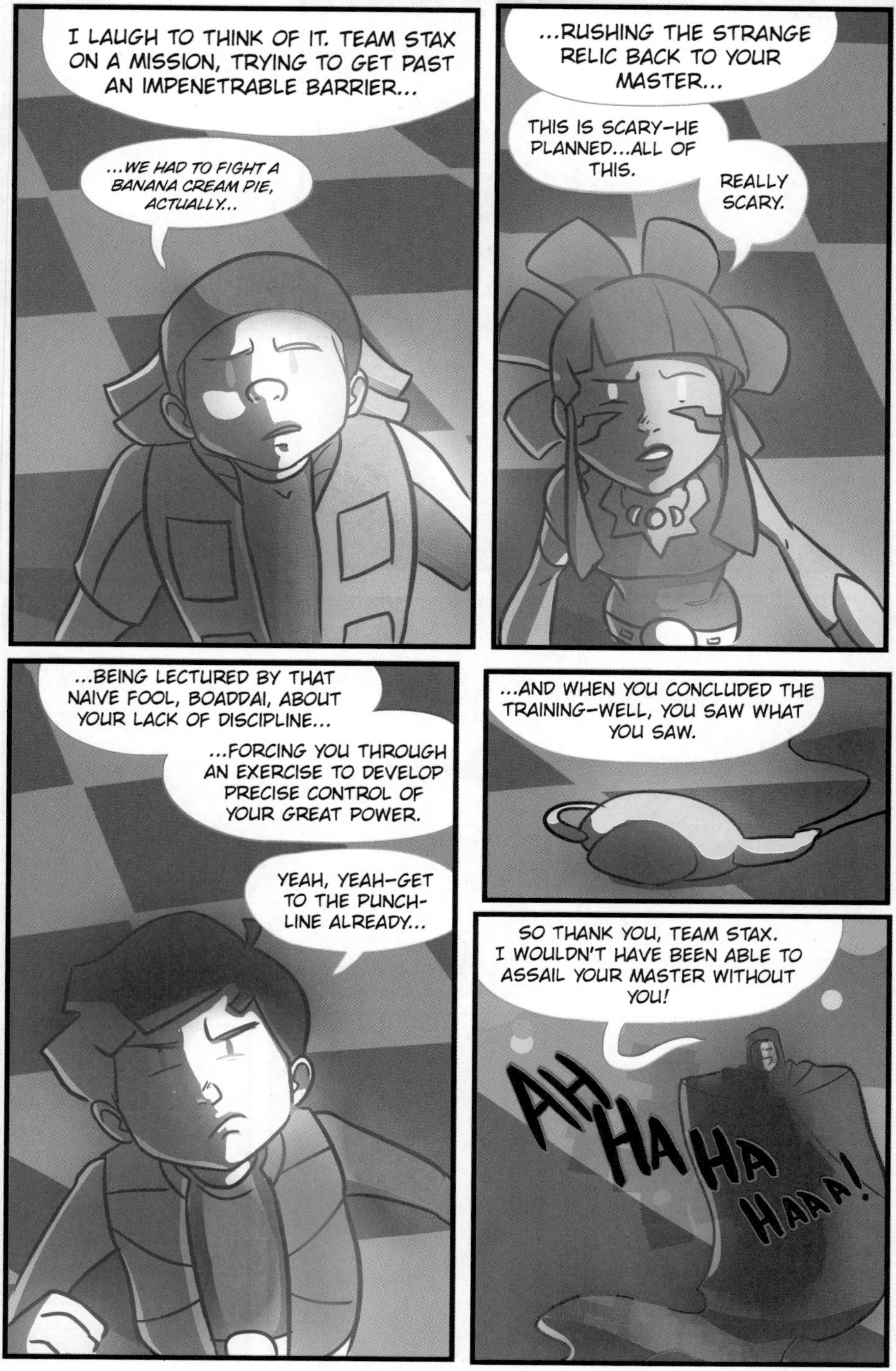
I LAUGH TO THINK OF IT. TEAM STAX ON A MISSION, TRYING TO GET PAST AN IMPENETRABLE BARRIER...
...WE HAD TO FIGHT A BANANA CREAM PIE, ACTUALLY...
...RUSHING THE STRANGE RELIC BACK TO YOUR MASTER...
THIS IS SCARY—HE PLANNED...ALL OF THIS.
REALLY SCARY.
...BEING LECTURED BY THAT NAIVE FOOL, BOADDAI, ABOUT YOUR LACK OF DISCIPLINE...
...FORCING YOU THROUGH AN EXERCISE TO DEVELOP PRECISE CONTROL OF YOUR GREAT POWER.
YEAH, YEAH—GET TO THE PUNCH-LINE ALREADY...
...AND WHEN YOU CONCLUDED THE TRAINING—WELL, YOU SAW WHAT YOU SAW.
SO THANK YOU, TEAM STAX. I WOULDN'T HAVE BEEN ABLE TO ASSAIL YOUR MASTER WITHOUT YOU!
AH HA HA HAAA!

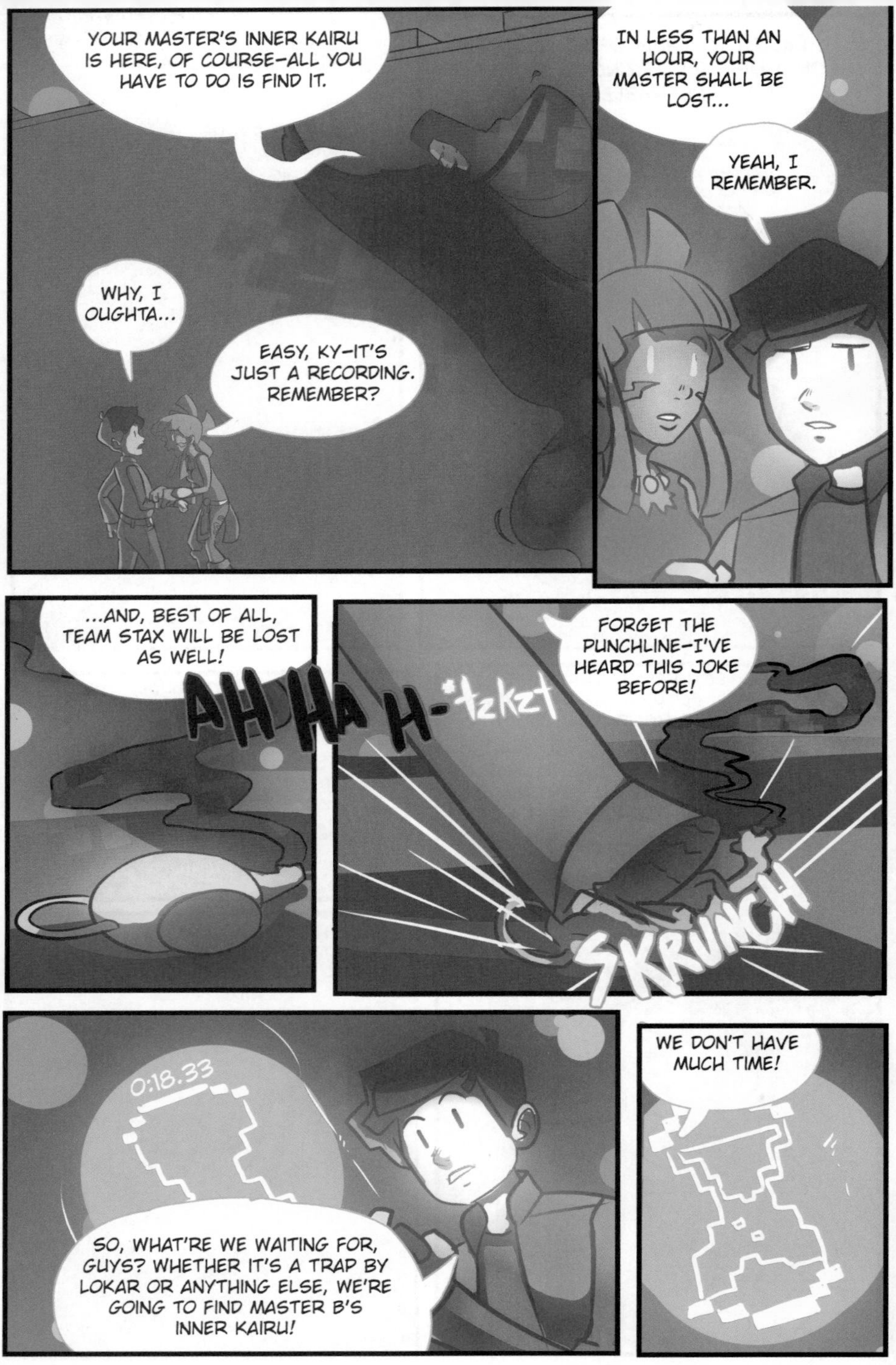
YOUR MASTER'S INNER KAIRU IS HERE, OF COURSE–ALL YOU HAVE TO DO IS FIND IT.
WHY, I OUGHTA...
EASY, KY–IT'S JUST A RECORDING. REMEMBER?
IN LESS THAN AN HOUR, YOUR MASTER SHALL BE LOST...
YEAH, I REMEMBER.
...AND, BEST OF ALL, TEAM STAX WILL BE LOST AS WELL!
AH HA H-*tzkzt
FORGET THE PUNCHLINE–I'VE HEARD THIS JOKE BEFORE!
SKRUNCH
0:18.33
SO, WHAT'RE WE WAITING FOR, GUYS? WHETHER IT'S A TRAP BY LOKAR OR ANYTHING ELSE, WE'RE GOING TO FIND MASTER B'S INNER KAIRU!
WE DON'T HAVE MUCH TIME!

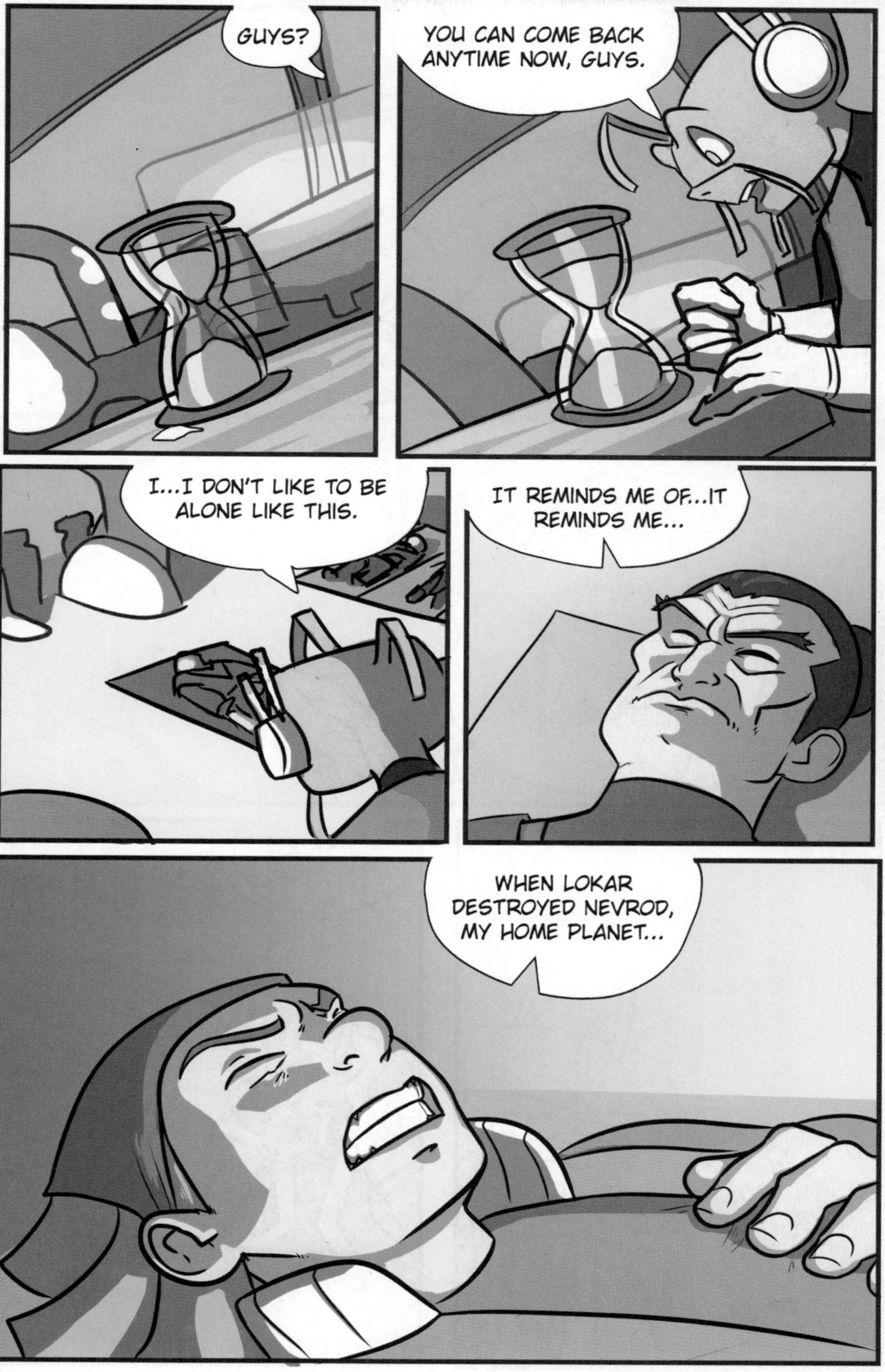
GUYS?
YOU CAN COME BACK ANYTIME NOW, GUYS.
I...I DON'T LIKE TO BE ALONE LIKE THIS.
IT REMINDS ME OF...IT REMINDS ME...
WHEN LOKAR DESTROYED NEVROD, MY HOME PLANET...

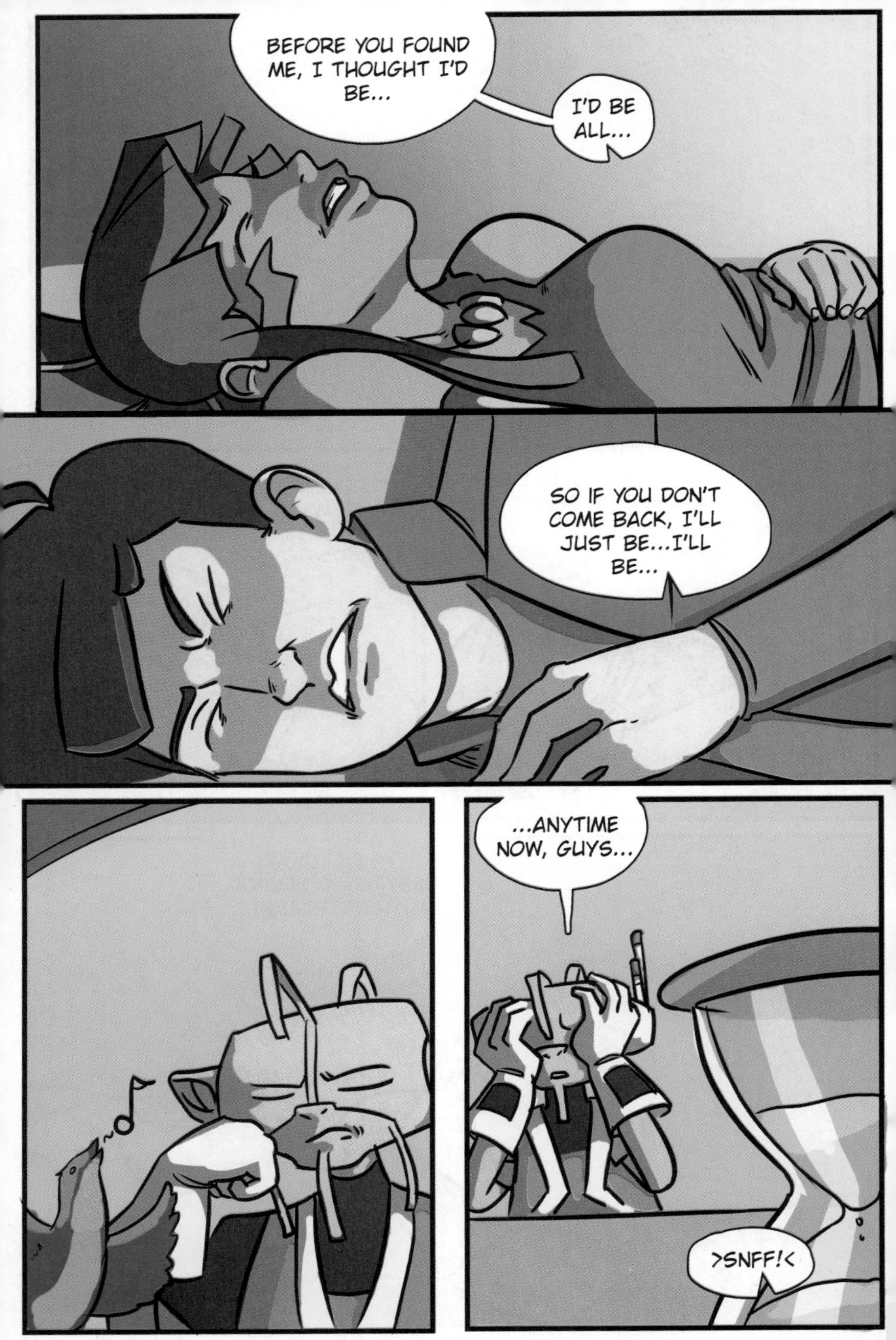
BEFORE YOU FOUND ME, I THOUGHT I'D BE...
I'D BE ALL...
SO IF YOU DON'T COME BACK, I'LL JUST BE...I'LL BE...
...ANYTIME NOW, GUYS...
>SNFF!<

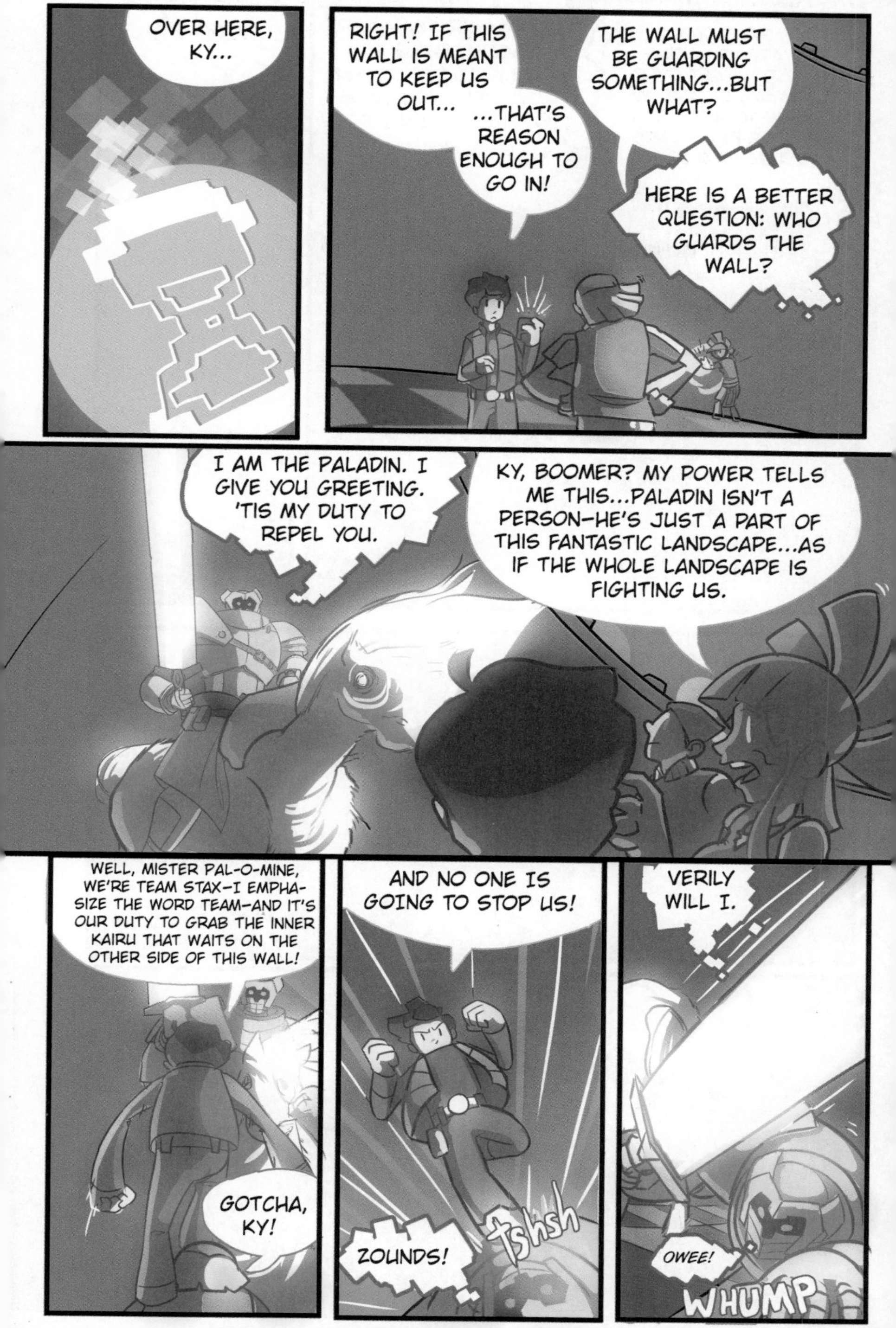
OVER HERE, KY...
RIGHT! IF THIS WALL IS MEANT TO KEEP US OUT...
...THAT'S REASON ENOUGH TO GO IN!
THE WALL MUST BE GUARDING SOMETHING...BUT WHAT?
HERE IS A BETTER QUESTION: WHO GUARDS THE WALL?
I AM THE PALADIN. I GIVE YOU GREETING. 'TIS MY DUTY TO REPEL YOU.
KY, BOOMER? MY POWER TELLS ME THIS...PALADIN ISN'T A PERSON—HE'S JUST A PART OF THIS FANTASTIC LANDSCAPE...AS IF THE WHOLE LANDSCAPE IS FIGHTING US.
WELL, MISTER PAL-O-MINE, WE'RE TEAM STAX—I EMPHASIZE THE WORD TEAM—AND IT'S OUR DUTY TO GRAB THE INNER KAIRU THAT WAITS ON THE OTHER SIDE OF THIS WALL!
GOTCHA, KY!
AND NO ONE IS GOING TO STOP US!
ZOUNDS!
tshsh
VERILY WILL I.
OWEE!
WHUMP

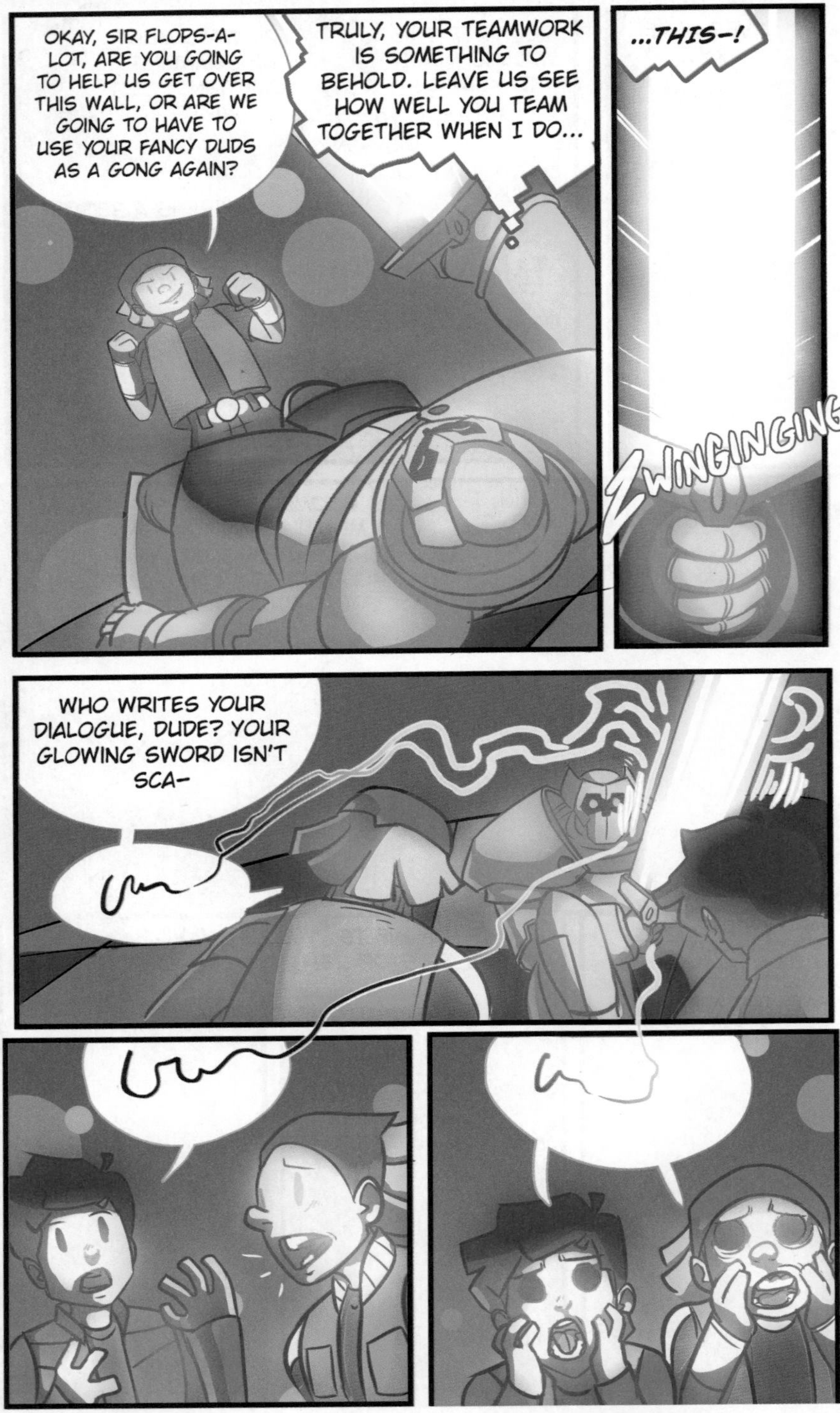

OKAY, SIR FLOPS-A-LOT, ARE YOU GOING TO HELP US GET OVER THIS WALL, OR ARE WE GOING TO HAVE TO USE YOUR FANCY DUDS AS A GONG AGAIN?
TRULY, YOUR TEAMWORK IS SOMETHING TO BEHOLD. LEAVE US SEE HOW WELL YOU TEAM TOGETHER WHEN I DO...
...THIS-!
ZWINGINGING
WHO WRITES YOUR DIALOGUE, DUDE? YOUR GLOWING SWORD ISN'T SCA-

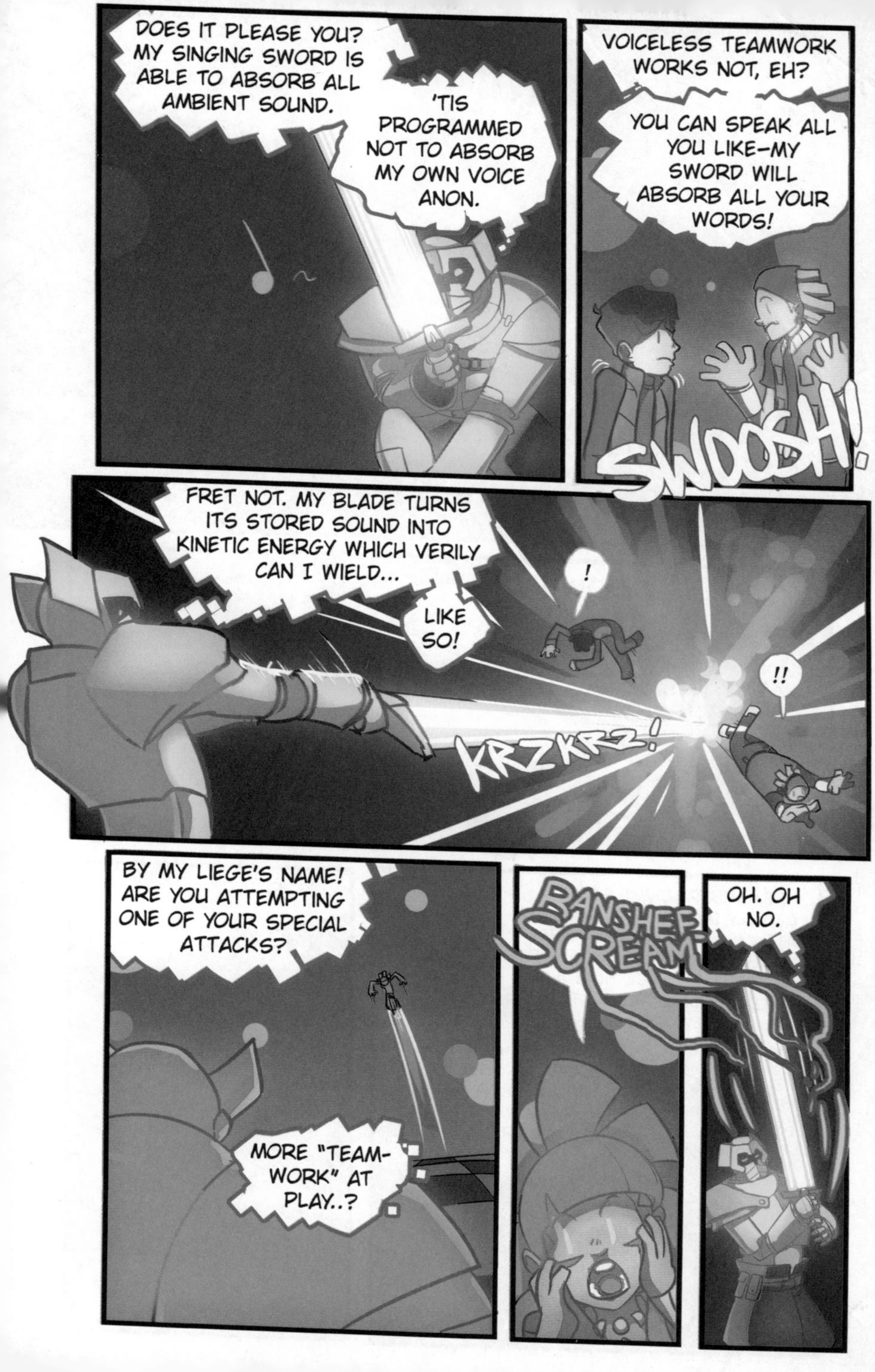
DOES IT PLEASE YOU? MY SINGING SWORD IS ABLE TO ABSORB ALL AMBIENT SOUND.
'TIS PROGRAMMED NOT TO ABSORB MY OWN VOICE ANON.
VOICELESS TEAMWORK WORKS NOT, EH?
YOU CAN SPEAK ALL YOU LIKE—MY SWORD WILL ABSORB ALL YOUR WORDS!
SWOOSH!
FRET NOT. MY BLADE TURNS ITS STORED SOUND INTO KINETIC ENERGY WHICH VERILY CAN I WIELD...
LIKE SO!
!
!!
KRZKRZ!
BY MY LIEGE'S NAME! ARE YOU ATTEMPTING ONE OF YOUR SPECIAL ATTACKS?
MORE "TEAM-WORK" AT PLAY..?
BANSHEE SCREAM
OH. OH NO.

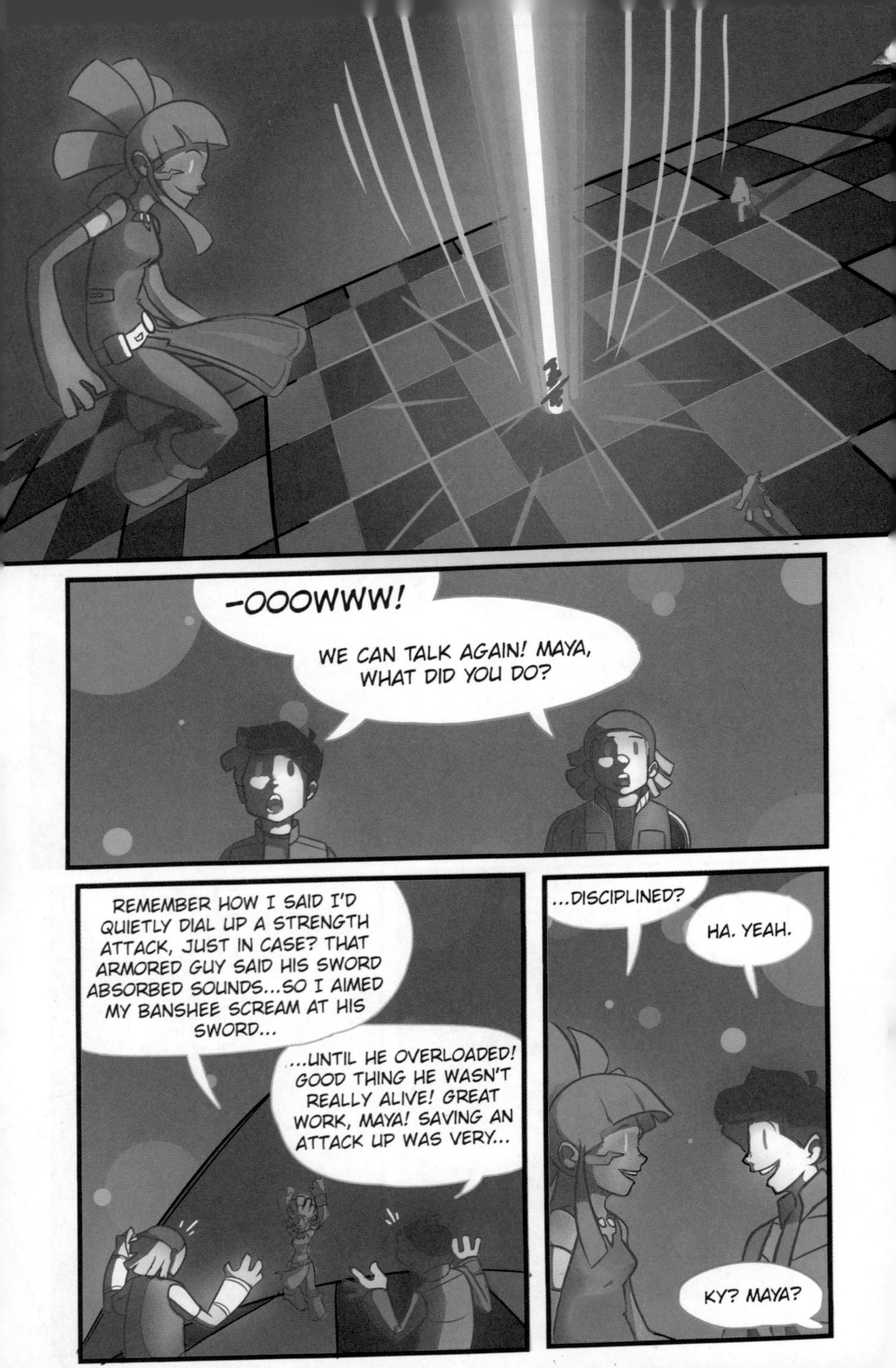
-OOOWWW!
WE CAN TALK AGAIN! MAYA, WHAT DID YOU DO?
REMEMBER HOW I SAID I'D QUIETLY DIAL UP A STRENGTH ATTACK, JUST IN CASE? THAT ARMORED GUY SAID HIS SWORD ABSORBED SOUNDS...SO I AIMED MY BANSHEE SCREAM AT HIS SWORD...
...UNTIL HE OVERLOADED! GOOD THING HE WASN'T REALLY ALIVE! GREAT WORK, MAYA! SAVING AN ATTACK UP WAS VERY...
...DISCIPLINED?
HA. YEAH.
KY? MAYA?

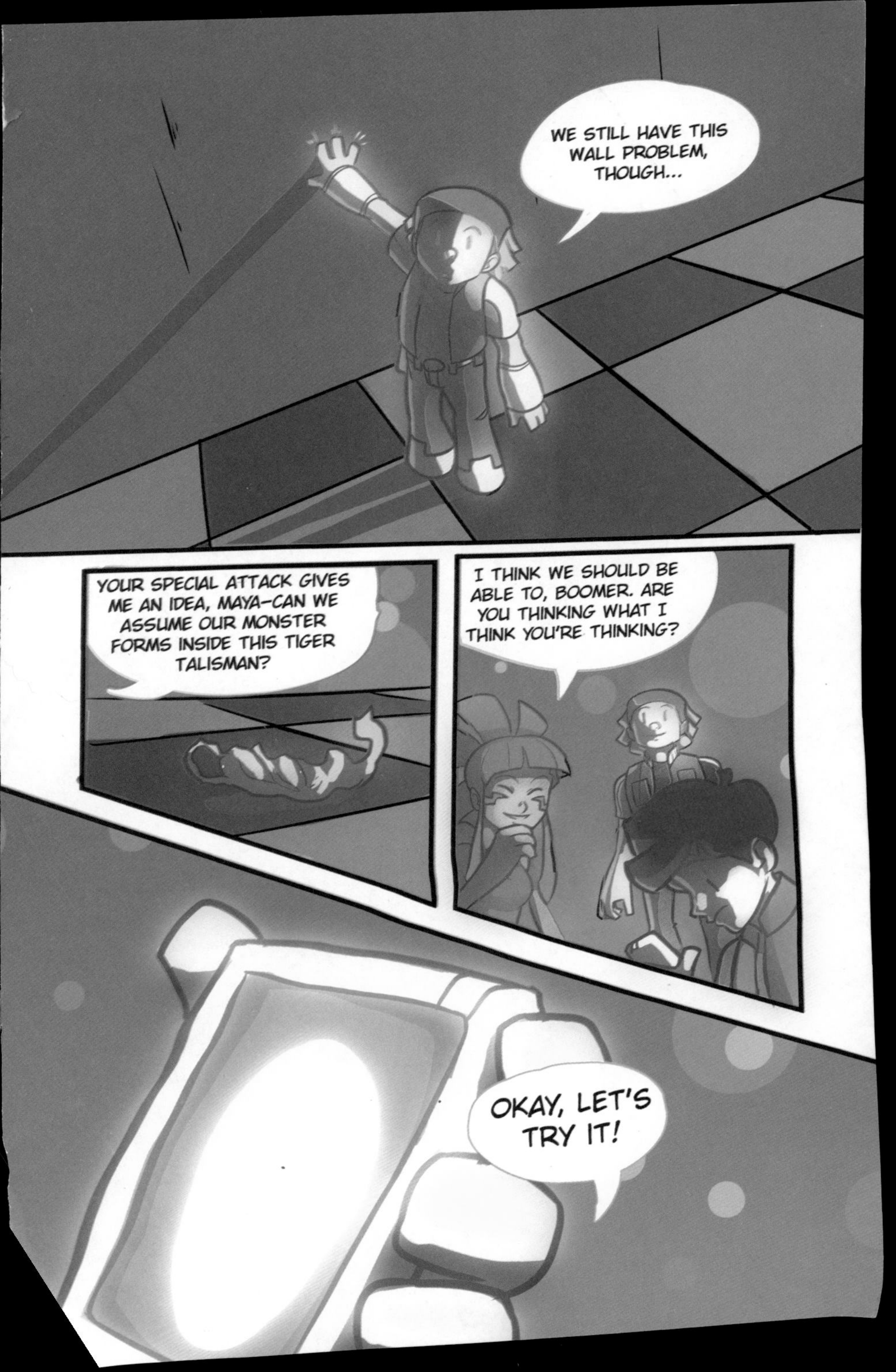
WE STILL HAVE THIS WALL PROBLEM, THOUGH...
YOUR SPECIAL ATTACK GIVES ME AN IDEA, MAYA—CAN WE ASSUME OUR MONSTER FORMS INSIDE THIS TIGER TALISMAN?
I THINK WE SHOULD BE ABLE TO, BOOMER. ARE YOU THINKING WHAT I THINK YOU'RE THINKING?
OKAY, LET'S TRY IT!

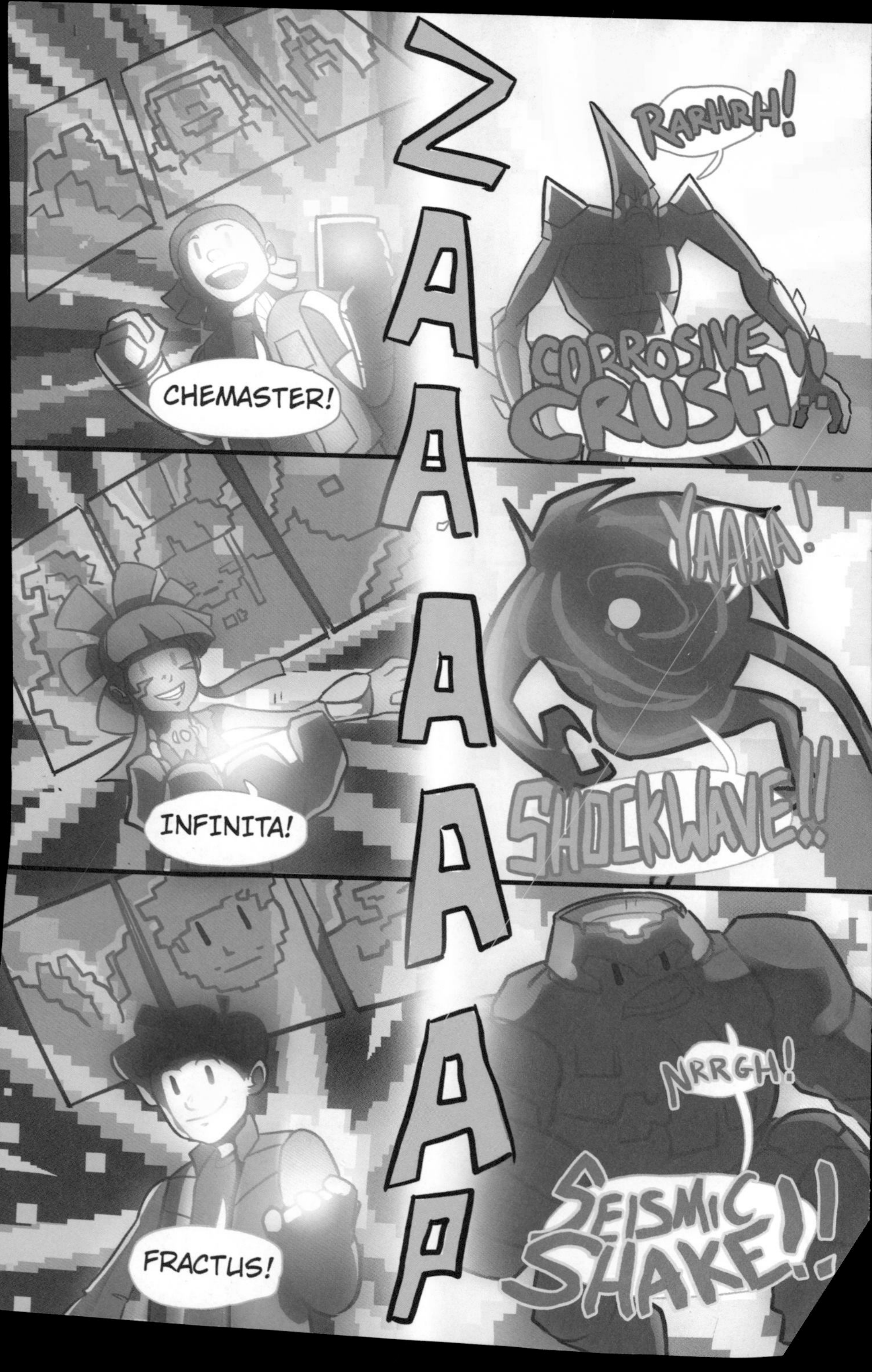

ZAAAAAAAP
RARHRH!
CHEMASTER!
CORROSIVE CRUSH!!
YAAAA!
INFINITA!
SHOCKWAVE!!
NRRGH!
FRACTUS!
SEISMIC SHAKE!!

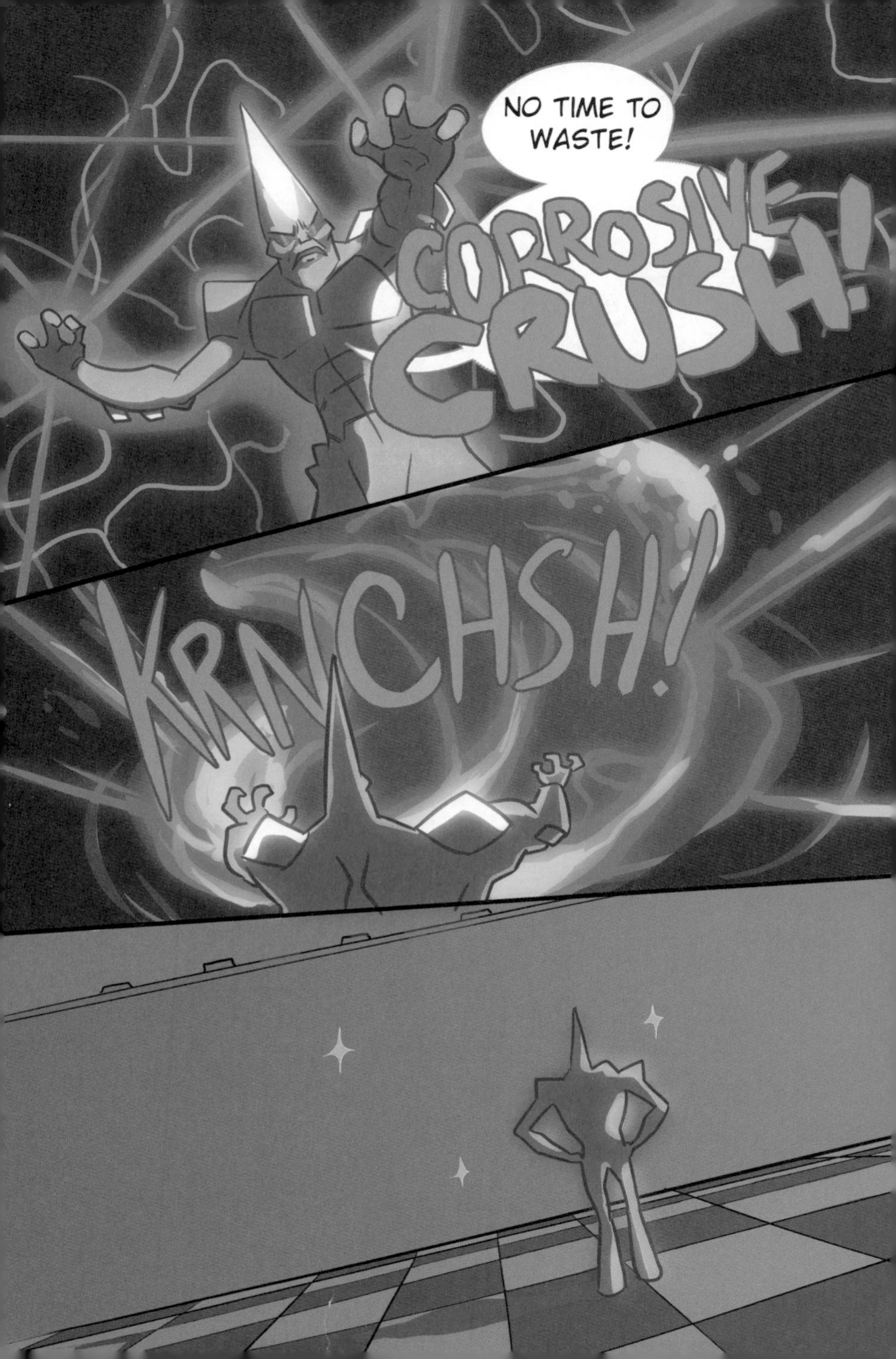
NO TIME TO WASTE!
CORROSIVE CRUSH!
KRNCHSH!

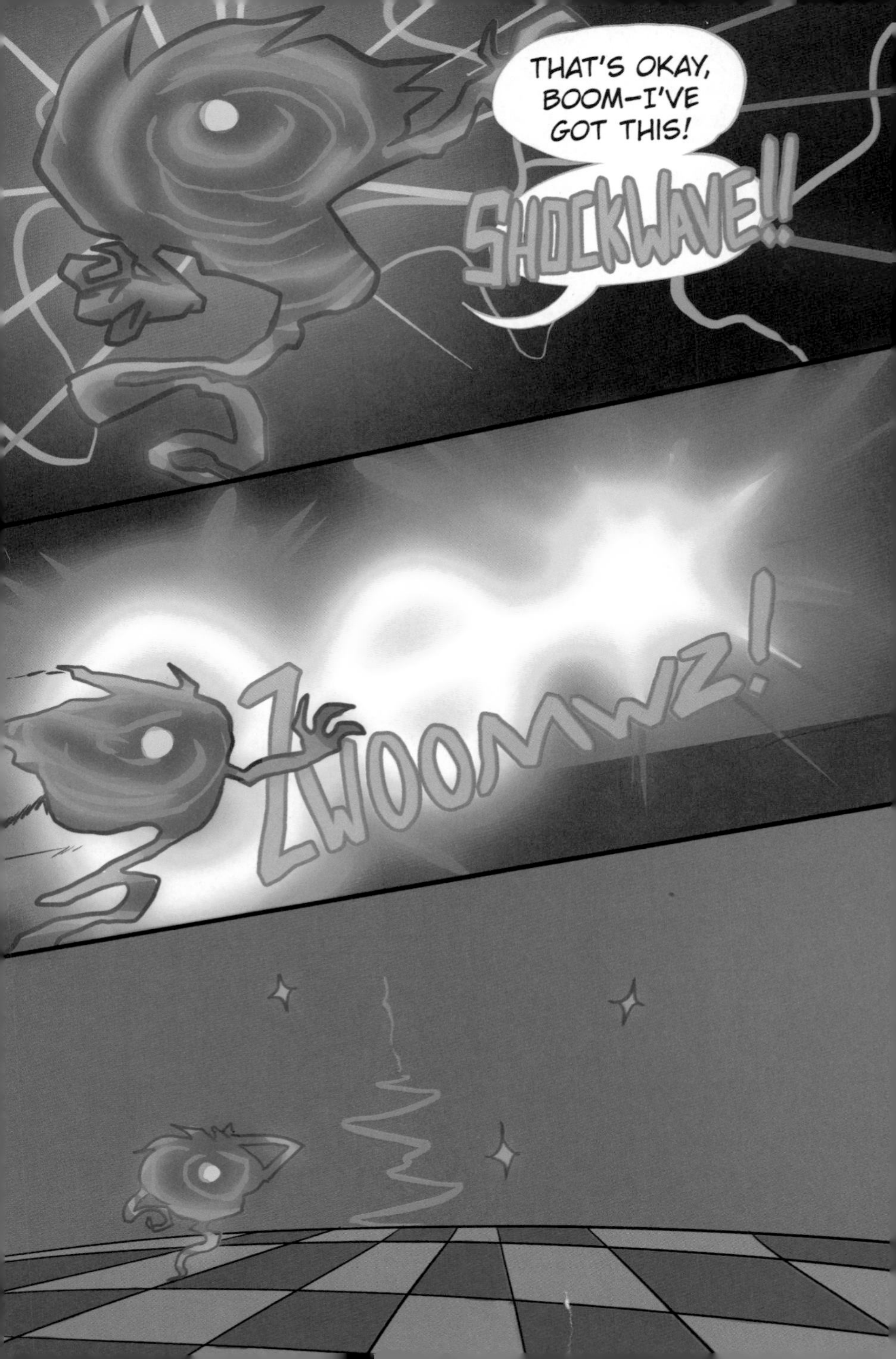
THAT'S OKAY, BOOM–I'VE GOT THIS!
SHOCKWAVE!!
ZWOOMWZ!

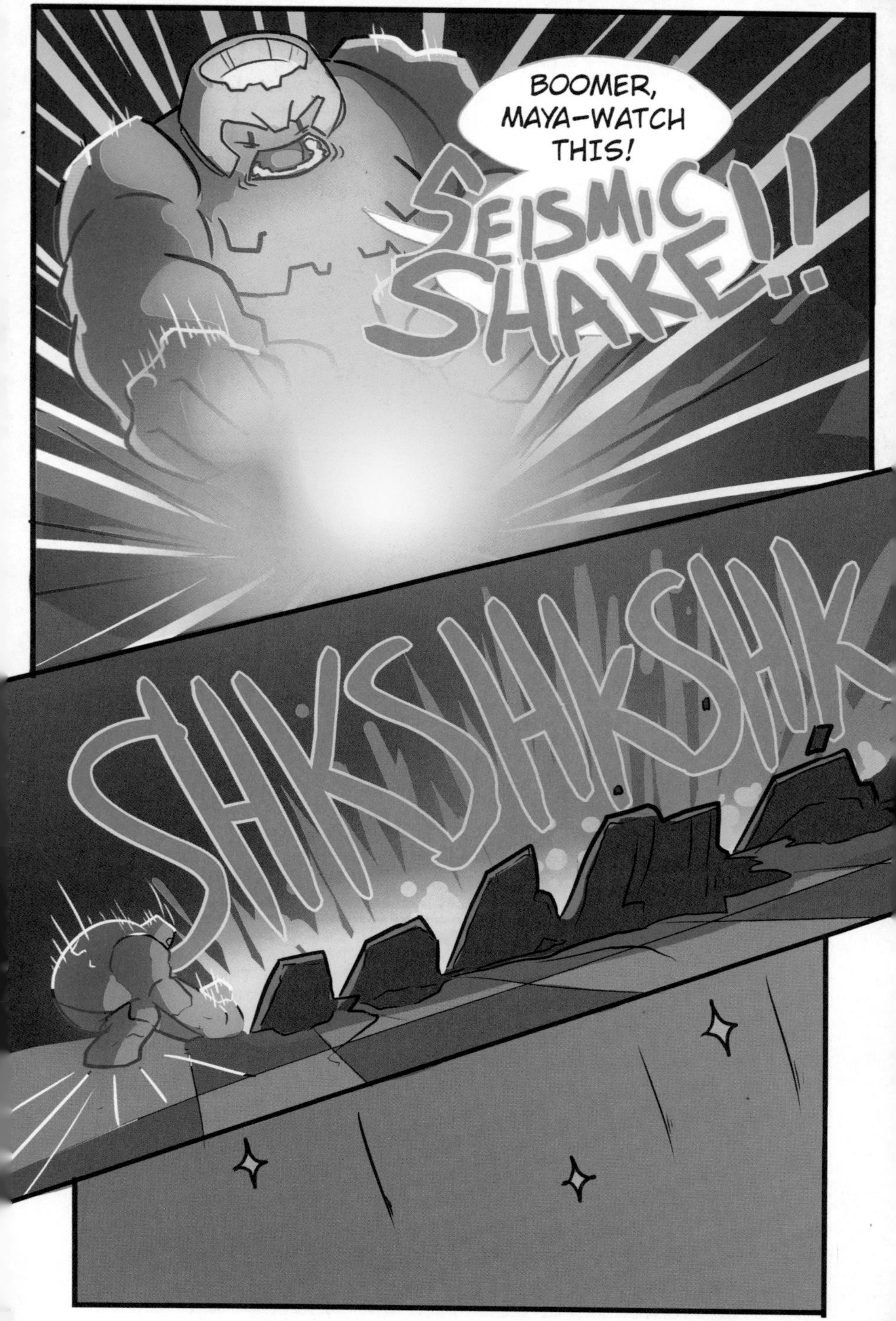
BOOMER, MAYA-WATCH THIS!
SEISMIC SHAKE!!
SHKSHKSHKSHK

>AHIH!< NONE OF OUR SPECIAL ATTACKS WORK. ALL THAT ENERGY WASTED...

YEAH, BUT WASTING THAT ENERGY SURE WAS FUN. >HIHHH!<

NOT VERY DISCIPLINED, THOUGH... >AH-HUH!<

IT DUH->AH-HUH<-DOESN'T MAKE SENSE? WHY DID MAYA'S BANSHEE SCREAM WORK ON THE PALADIN BUT NONE OF OUR SPECIAL ATTACKS?

WAIT A MINUTE. I MIGHT GET IT.

GET WHAT?

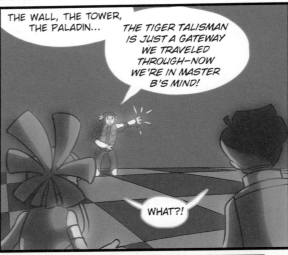

THE WALL, THE TOWER, THE PALADIN...

THE TIGER TALISMAN IS JUST A GATEWAY WE TRAVELED THROUGH—NOW WE'RE IN MASTER B'S MIND!

WHAT?!

WELL, YOU KNOW HOW HE'S ALWAYS SO INTERESTED IN CHATURANJI?

COULD BE THAT HE PROTECTS HIS INNER KAIRU BY USING A COSMIC CHATURANJI GAME! WE MUST BE CLOSE! HIS INNER KAIRU IS HIDDEN SOMEWHERE IN THIS REALITY.

THAT'S WHY OUR SPECIAL ATTACKS DON'T WORK ON THE WALL: WE'RE APPLYING THE WRONG METHOD, JUST LIKE MASTER B SAID! MAYBE WE'RE JUST PLAYING THIS COSMIC INTERDIMENSIONAL VERSION OF CHATURANJI!

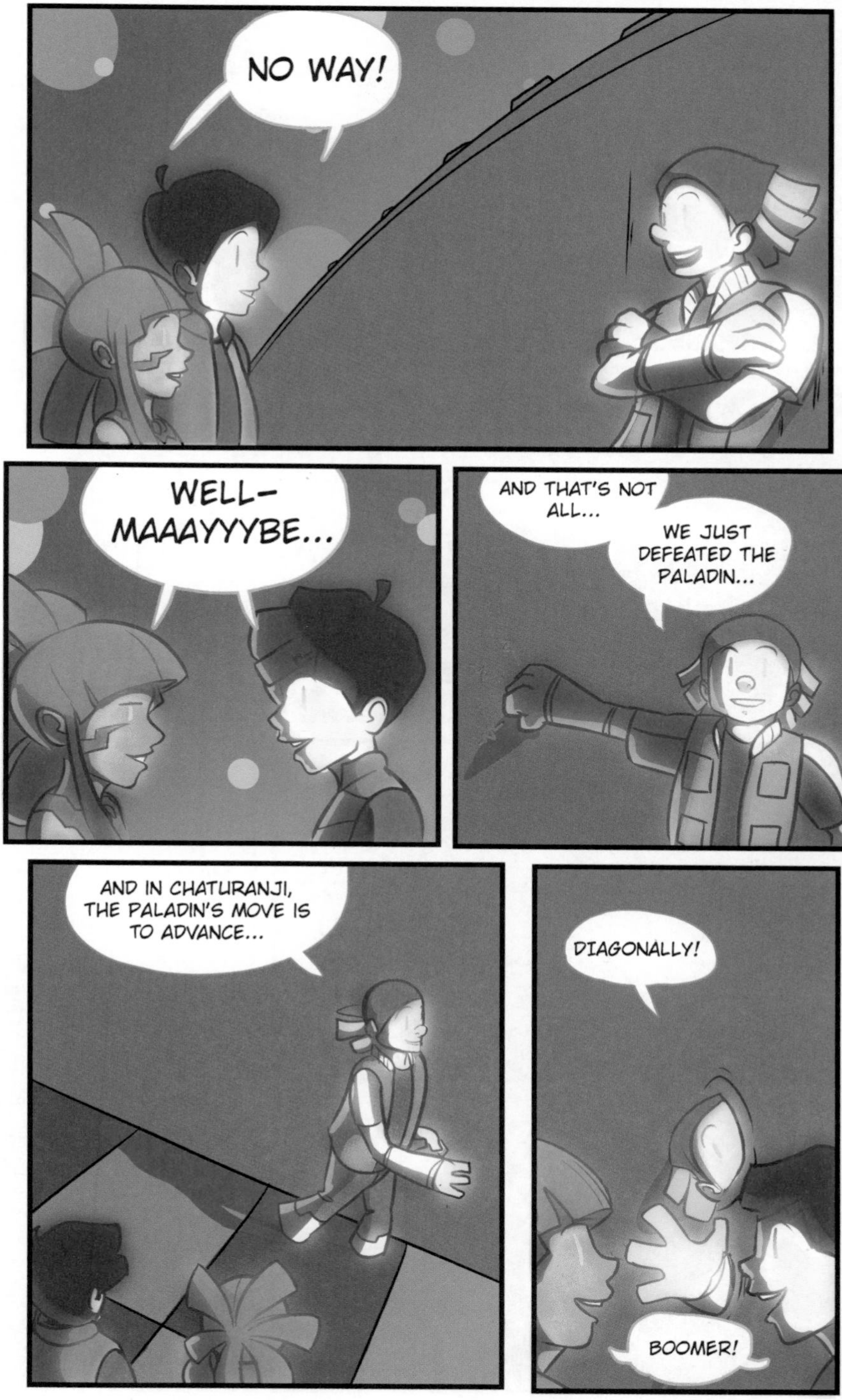
NO WAY!
WELL-
MAAAYYYBE...
AND THAT'S NOT ALL...
WE JUST DEFEATED THE PALADIN...
AND IN CHATURANJI, THE PALADIN'S MOVE IS TO ADVANCE...
DIAGONALLY!
BOOMER!

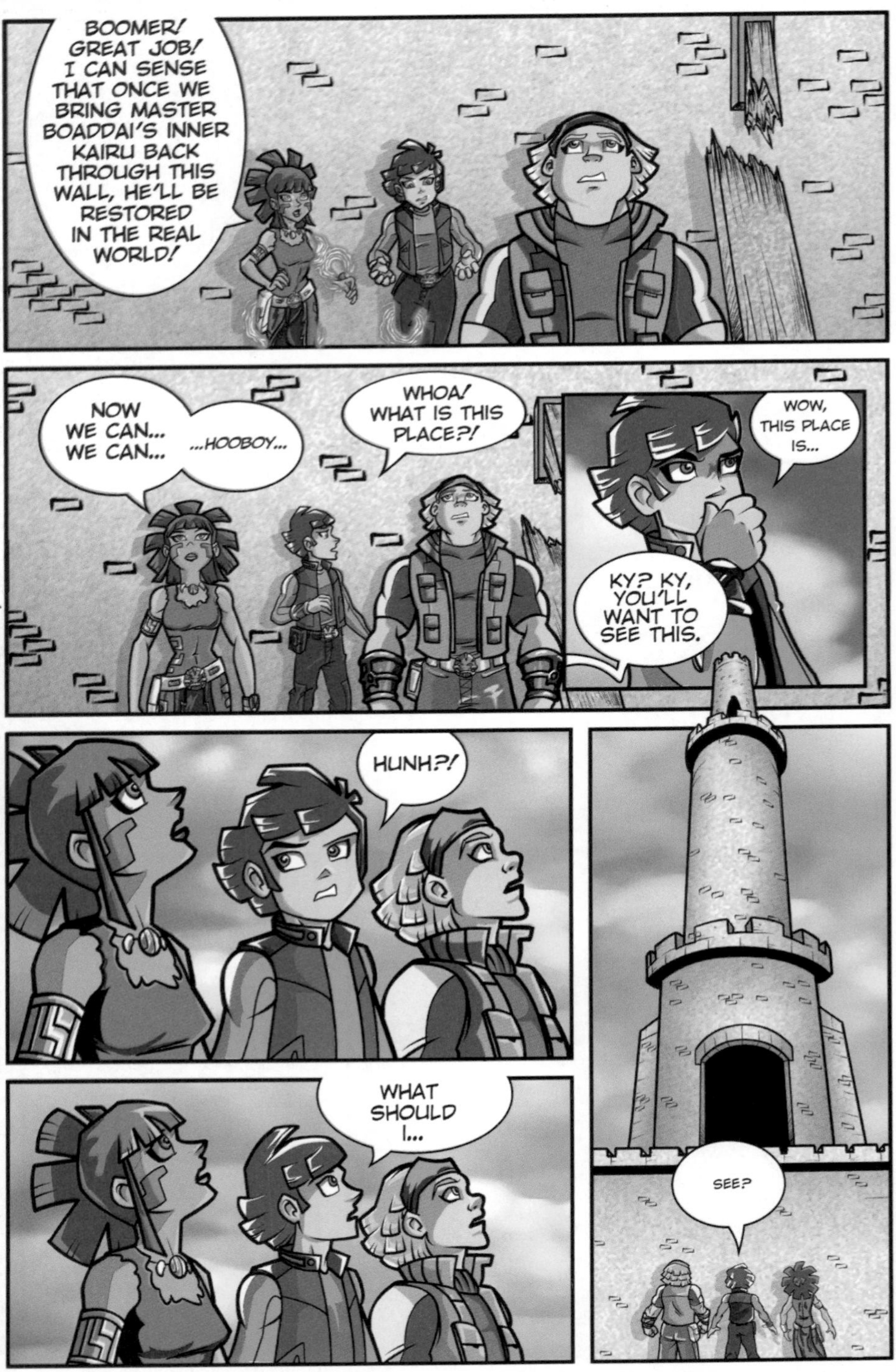
BOOMER! GREAT JOB! I CAN SENSE THAT ONCE WE BRING MASTER BOADDAI'S INNER KAIRU BACK THROUGH THIS WALL, HE'LL BE RESTORED IN THE REAL WORLD!
NOW WE CAN... WE CAN...
...HOOBOY...
WHOA! WHAT IS THIS PLACE?!
WOW, THIS PLACE IS...
KY? KY, YOU'LL WANT TO SEE THIS.
HUNH?!
WHAT SHOULD I...
SEE?

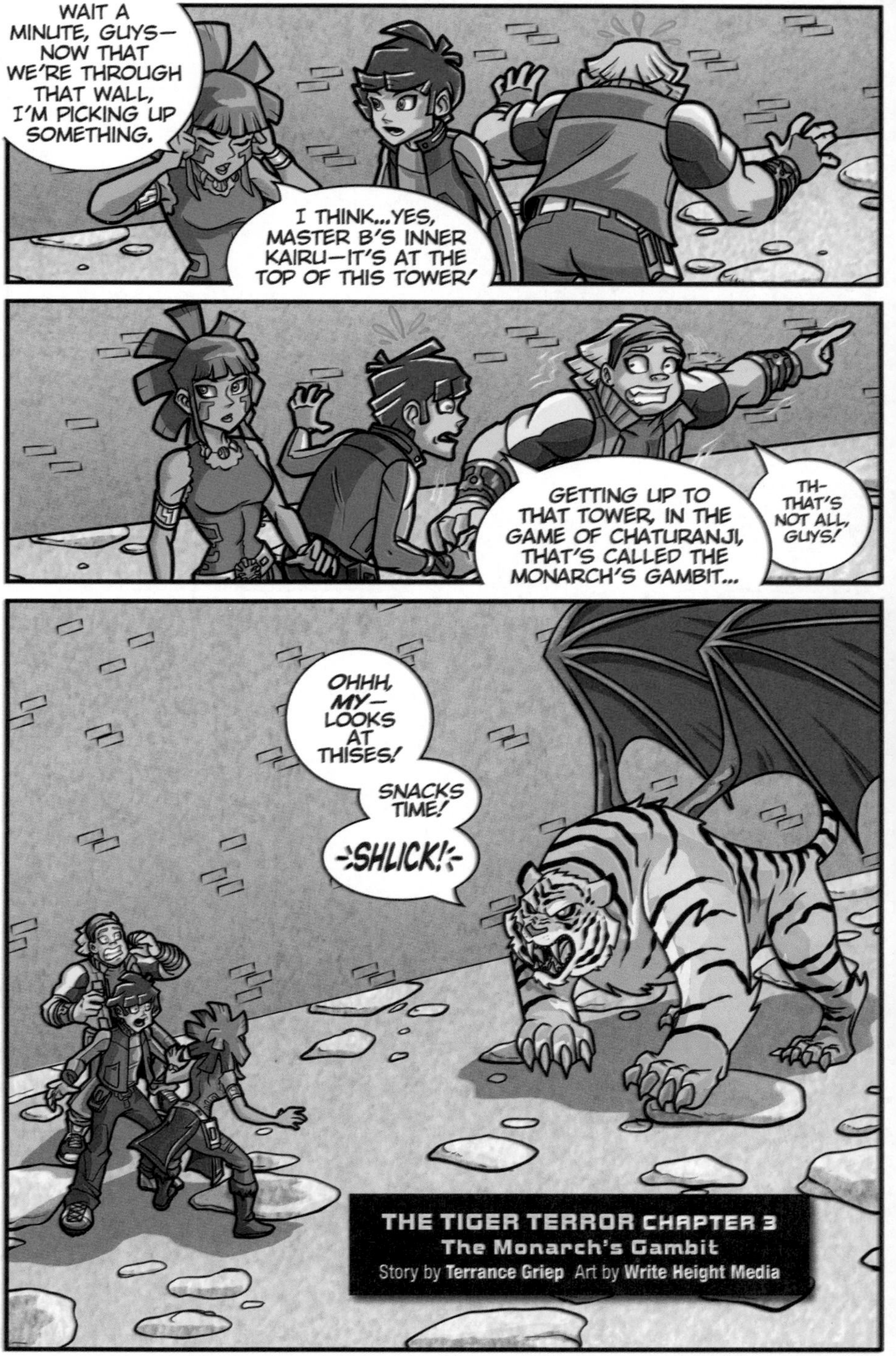
WAIT A MINUTE, GUYS— NOW THAT WE'RE THROUGH THAT WALL, I'M PICKING UP SOMETHING.
I THINK...YES, MASTER B'S INNER KAIRU—IT'S AT THE TOP OF THIS TOWER!
GETTING UP TO THAT TOWER, IN THE GAME OF CHATURANJI, THAT'S CALLED THE MONARCH'S GAMBIT...
TH- THAT'S NOT ALL, GUYS!
OHHH, MY— LOOKS AT THISES!
SNACKS TIME!
-SHLICK!-
THE TIGER TERROR CHAPTER 3
The Monarch's Gambit
Story by Terrance Griep Art by Write Height Media

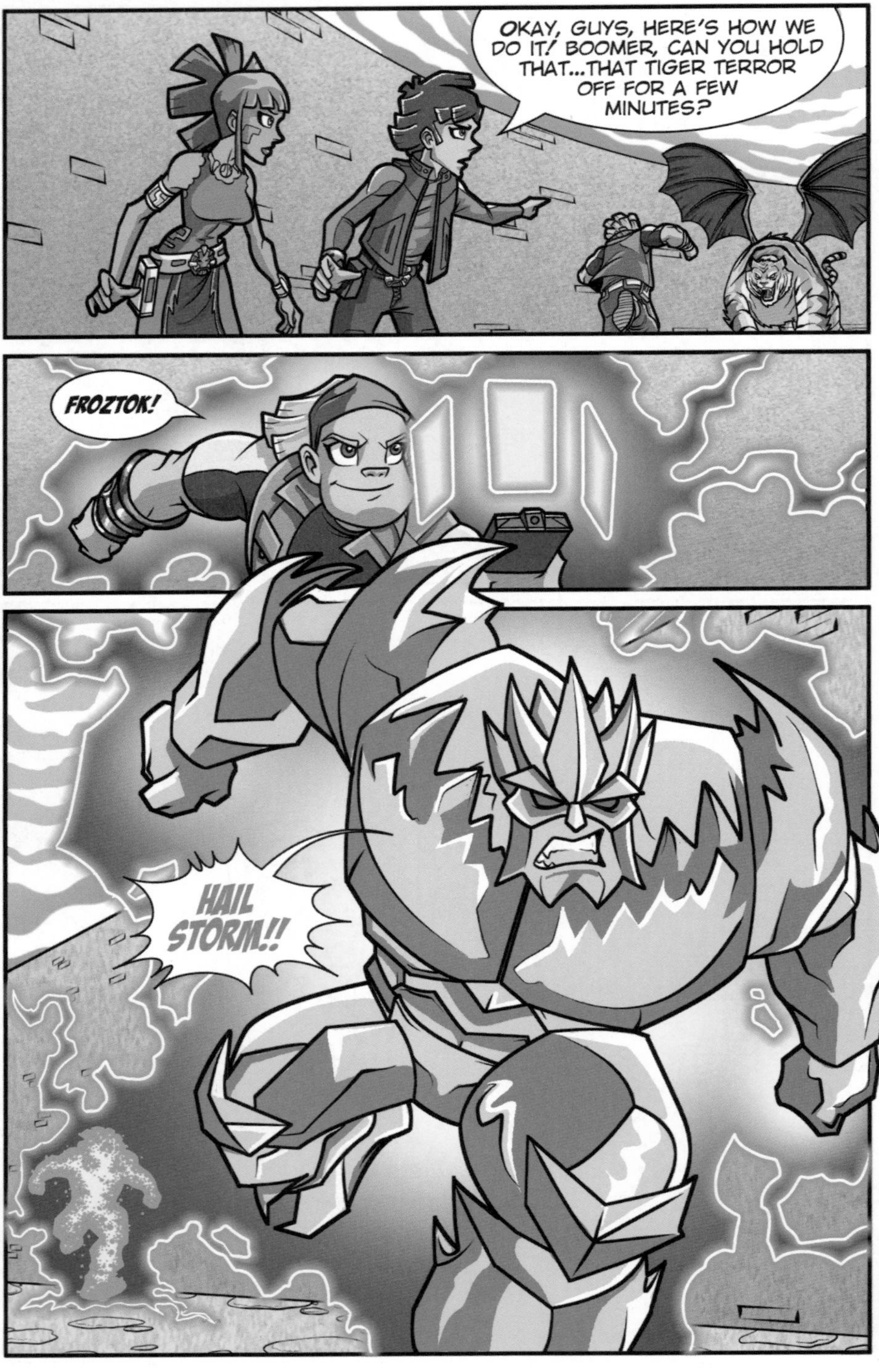
OKAY, GUYS, HERE'S HOW WE DO IT! BOOMER, CAN YOU HOLD THAT...THAT TIGER TERROR OFF FOR A FEW MINUTES?
FROZTOK!
HAIL STORM!!

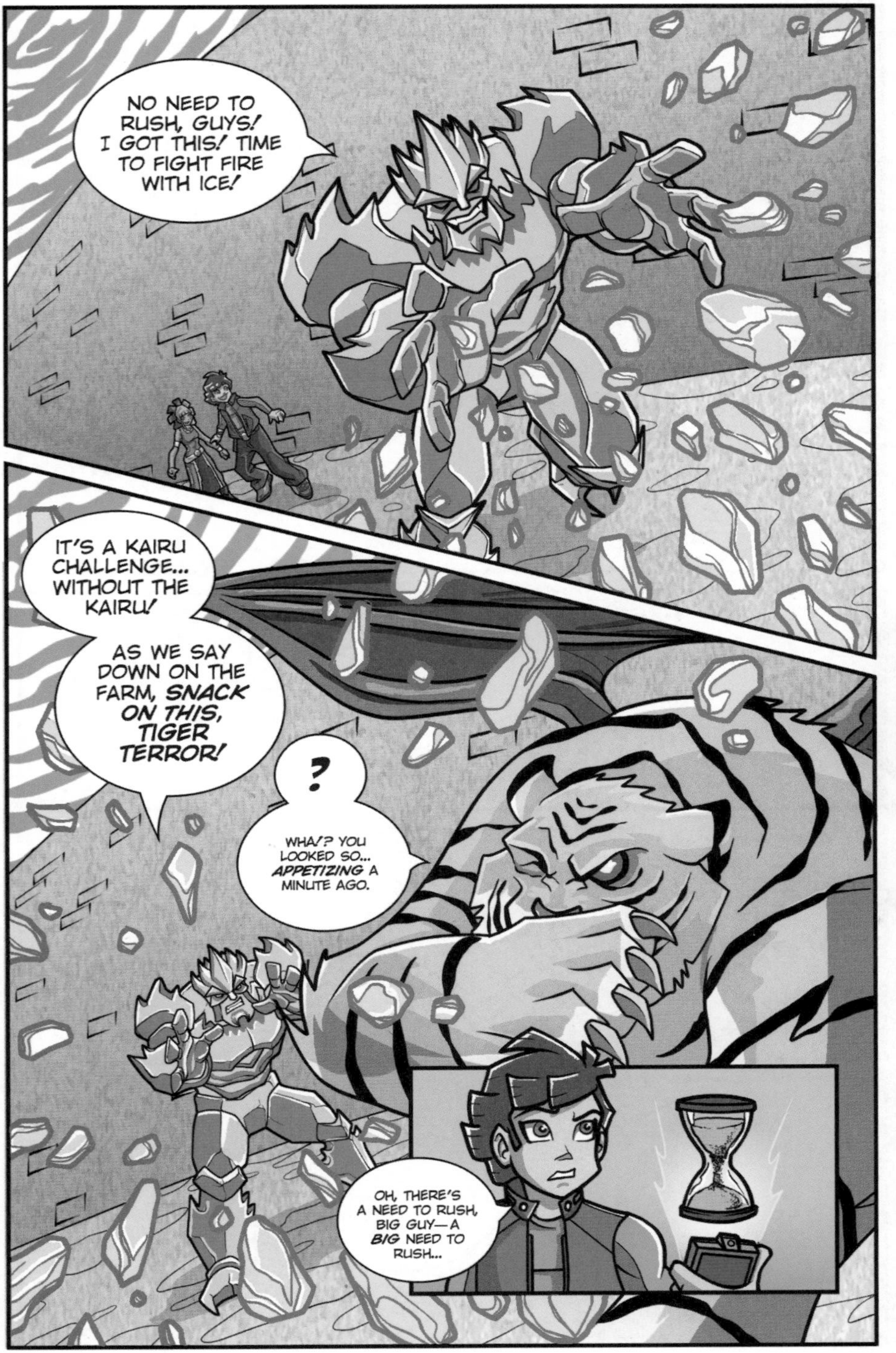
NO NEED TO RUSH, GUYS! I GOT THIS! TIME TO FIGHT FIRE WITH ICE!
IT'S A KAIRU CHALLENGE... WITHOUT THE KAIRU!
AS WE SAY DOWN ON THE FARM, SNACK ON THIS, TIGER TERROR!
?
WHA!? YOU LOOKED SO... APPETIZING A MINUTE AGO.
OH, THERE'S A NEED TO RUSH, BIG GUY—A BIG NEED TO RUSH...

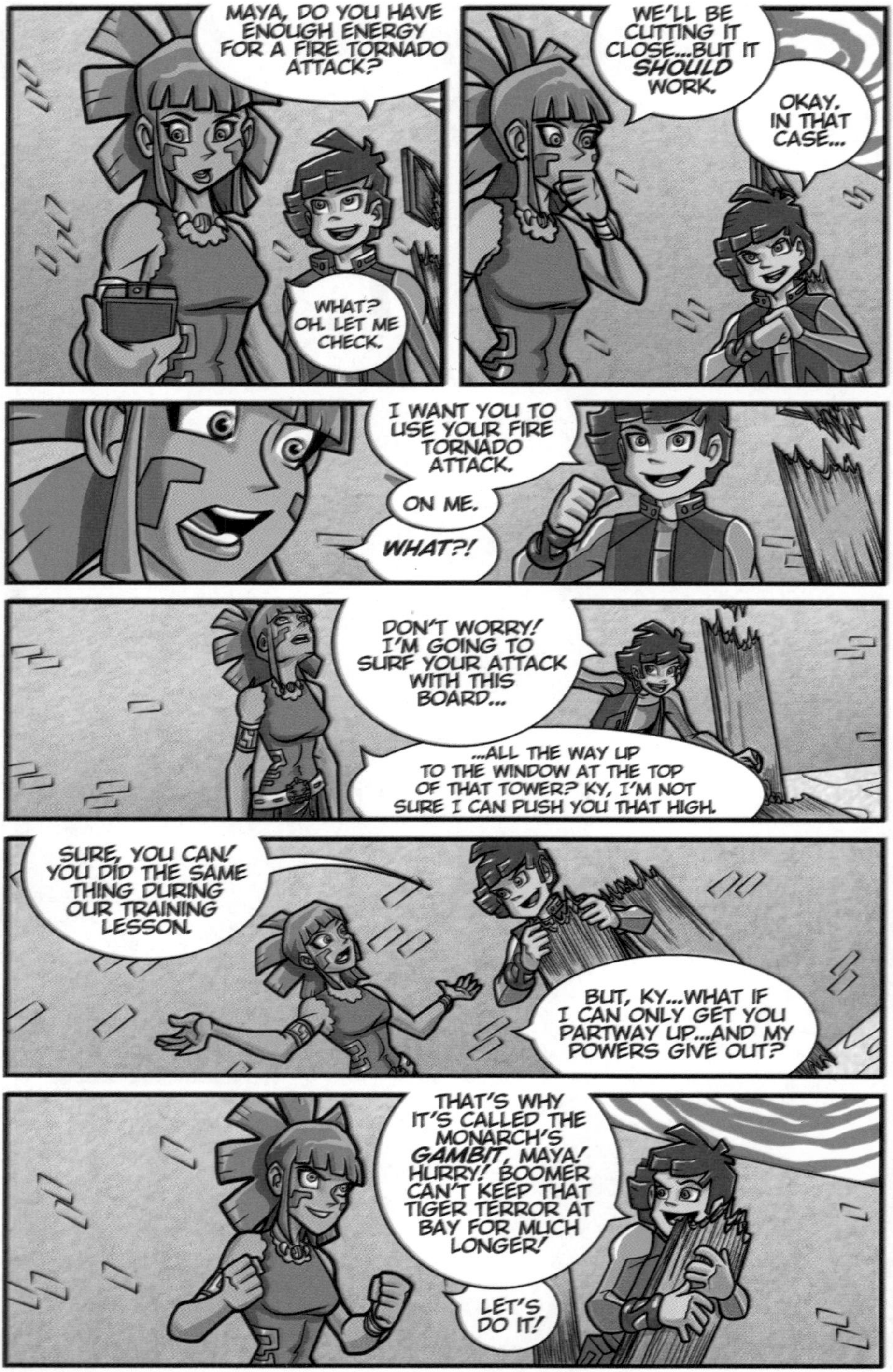
MAYA, DO YOU HAVE ENOUGH ENERGY FOR A FIRE TORNADO ATTACK?
WHAT? OH. LET ME CHECK.
WE'LL BE CUTTING IT CLOSE...BUT IT *SHOULD* WORK.
OKAY. IN THAT CASE...
I WANT YOU TO USE YOUR FIRE TORNADO ATTACK.
ON ME.
WHAT?!
DON'T WORRY! I'M GOING TO SURF YOUR ATTACK WITH THIS BOARD...
...ALL THE WAY UP TO THE WINDOW AT THE TOP OF THAT TOWER? KY, I'M NOT SURE I CAN PUSH YOU THAT HIGH.
SURE, YOU CAN! YOU DID THE SAME THING DURING OUR TRAINING LESSON.
BUT, KY...WHAT IF I CAN ONLY GET YOU PARTWAY UP...AND MY POWERS GIVE OUT?
THAT'S WHY IT'S CALLED THE MONARCH'S *GAMBIT*, MAYA! HURRY! BOOMER CAN'T KEEP THAT TIGER TERROR AT BAY FOR MUCH LONGER!
LET'S DO IT!

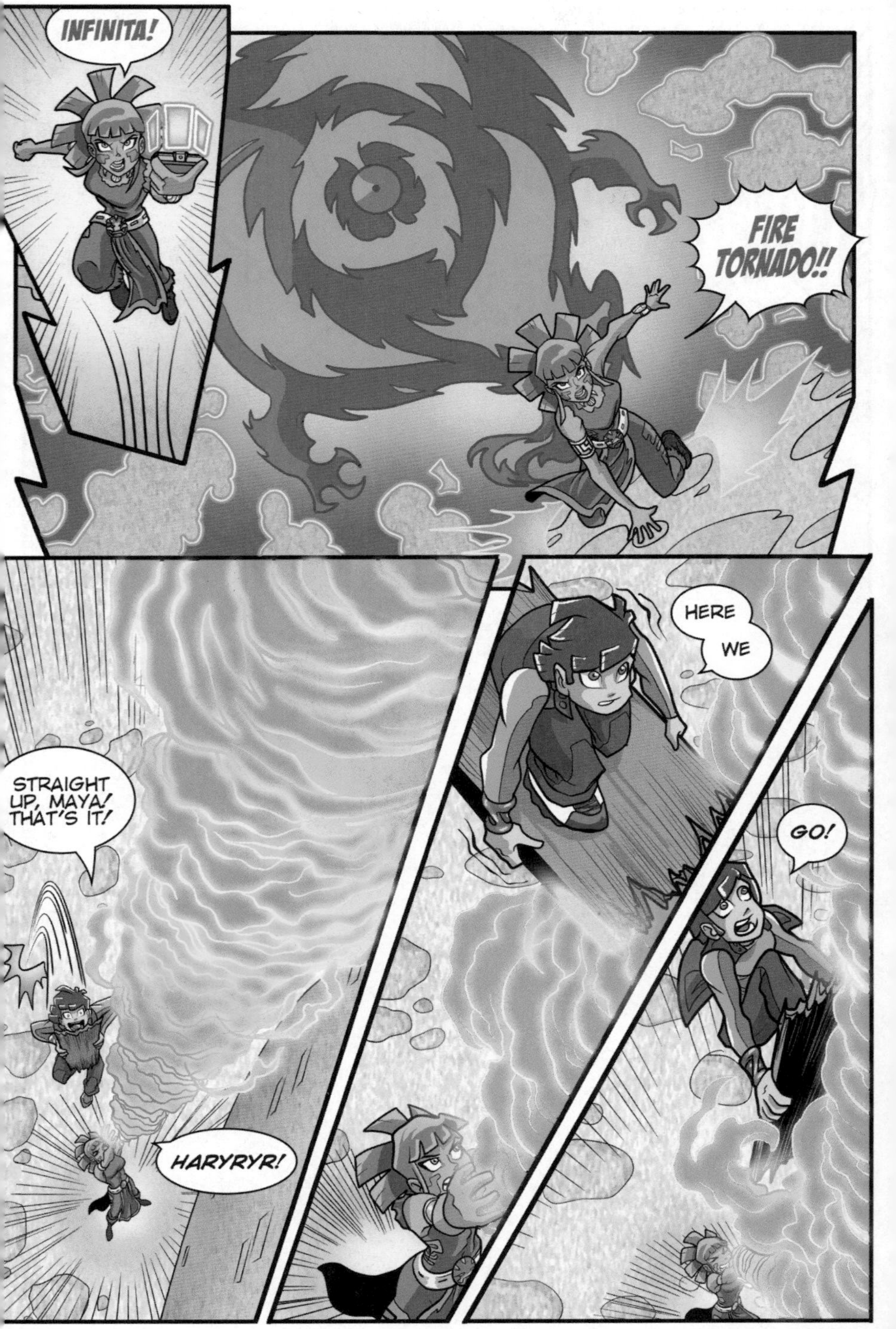
INFINITA!
FIRE TORNADO!!
STRAIGHT UP, MAYA! THAT'S IT!
HARYRYR!
HERE WE
GO!

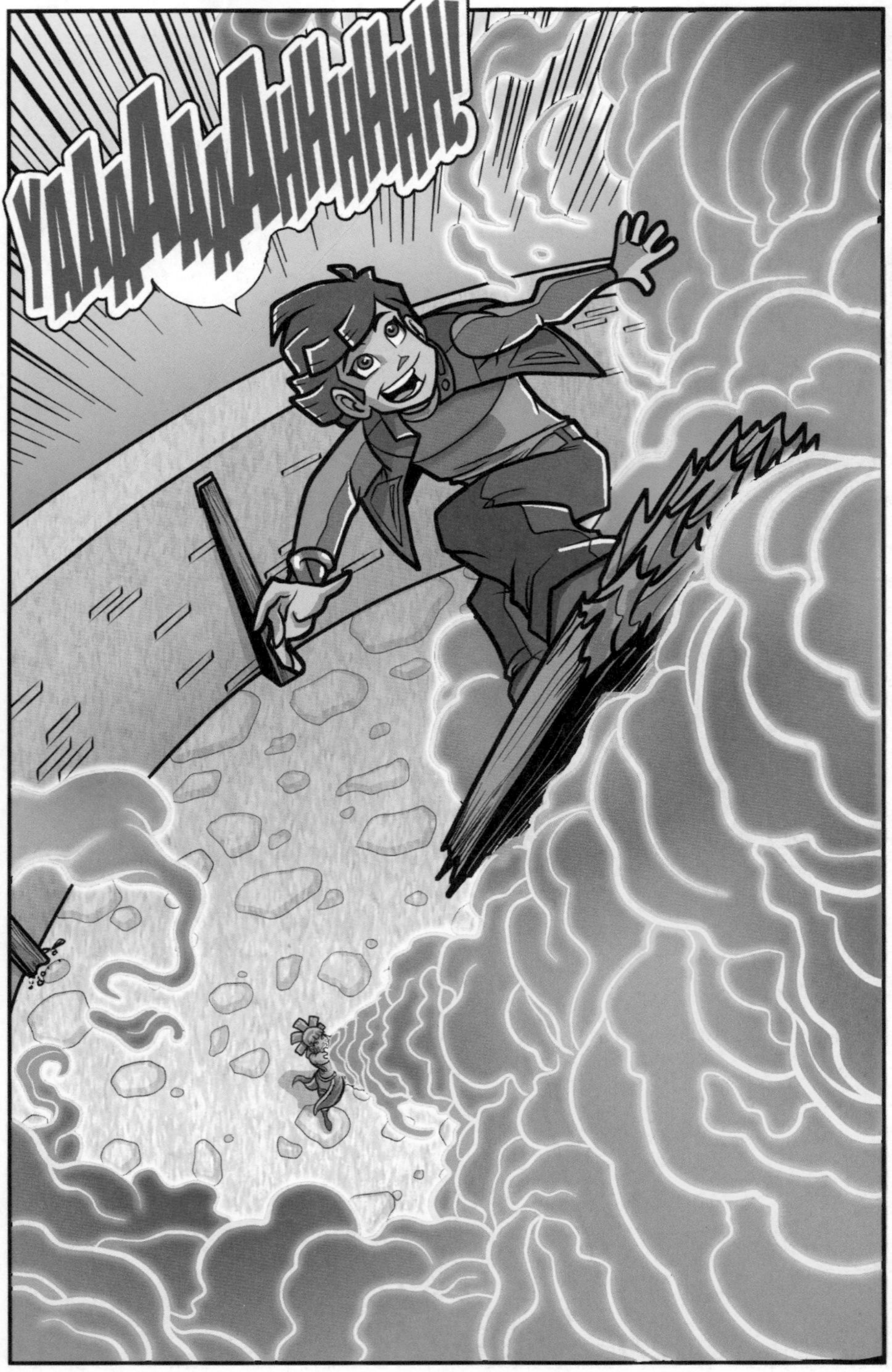
YAAAAAAHHHHHH!

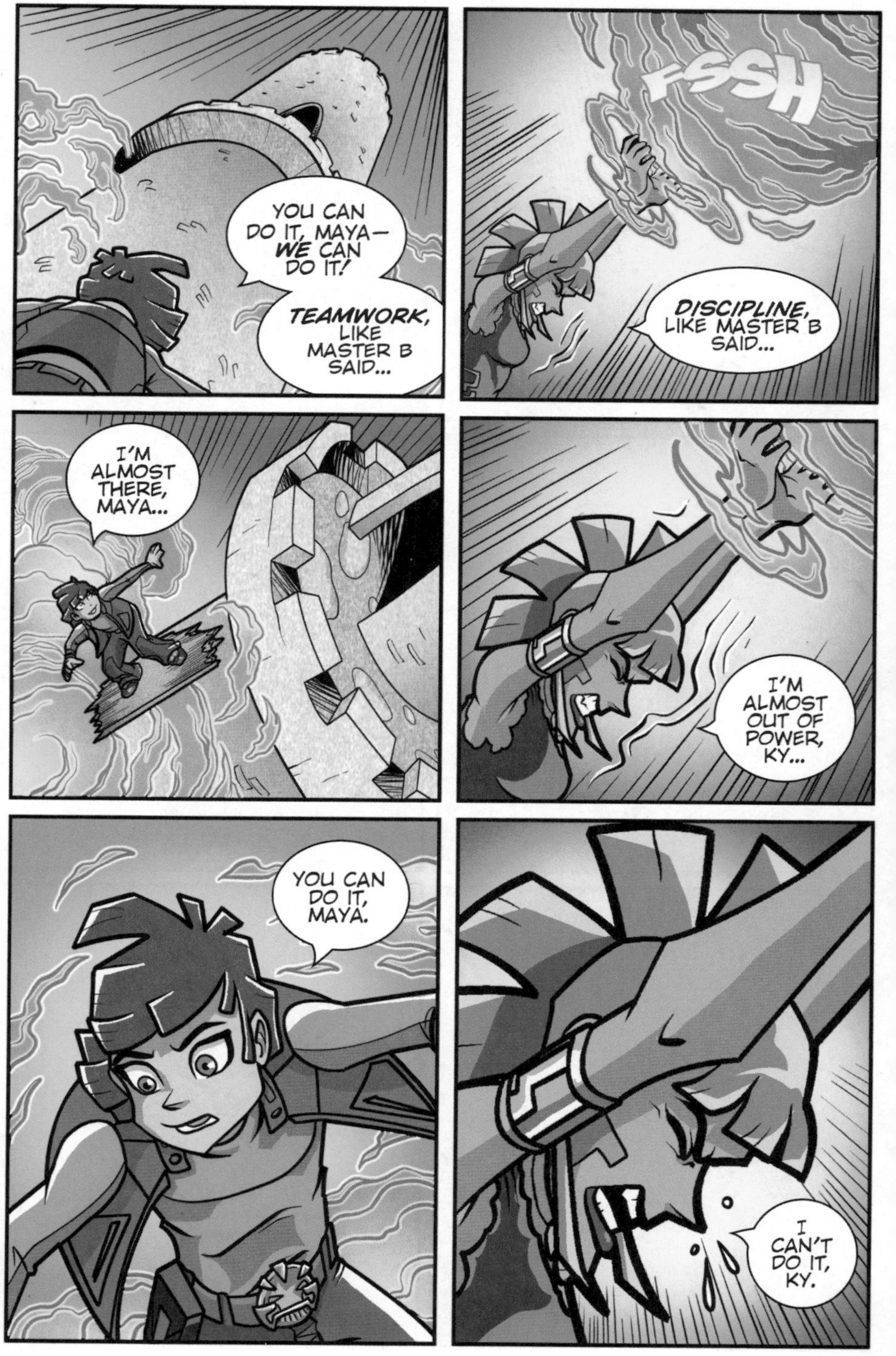
YOU CAN DO IT, MAYA— WE CAN DO IT!
TEAMWORK, LIKE MASTER B SAID...
FSSH
DISCIPLINE, LIKE MASTER B SAID...
I'M ALMOST THERE, MAYA...
I'M ALMOST OUT OF POWER, KY...
YOU CAN DO IT, MAYA.
I CAN'T DO IT, KY.

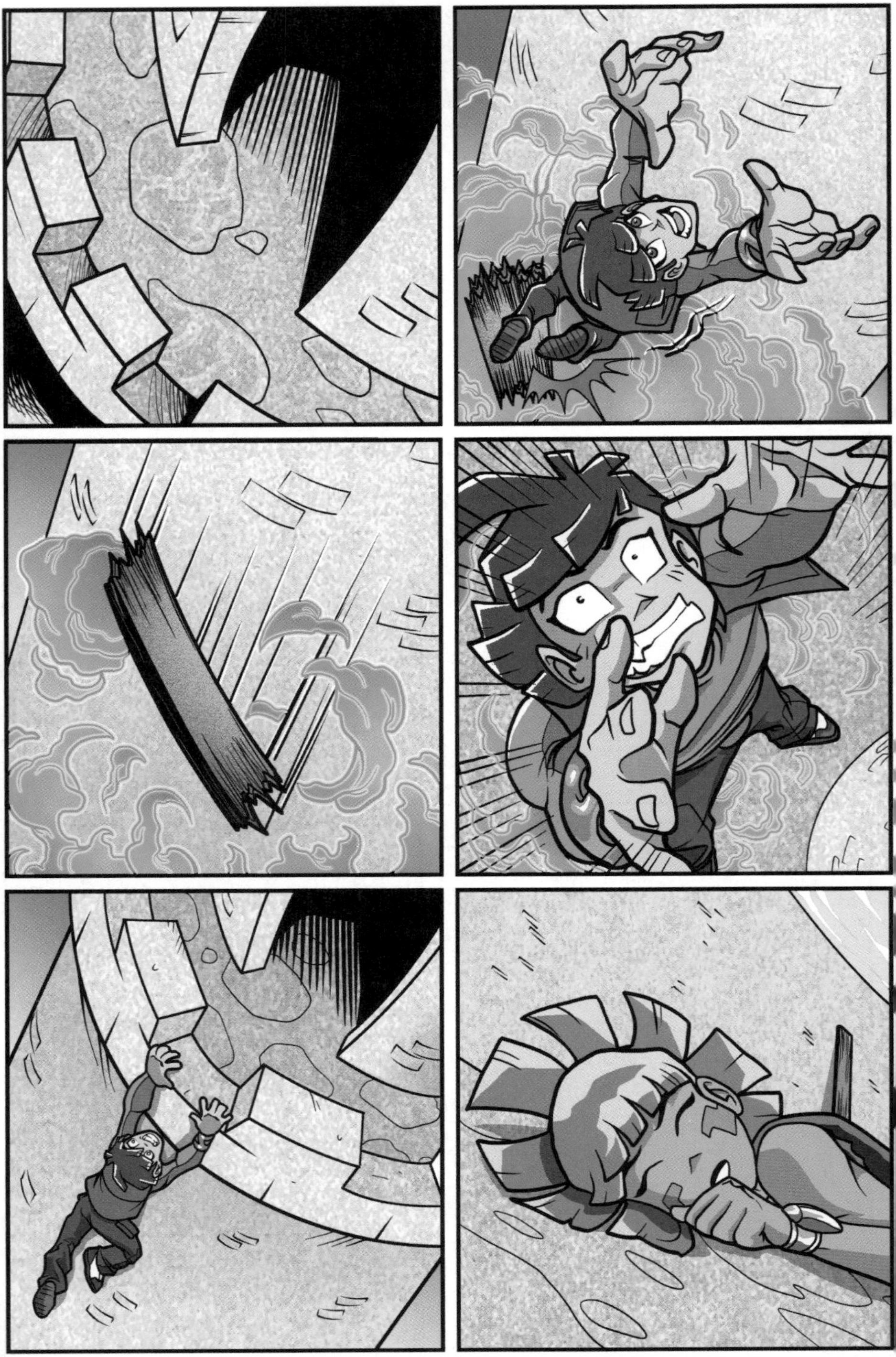

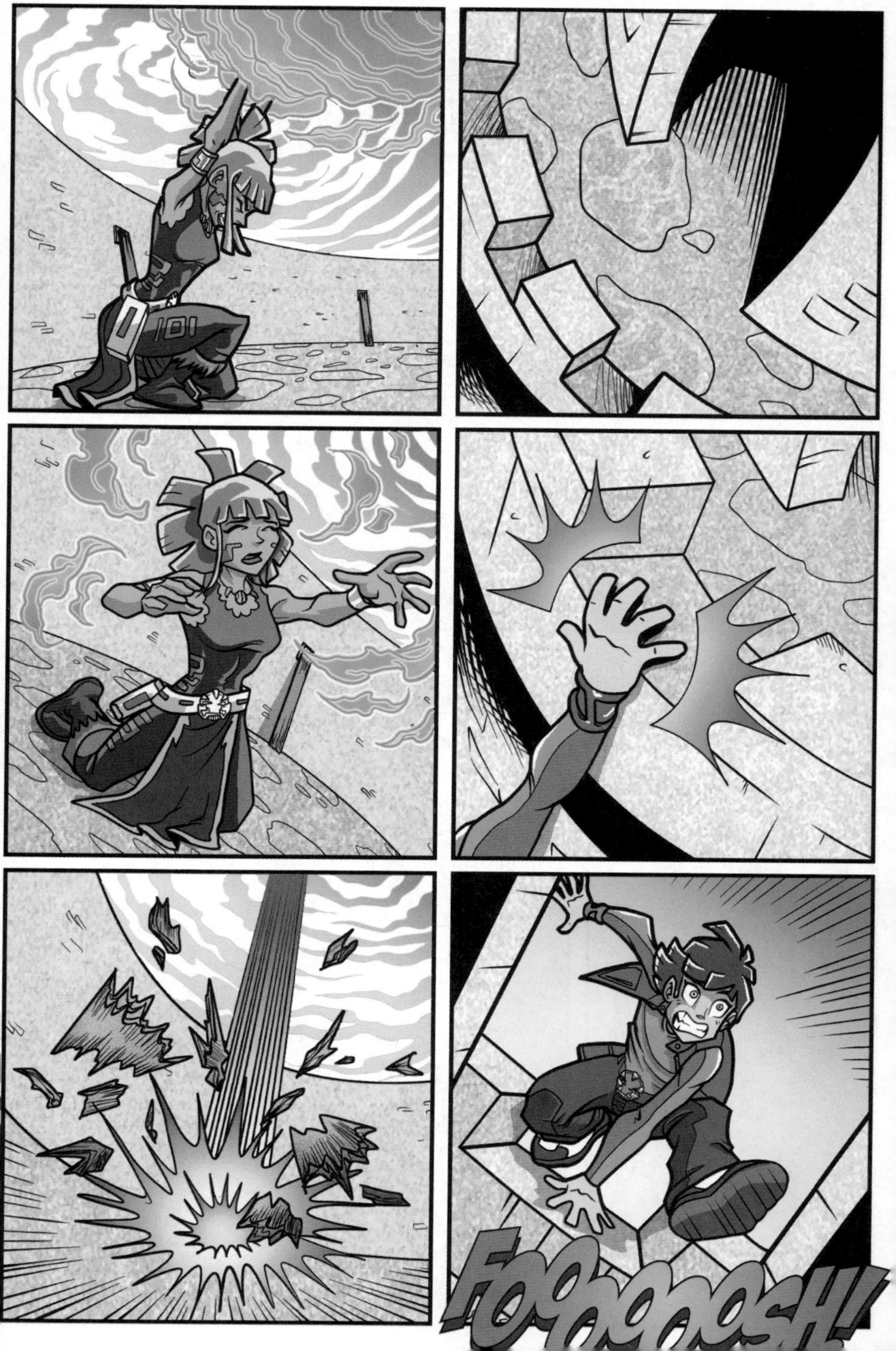
FOOOOOSH!

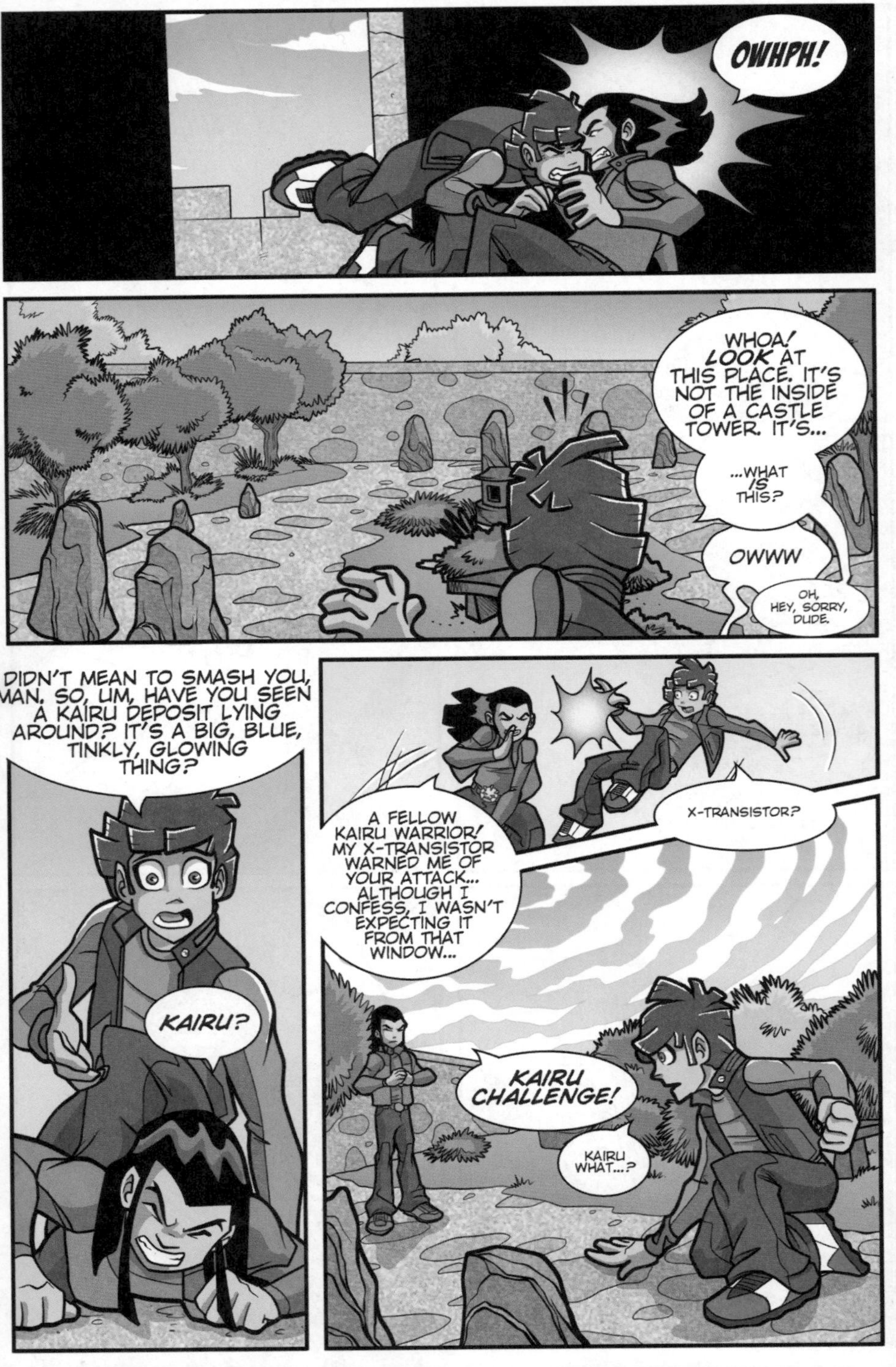
OWHPH!
WHOA! LOOK AT THIS PLACE. IT'S NOT THE INSIDE OF A CASTLE TOWER. IT'S...
...WHAT IS THIS?
OWWW
OH, HEY, SORRY, DUDE.
DIDN'T MEAN TO SMASH YOU, MAN. SO, UM, HAVE YOU SEEN A KAIRU DEPOSIT LYING AROUND? IT'S A BIG, BLUE, TINKLY, GLOWING THING?
KAIRU?
A FELLOW KAIRU WARRIOR! MY X-TRANSISTOR WARNED ME OF YOUR ATTACK... ALTHOUGH I CONFESS, I WASN'T EXPECTING IT FROM THAT WINDOW...
X-TRANSISTOR?
KAIRU CHALLENGE!
KAIRU WHAT...?

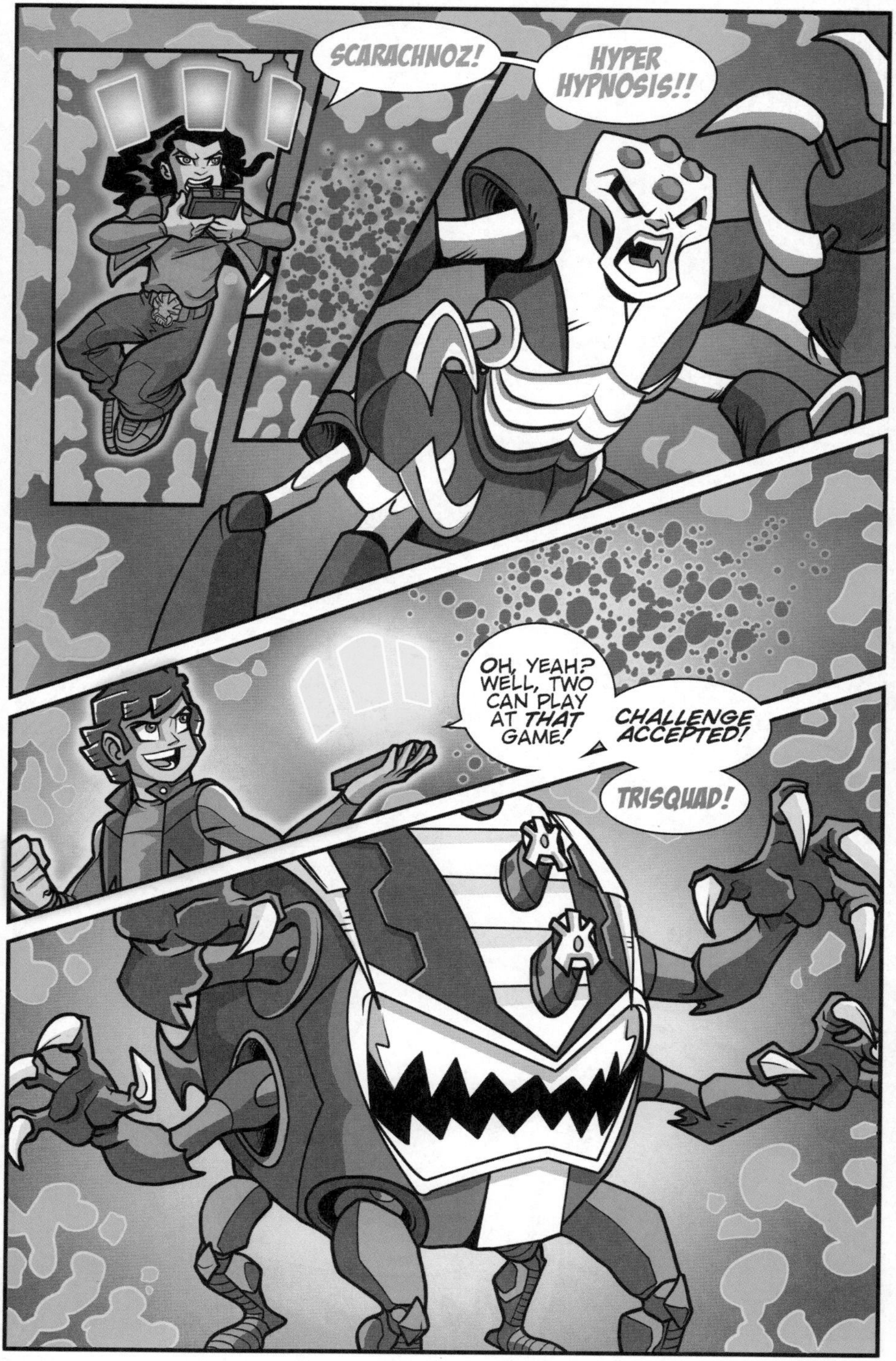
SCARACHNOZ!
HYPER HYPNOSIS!!
OH, YEAH? WELL, TWO CAN PLAY AT *THAT* GAME!
CHALLENGE ACCEPTED!
TRISQUAD!

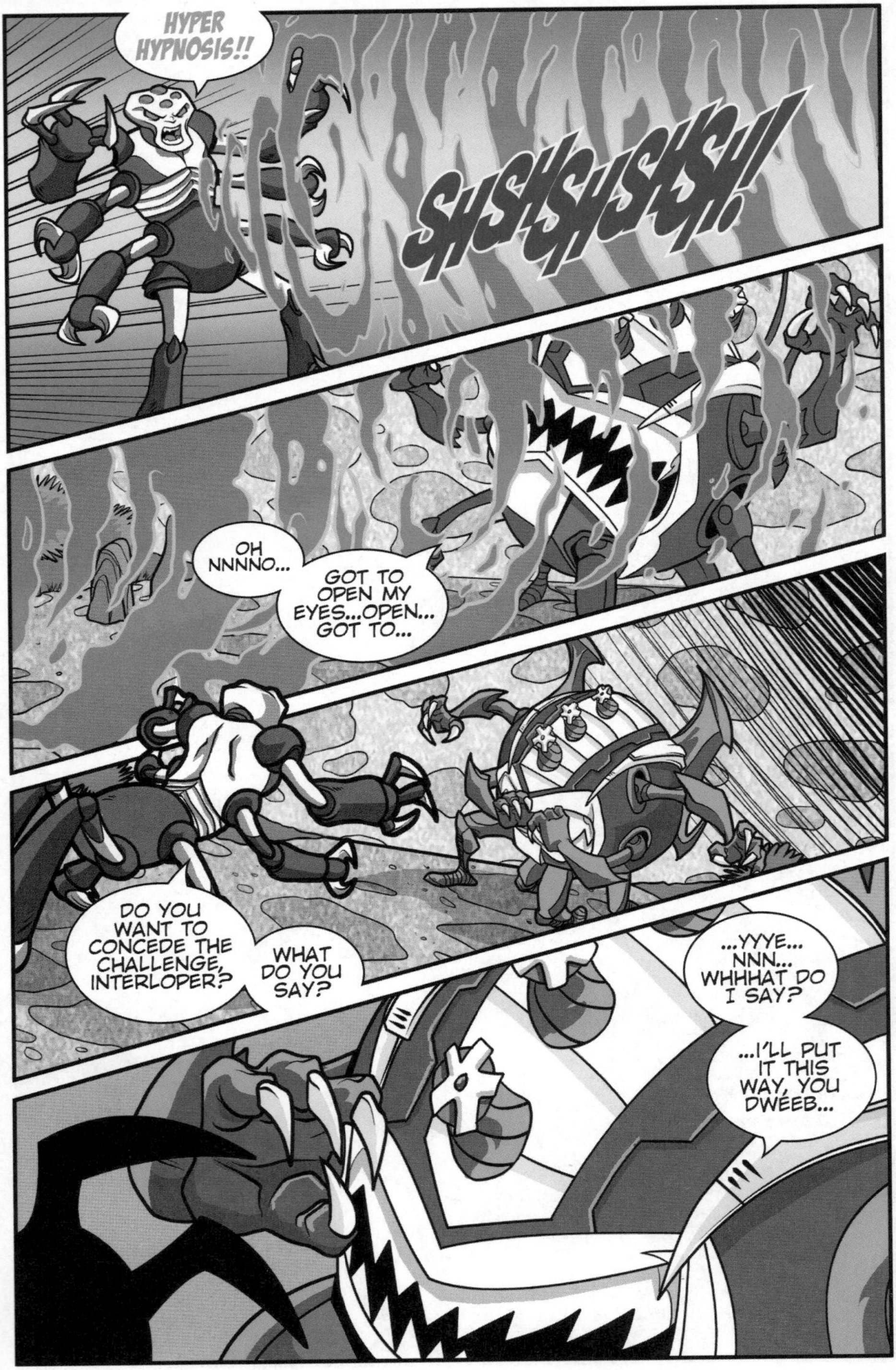
HYPER HYPNOSIS!!
SHSHSHSHSH!!
OH NNNNO...
GOT TO OPEN MY EYES...OPEN... GOT TO...
DO YOU WANT TO CONCEDE THE CHALLENGE, INTERLOPER?
WHAT DO YOU SAY?
...YYYE... NNN... WHHHAT DO I SAY?
...I'LL PUT IT THIS WAY, YOU DWEEB...

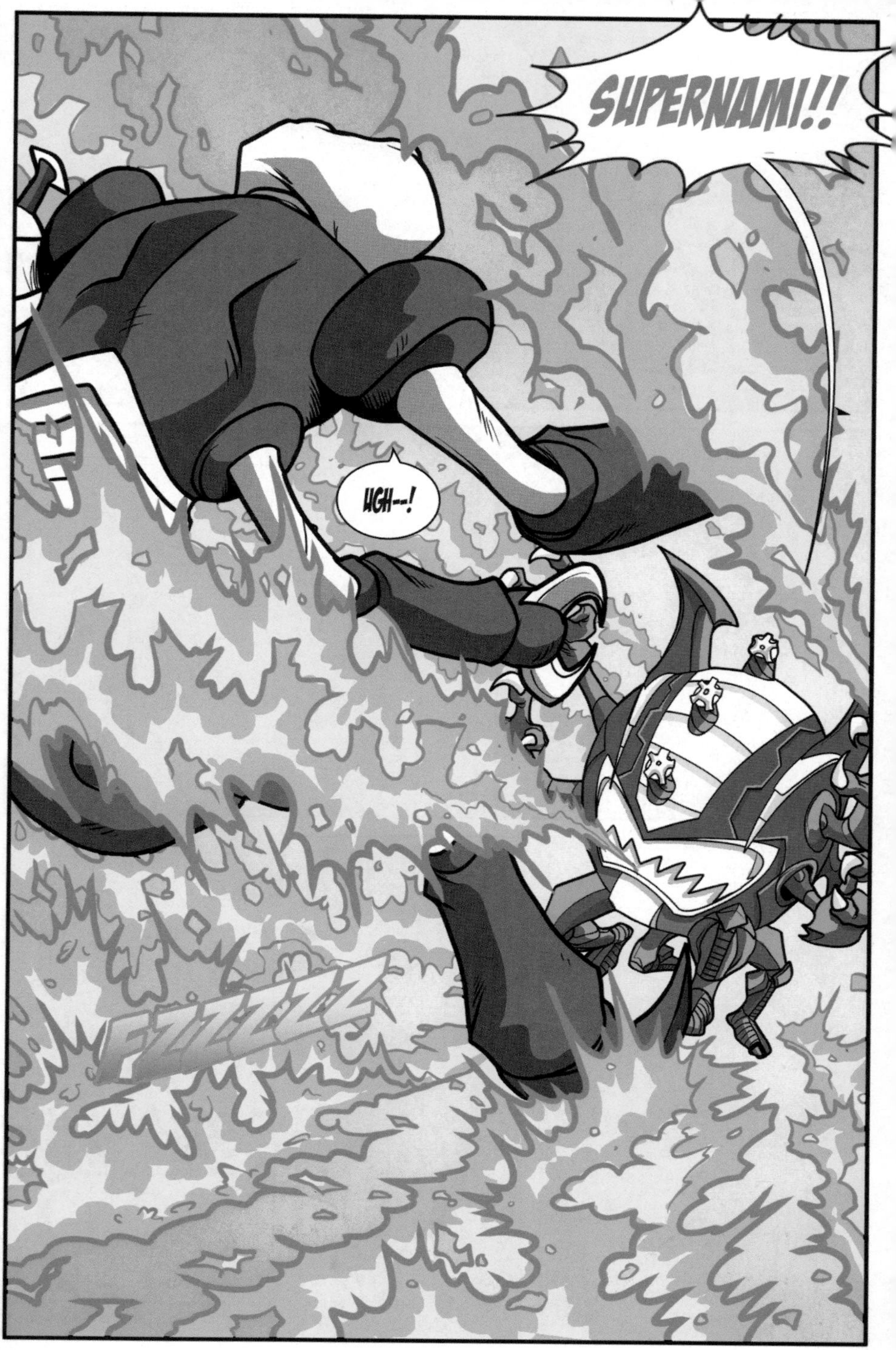
SUPERNAMI!!
UGH--!
FZZZZZ

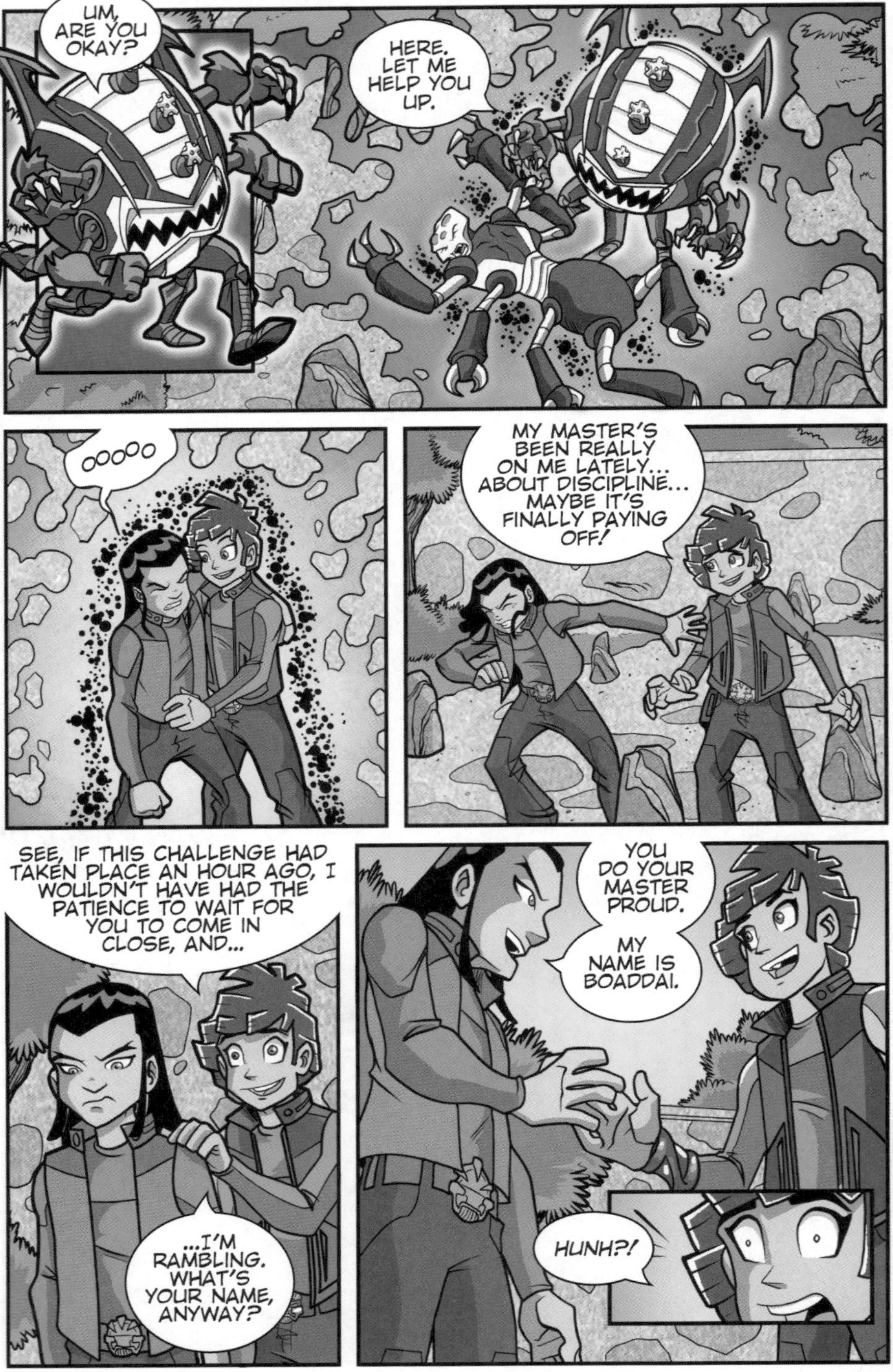
UM, ARE YOU OKAY?
HERE. LET ME HELP YOU UP.
OOOOO
MY MASTER'S BEEN REALLY ON ME LATELY... ABOUT DISCIPLINE... MAYBE IT'S FINALLY PAYING OFF!
SEE, IF THIS CHALLENGE HAD TAKEN PLACE AN HOUR AGO, I WOULDN'T HAVE HAD THE PATIENCE TO WAIT FOR YOU TO COME IN CLOSE, AND...
...I'M RAMBLING. WHAT'S YOUR NAME, ANYWAY?
YOU DO YOUR MASTER PROUD.
MY NAME IS BOADDAI.
HUNH?!

Early sketch by Zack Turner of
Mawdi the Gilfreem from REDAKAI Vol. 1!

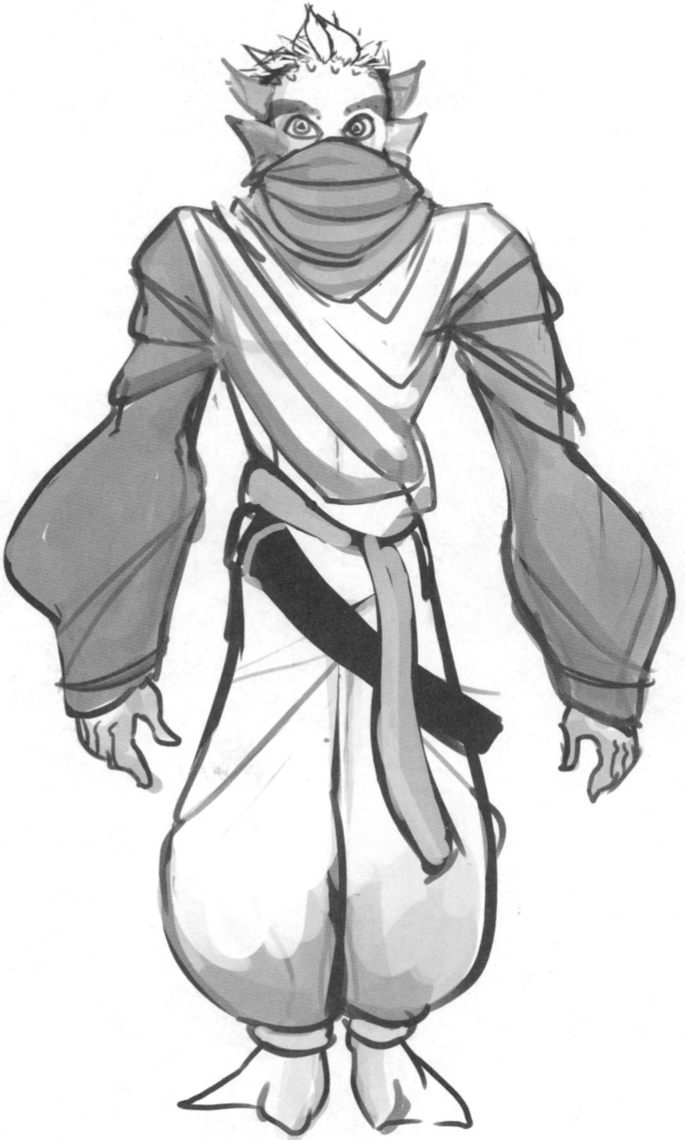

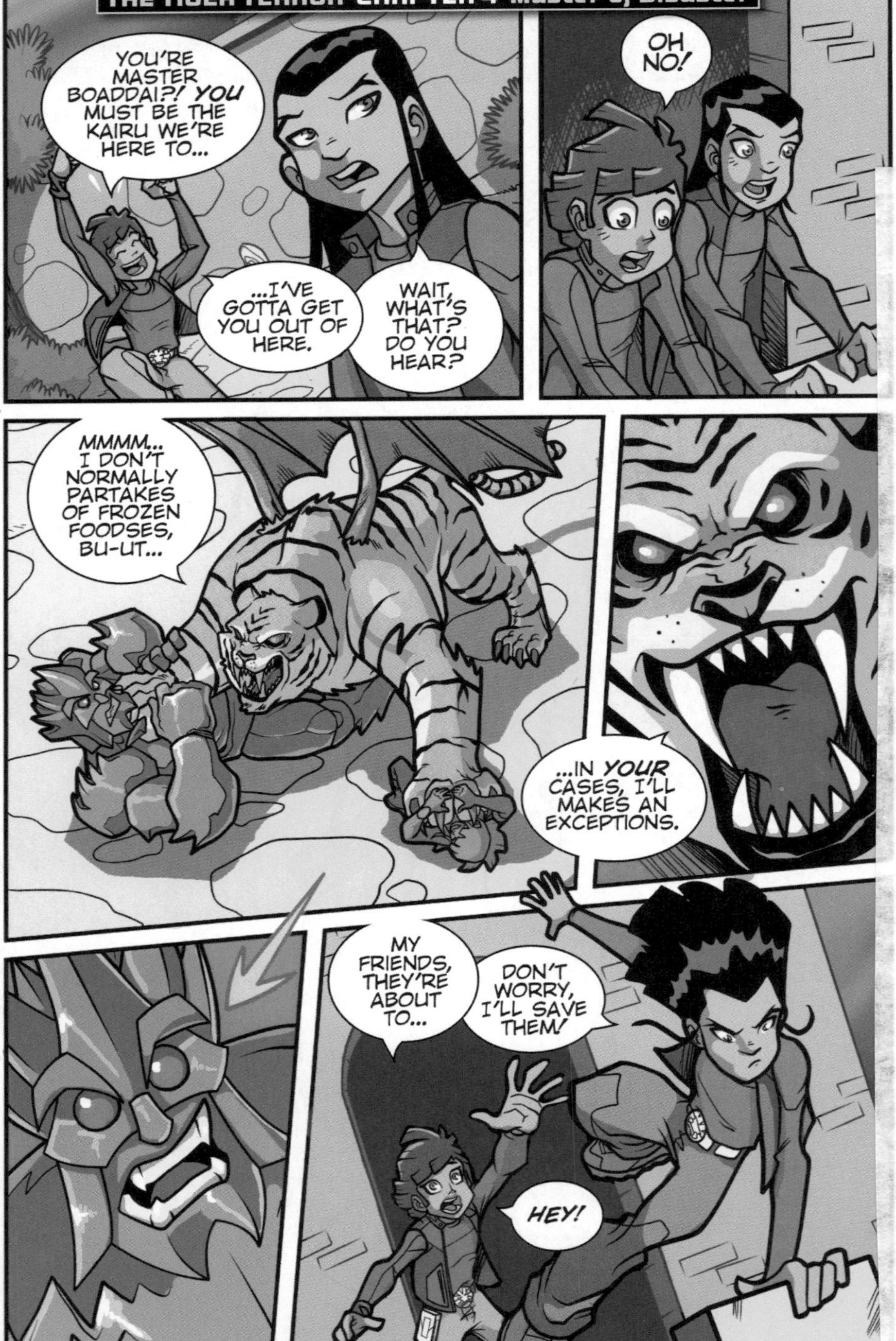
YOU'RE MASTER BOADDAI?! YOU MUST BE THE KAIRU WE'RE HERE TO...
...I'VE GOTTA GET YOU OUT OF HERE.
WAIT, WHAT'S THAT? DO YOU HEAR?
OH NO!
MMMM... I DON'T NORMALLY PARTAKES OF FROZEN FOODSES, BU-UT...
...IN YOUR CASES, I'LL MAKES AN EXCEPTIONS.
MY FRIENDS, THEY'RE ABOUT TO...
DON'T WORRY, I'LL SAVE THEM!
HEY!

Story by **Terrance Griep** Art by **Write Height Media** Colors by **Zack Turner**

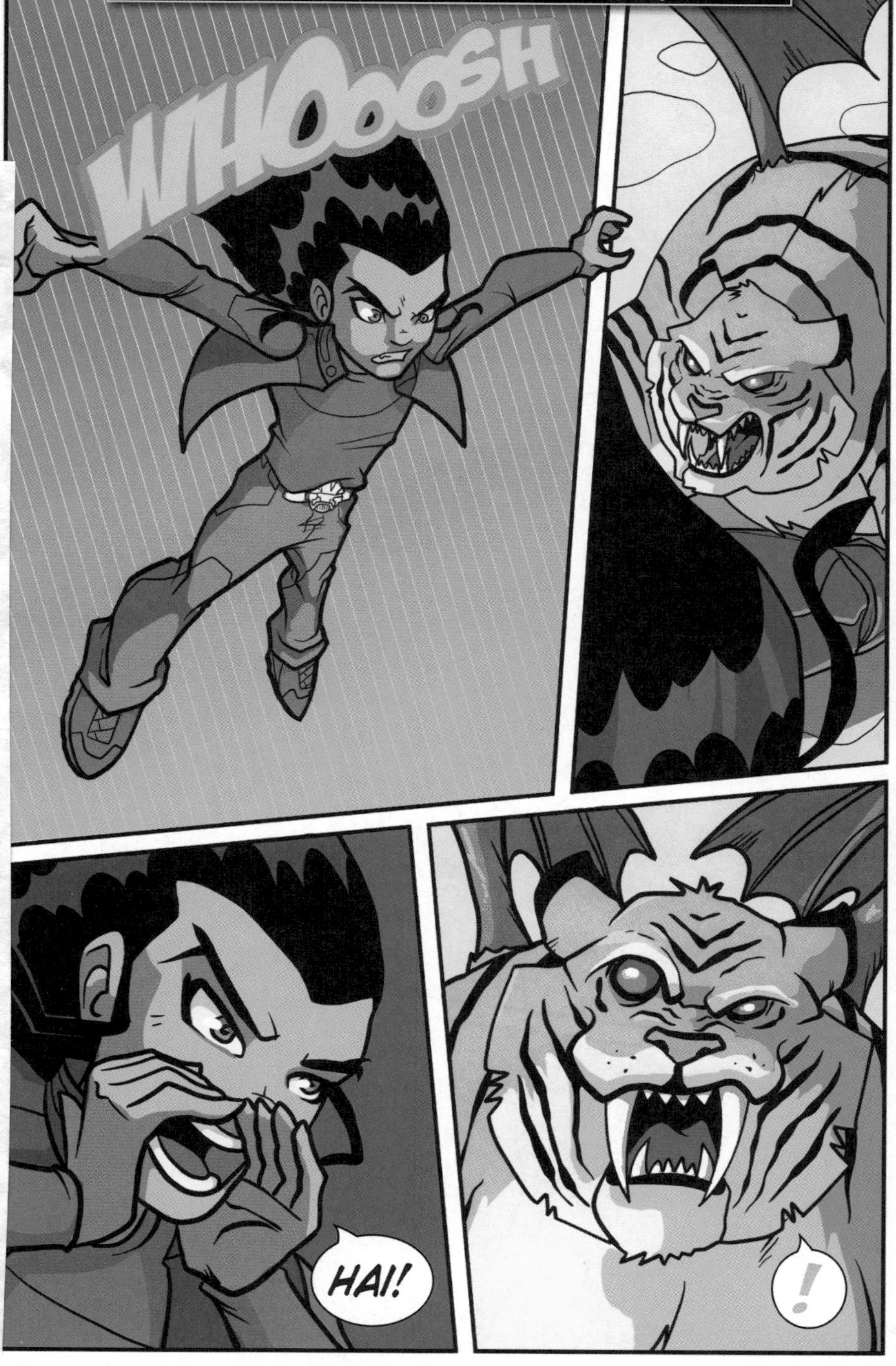
WHOOOOSH
HAI!
!

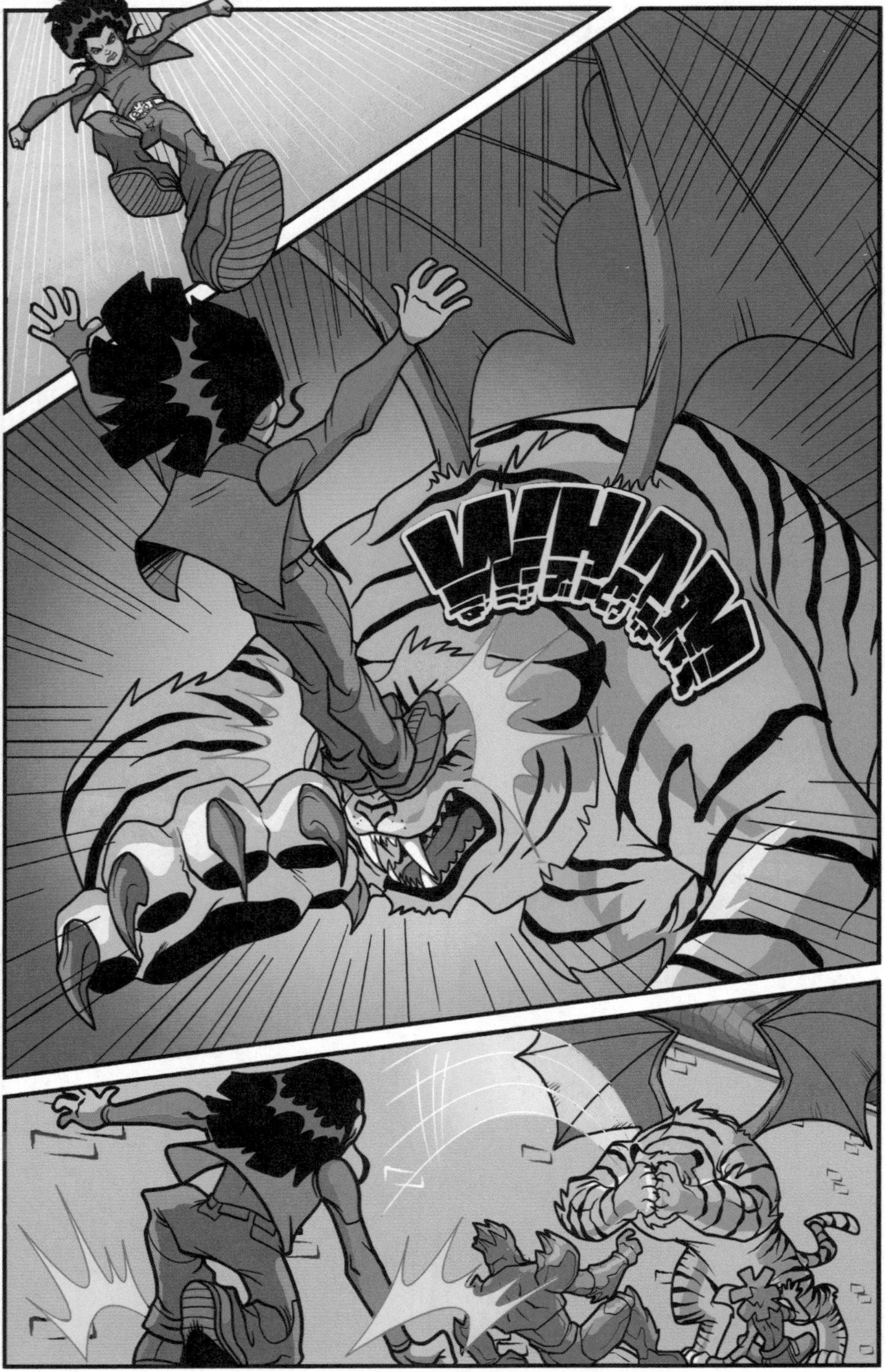
WHAM

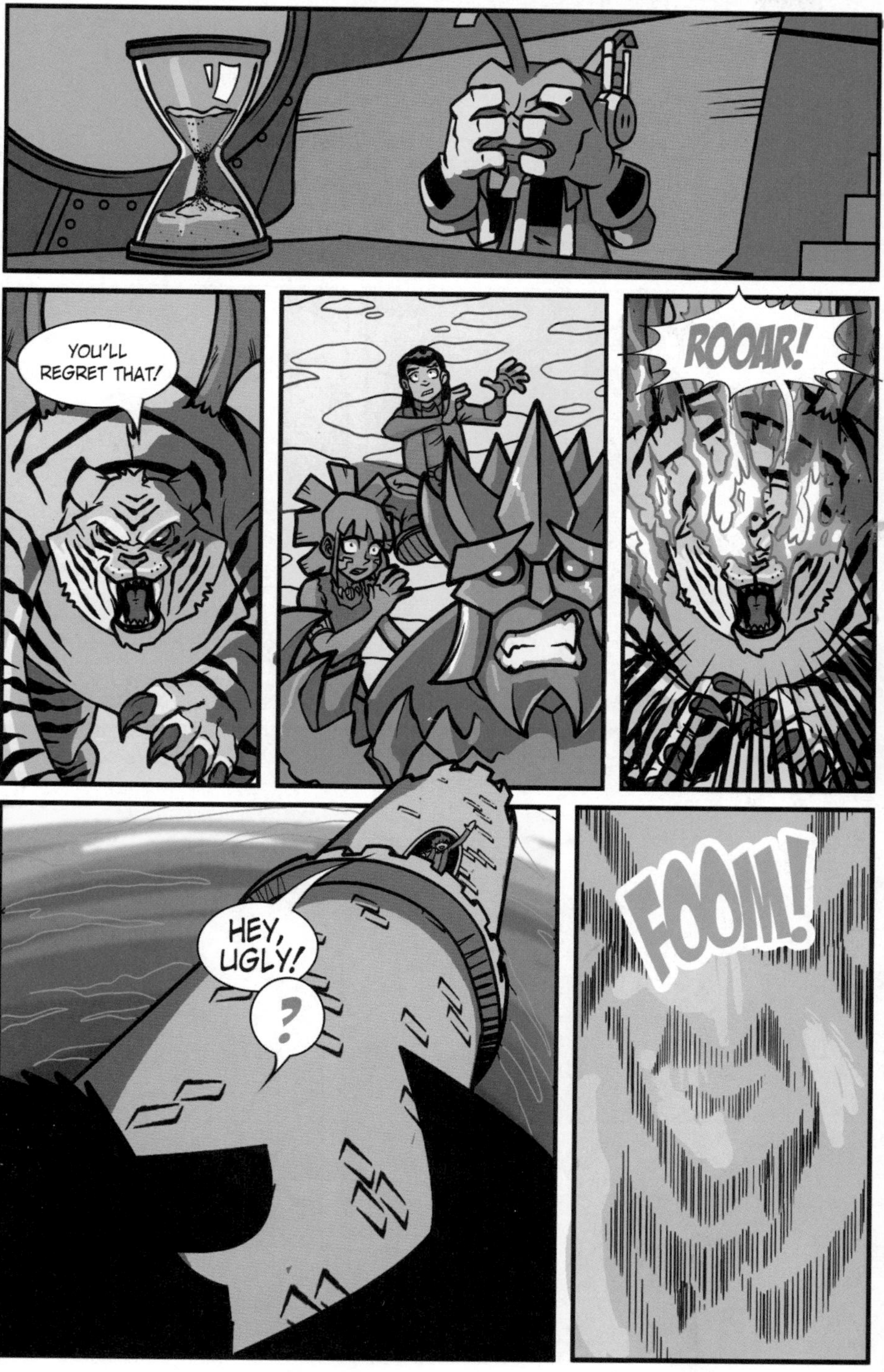
YOU'LL REGRET THAT!
ROOAR!
HEY, UGLY!
?
FOOM!

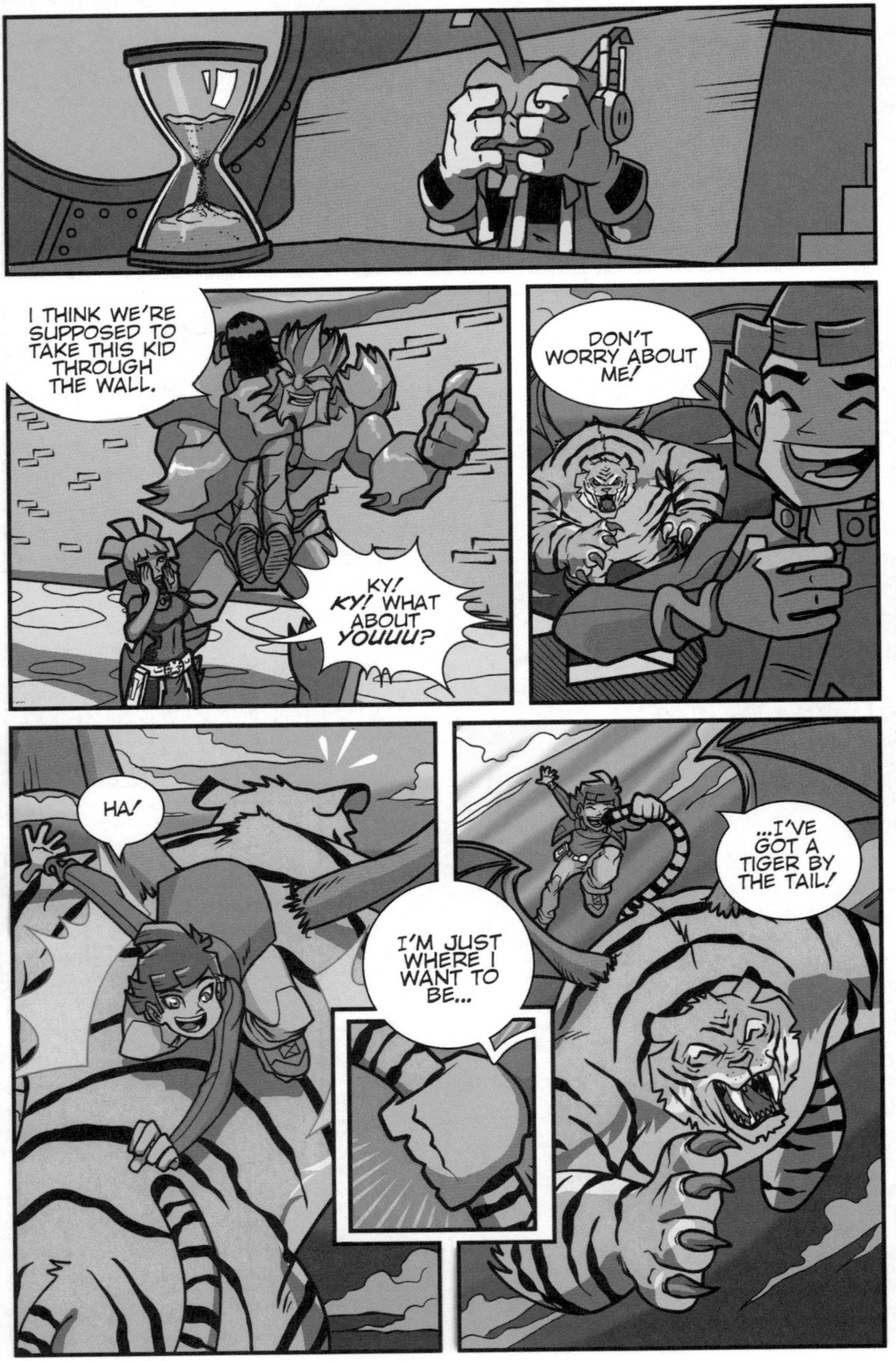
I THINK WE'RE SUPPOSED TO TAKE THIS KID THROUGH THE WALL.
KY! KY! WHAT ABOUT YOUUU?
DON'T WORRY ABOUT ME!
HA!
I'M JUST WHERE I WANT TO BE...
...I'VE GOT A TIGER BY THE TAIL!

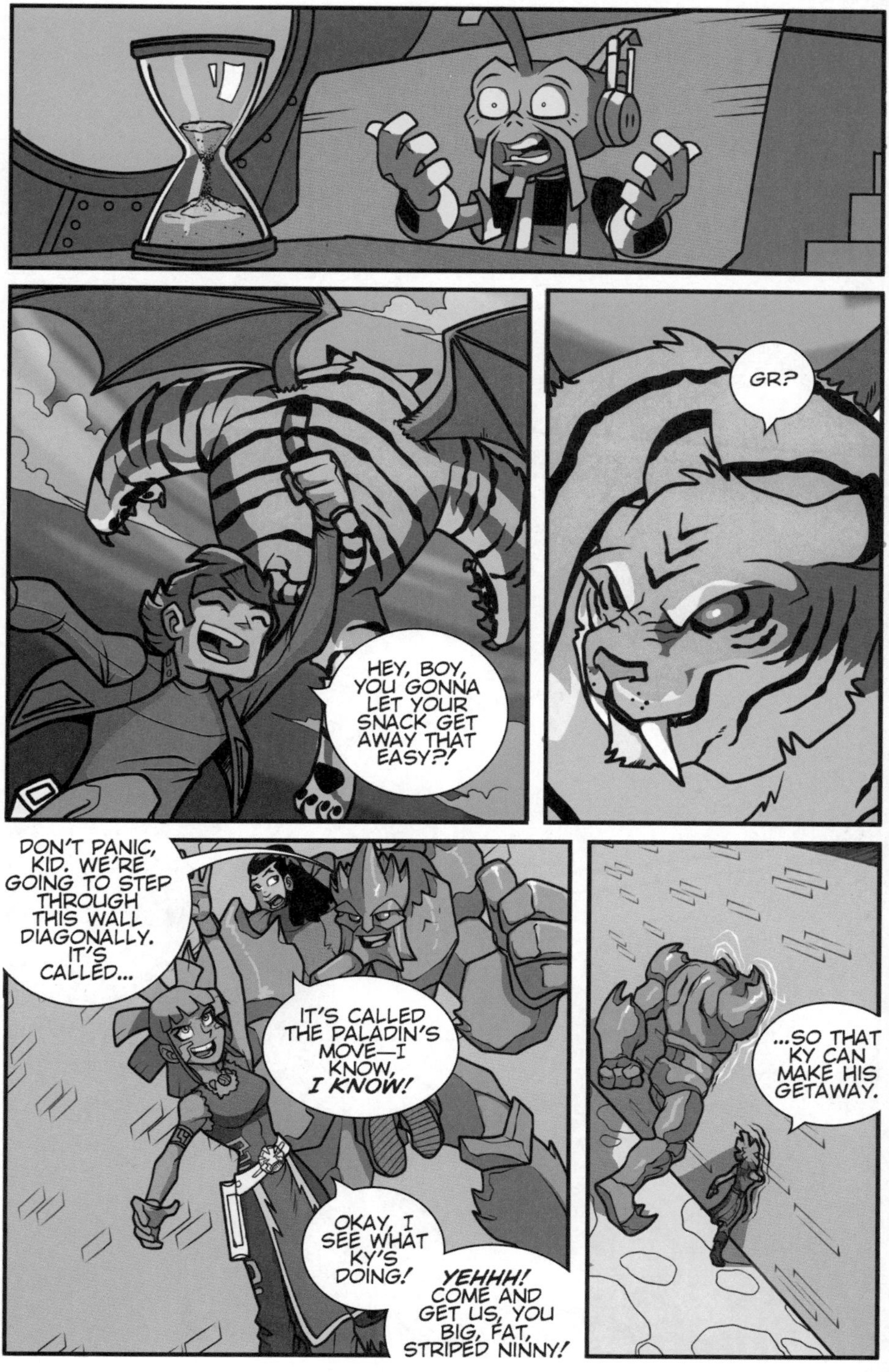
GR?
HEY, BOY, YOU GONNA LET YOUR SNACK GET AWAY THAT EASY?!
DON'T PANIC, KID. WE'RE GOING TO STEP THROUGH THIS WALL DIAGONALLY. IT'S CALLED...
IT'S CALLED THE PALADIN'S MOVE—I KNOW, I KNOW!
OKAY, I SEE WHAT KY'S DOING!
YEHHH! COME AND GET US, YOU BIG, FAT, STRIPED NINNY!
...SO THAT KY CAN MAKE HIS GETAWAY.

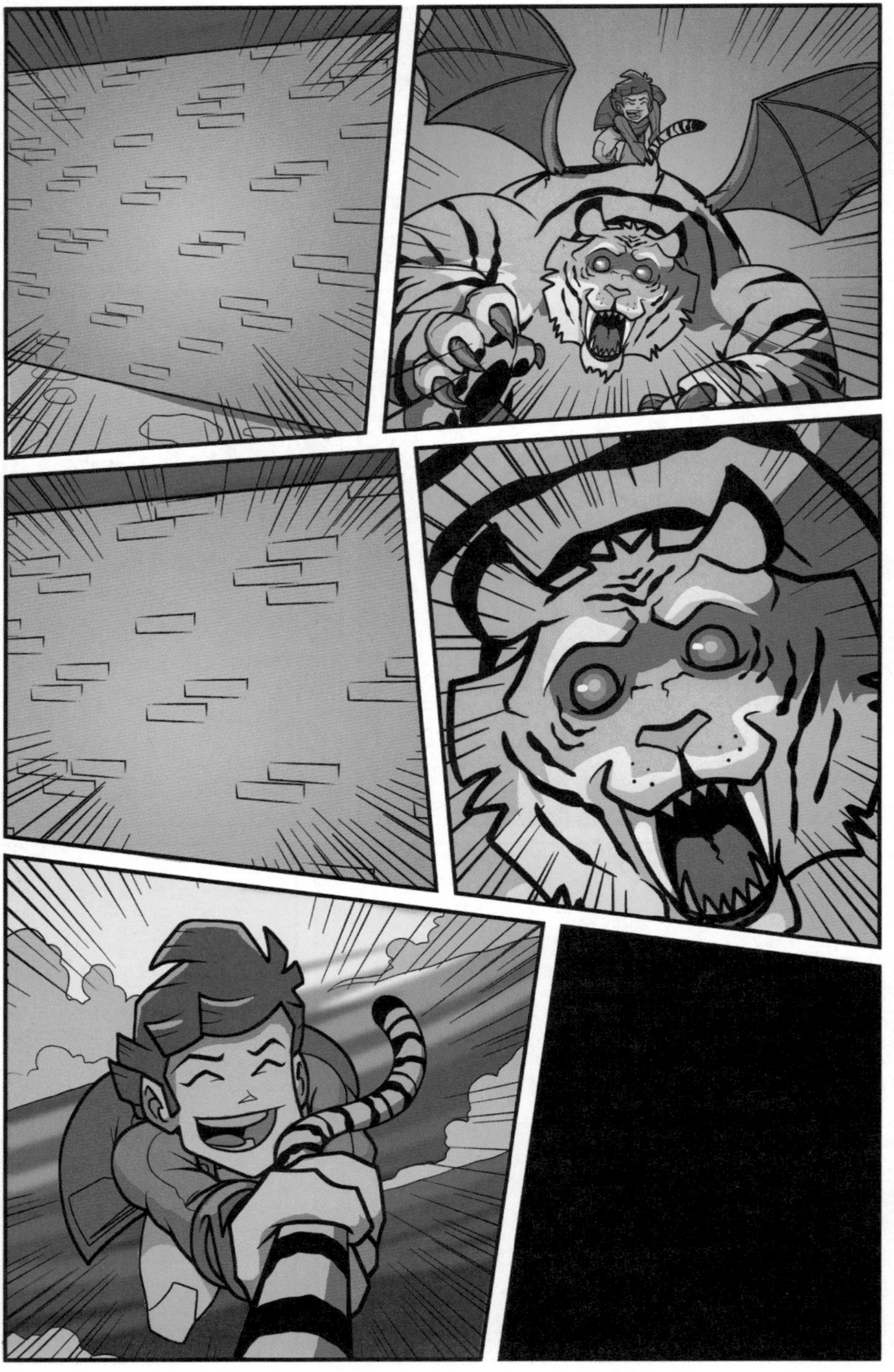

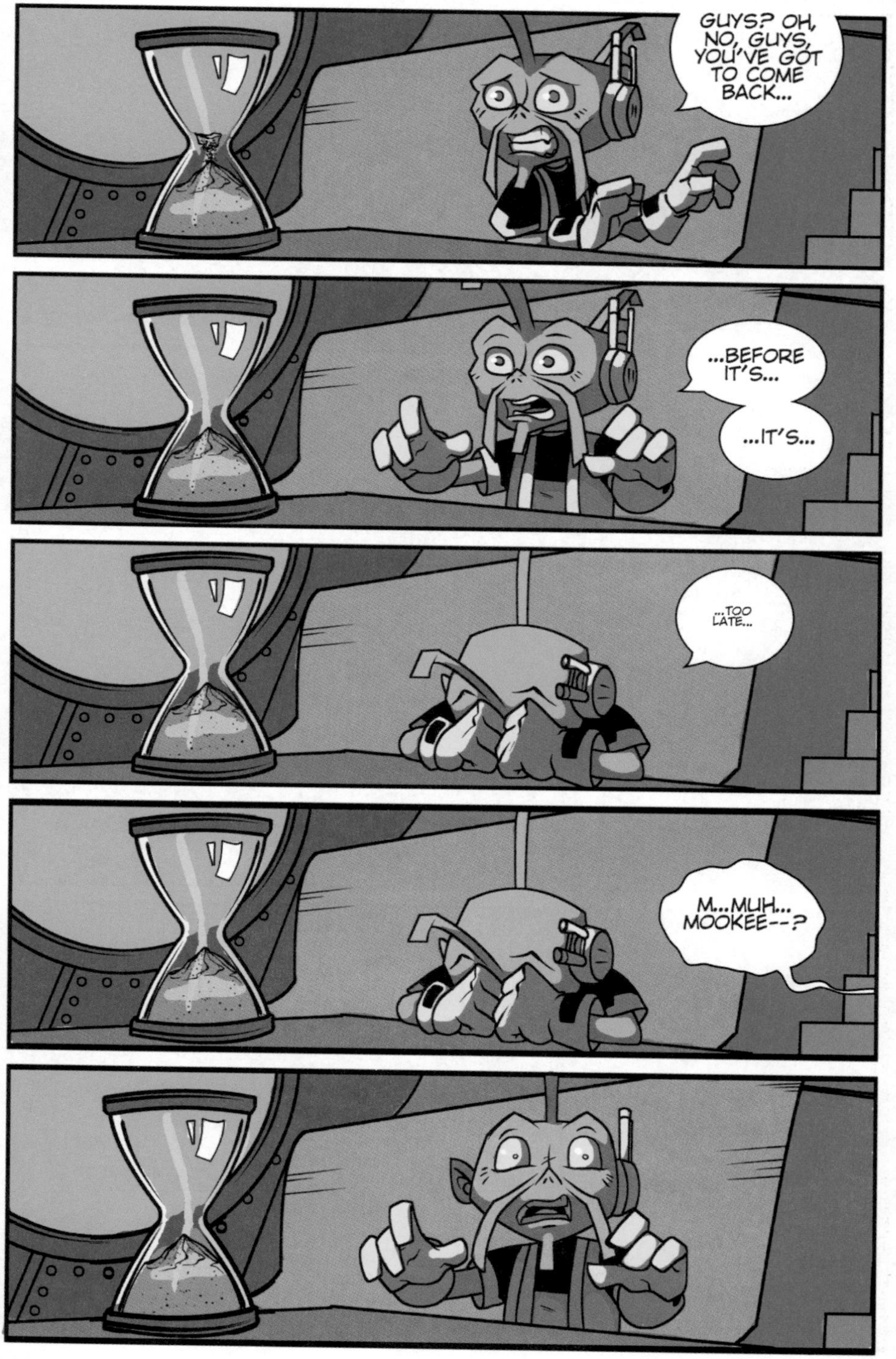
GUYS? OH, NO, GUYS, YOU'VE GOT TO COME BACK...
...BEFORE IT'S...
...IT'S...
...TOO LATE...
M...MUH... MOOKEE--?

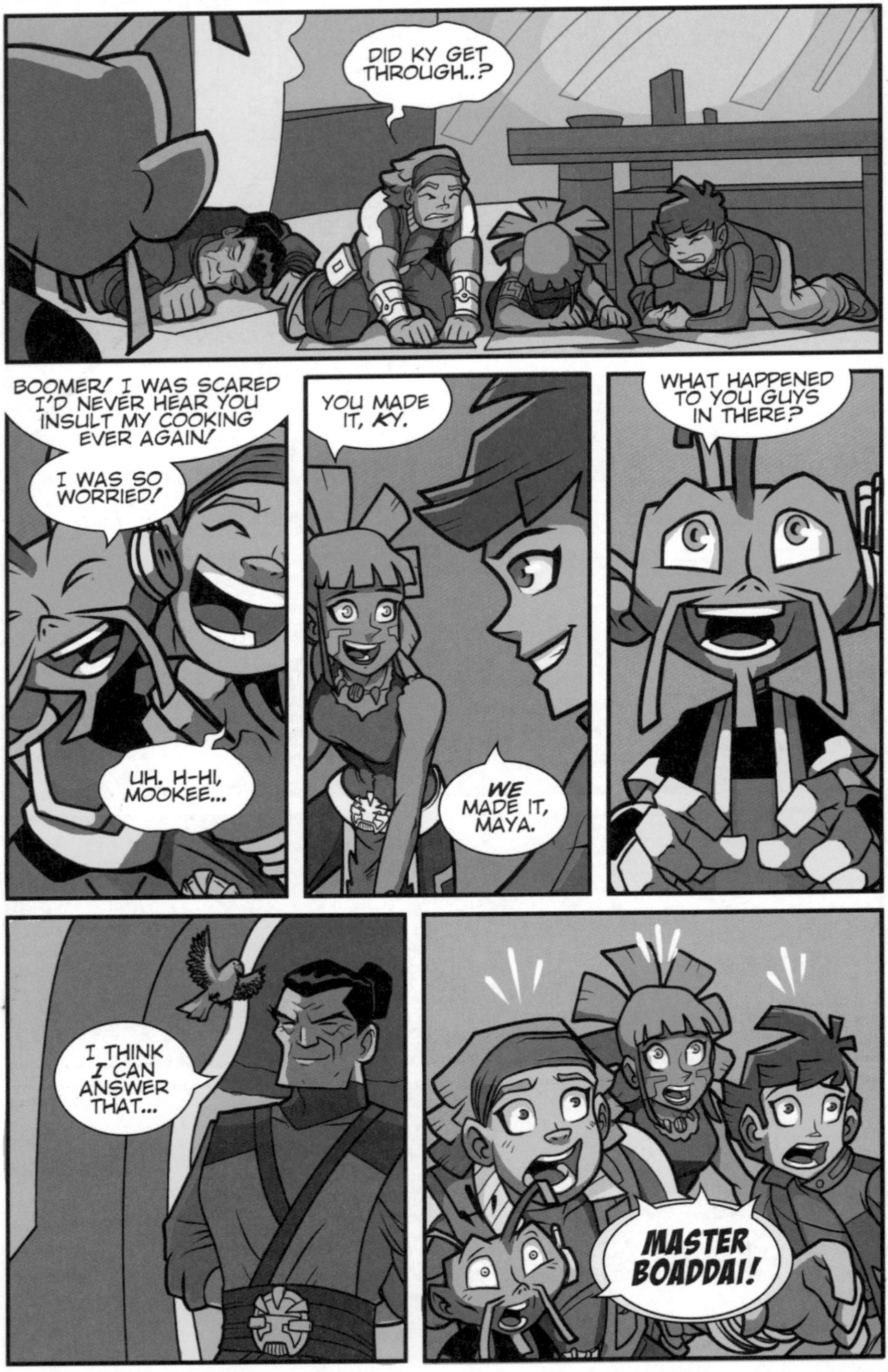

DID KY GET THROUGH..?
BOOMER! I WAS SCARED I'D NEVER HEAR YOU INSULT MY COOKING EVER AGAIN!
I WAS SO WORRIED!
UH. H-HI, MOOKEE...
YOU MADE IT, *KY*.
WE MADE IT, MAYA.
WHAT HAPPENED TO YOU GUYS IN THERE?
I THINK *I* CAN ANSWER THAT...
MASTER BOADDAI!

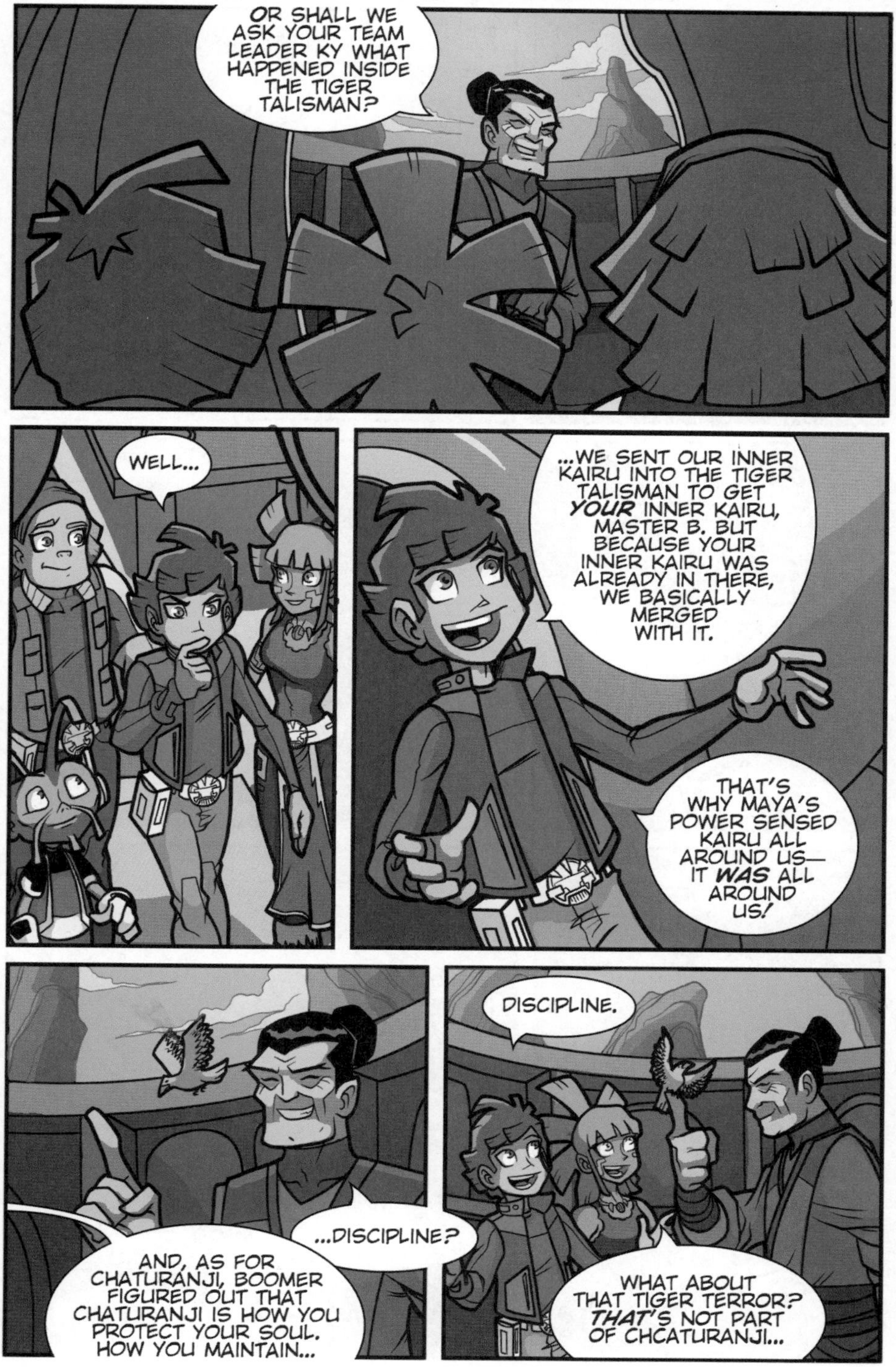
OR SHALL WE ASK YOUR TEAM LEADER KY WHAT HAPPENED INSIDE THE TIGER TALISMAN?
WELL...
...WE SENT OUR INNER KAIRU INTO THE TIGER TALISMAN TO GET ***YOUR*** INNER KAIRU, MASTER B. BUT BECAUSE YOUR INNER KAIRU WAS ALREADY IN THERE, WE BASICALLY MERGED WITH IT.
THAT'S WHY MAYA'S POWER SENSED KAIRU ALL AROUND US— IT ***WAS*** ALL AROUND US!
AND, AS FOR CHATURANJI, BOOMER FIGURED OUT THAT CHATURANJI IS HOW YOU PROTECT YOUR SOUL. HOW YOU MAINTAIN...
...DISCIPLINE?
DISCIPLINE.
WHAT ABOUT THAT TIGER TERROR? ***THAT***'S NOT PART OF CHCATURANJI...

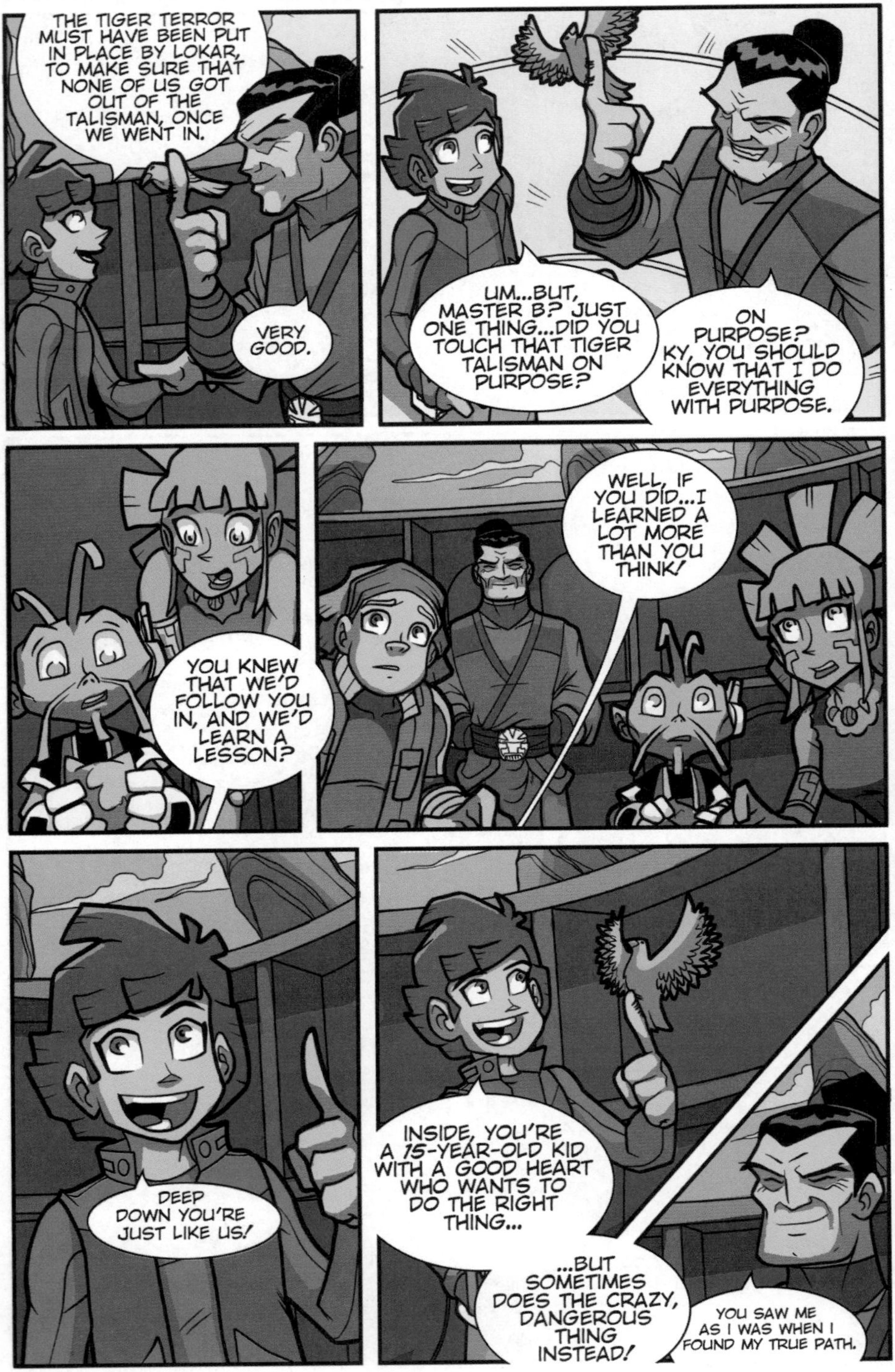
THE TIGER TERROR MUST HAVE BEEN PUT IN PLACE BY LOKAR, TO MAKE SURE THAT NONE OF US GOT OUT OF THE TALISMAN, ONCE WE WENT IN.
VERY GOOD.
UM...BUT, MASTER B? JUST ONE THING...DID YOU TOUCH THAT TIGER TALISMAN ON PURPOSE?
ON PURPOSE? KY, YOU SHOULD KNOW THAT I DO EVERYTHING WITH PURPOSE.
YOU KNEW THAT WE'D FOLLOW YOU IN, AND WE'D LEARN A LESSON?
WELL, IF YOU DID...I LEARNED A LOT MORE THAN YOU THINK!
DEEP DOWN YOU'RE JUST LIKE US!
INSIDE, YOU'RE A 15-YEAR-OLD KID WITH A GOOD HEART WHO WANTS TO DO THE RIGHT THING...
...BUT SOMETIMES DOES THE CRAZY, DANGEROUS THING INSTEAD!
YOU SAW ME AS I WAS WHEN I FOUND MY TRUE PATH.

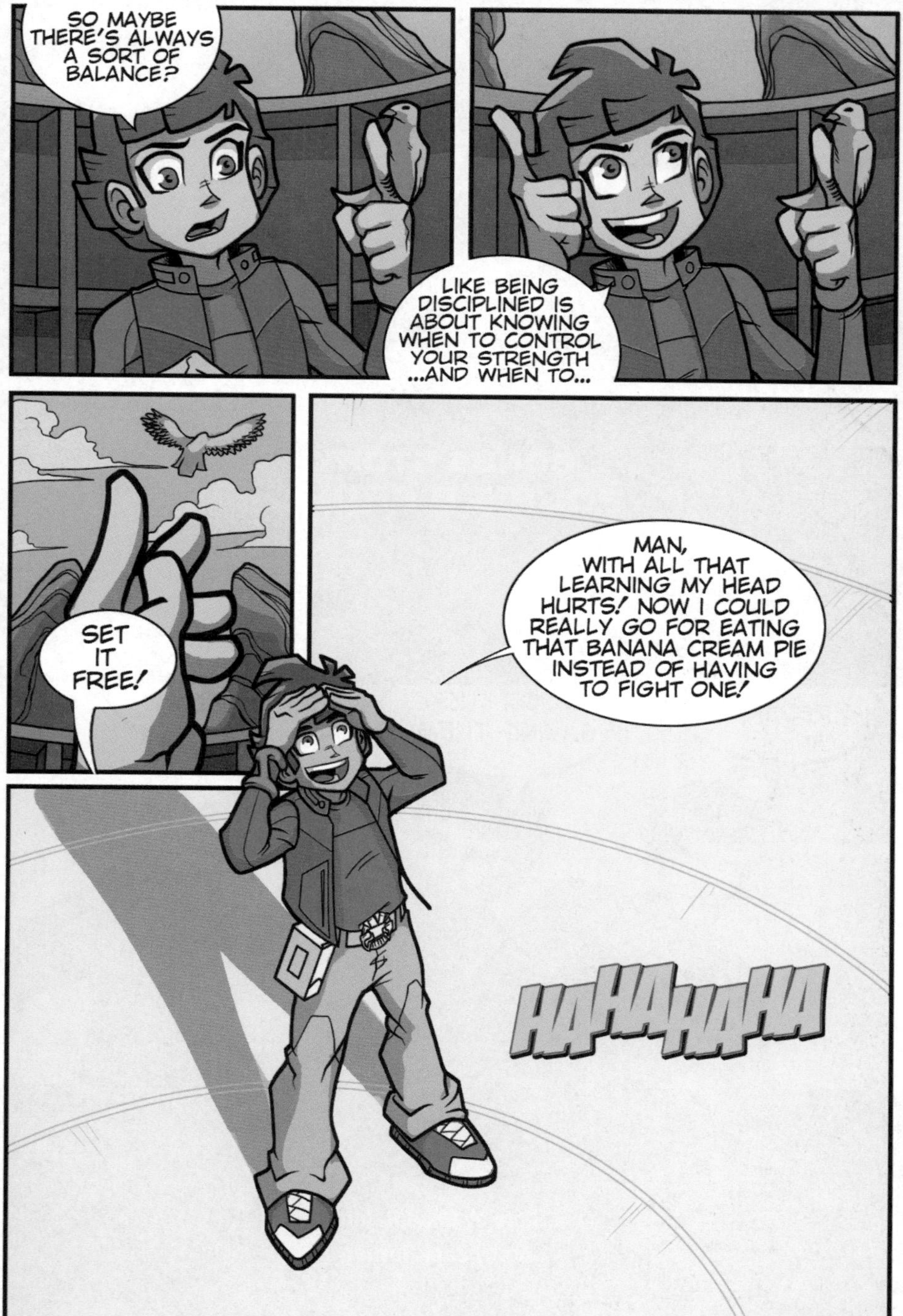
SO MAYBE THERE'S ALWAYS A SORT OF BALANCE?
LIKE BEING DISCIPLINED IS ABOUT KNOWING WHEN TO CONTROL YOUR STRENGTH ...AND WHEN TO...
SET IT FREE!
MAN, WITH ALL THAT LEARNING MY HEAD HURTS! NOW I COULD REALLY GO FOR EATING THAT BANANA CREAM PIE INSTEAD OF HAVING TO FIGHT ONE!
HAHAHAHA
END

BONUS STORY
FOUR'S A CROWD

A REDAKAI!
GOOD LUCK SAVING THEM!
YOU'LL NEED IT!

Story by **Mike Raicht**
Art by **Zack Turner**

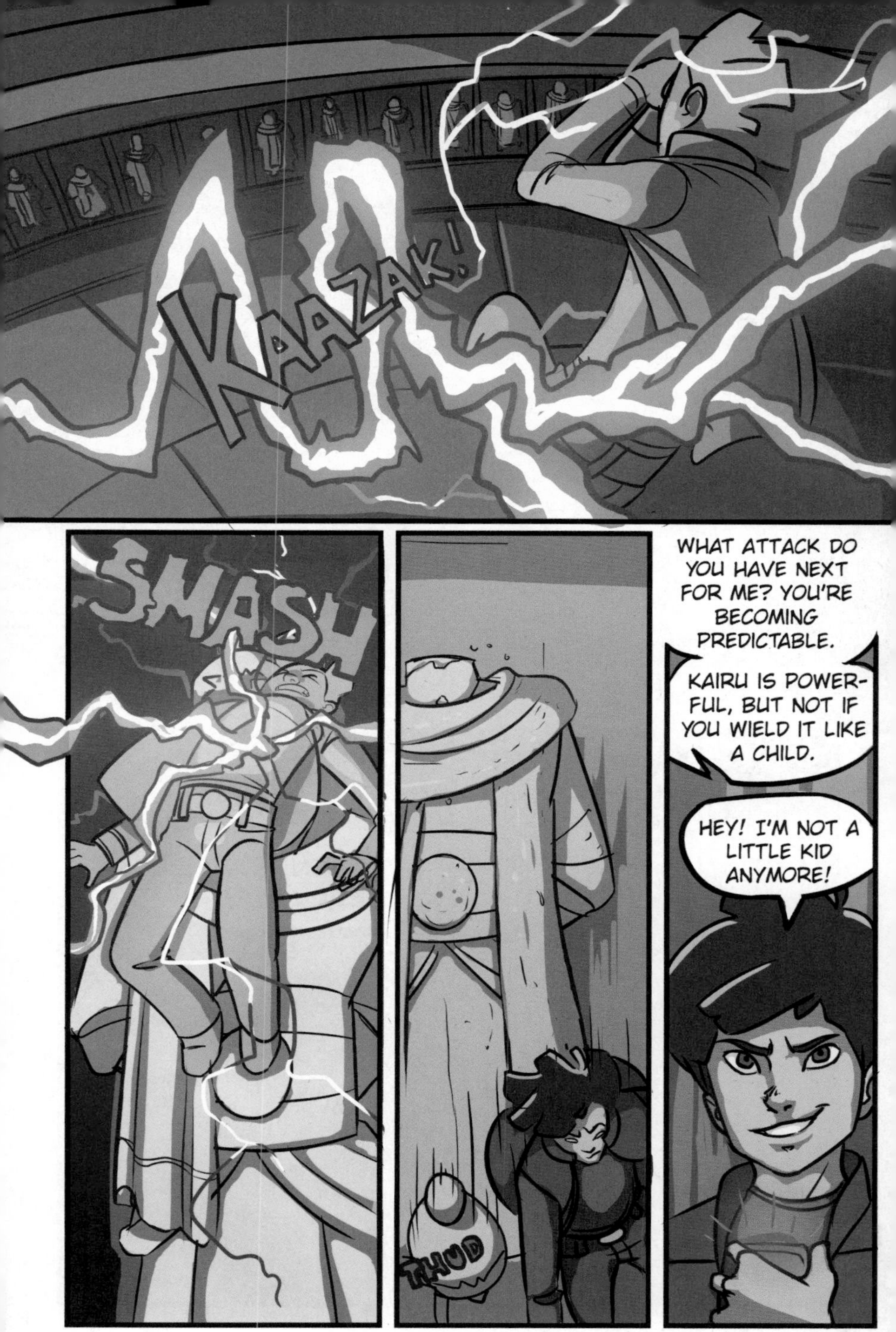
KAAZAK!
SMASH
THUD
WHAT ATTACK DO YOU HAVE NEXT FOR ME? YOU'RE BECOMING PREDICTABLE.
KAIRU IS POWER-FUL, BUT NOT IF YOU WIELD IT LIKE A CHILD.
HEY! I'M NOT A LITTLE KID ANYMORE!

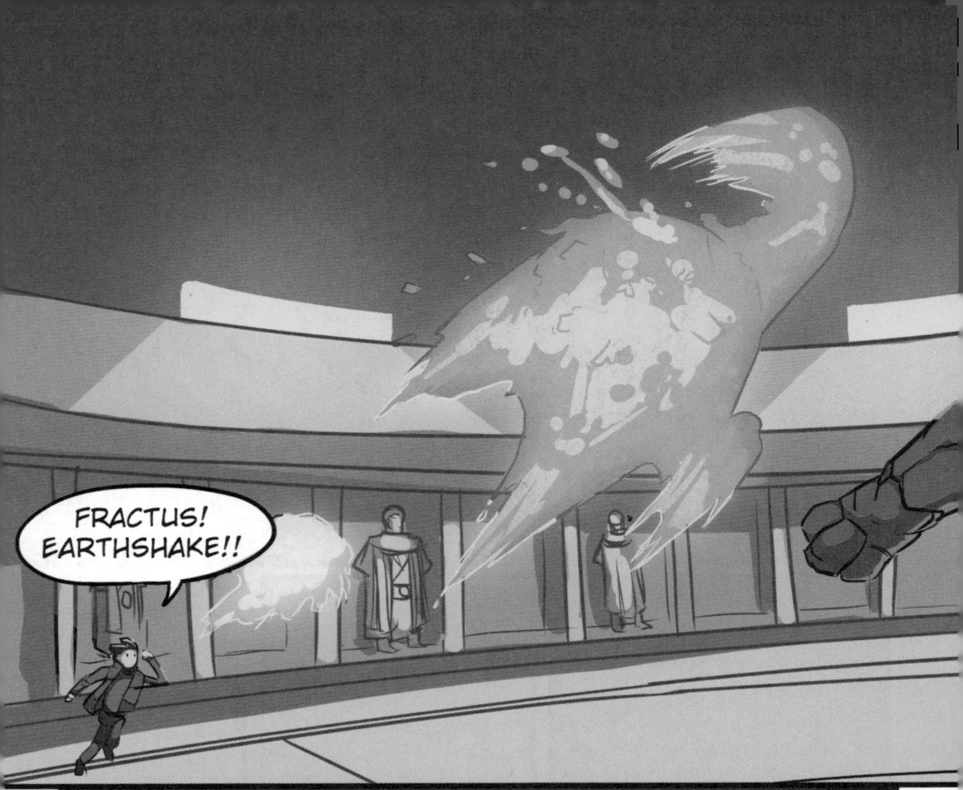
FRACTUS! EARTHSHAKE!!

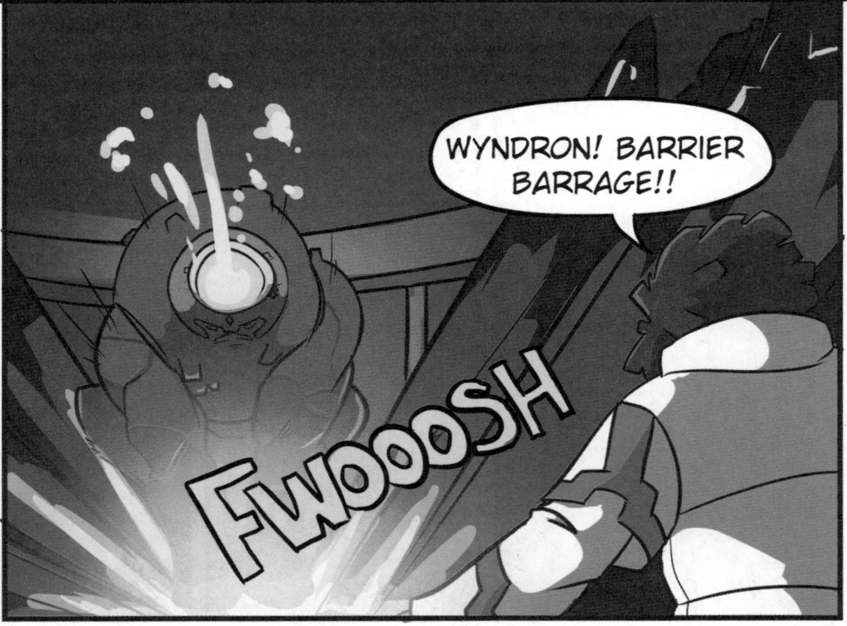
WYNDRON! BARRIER BARRAGE!!
FWOOOSH

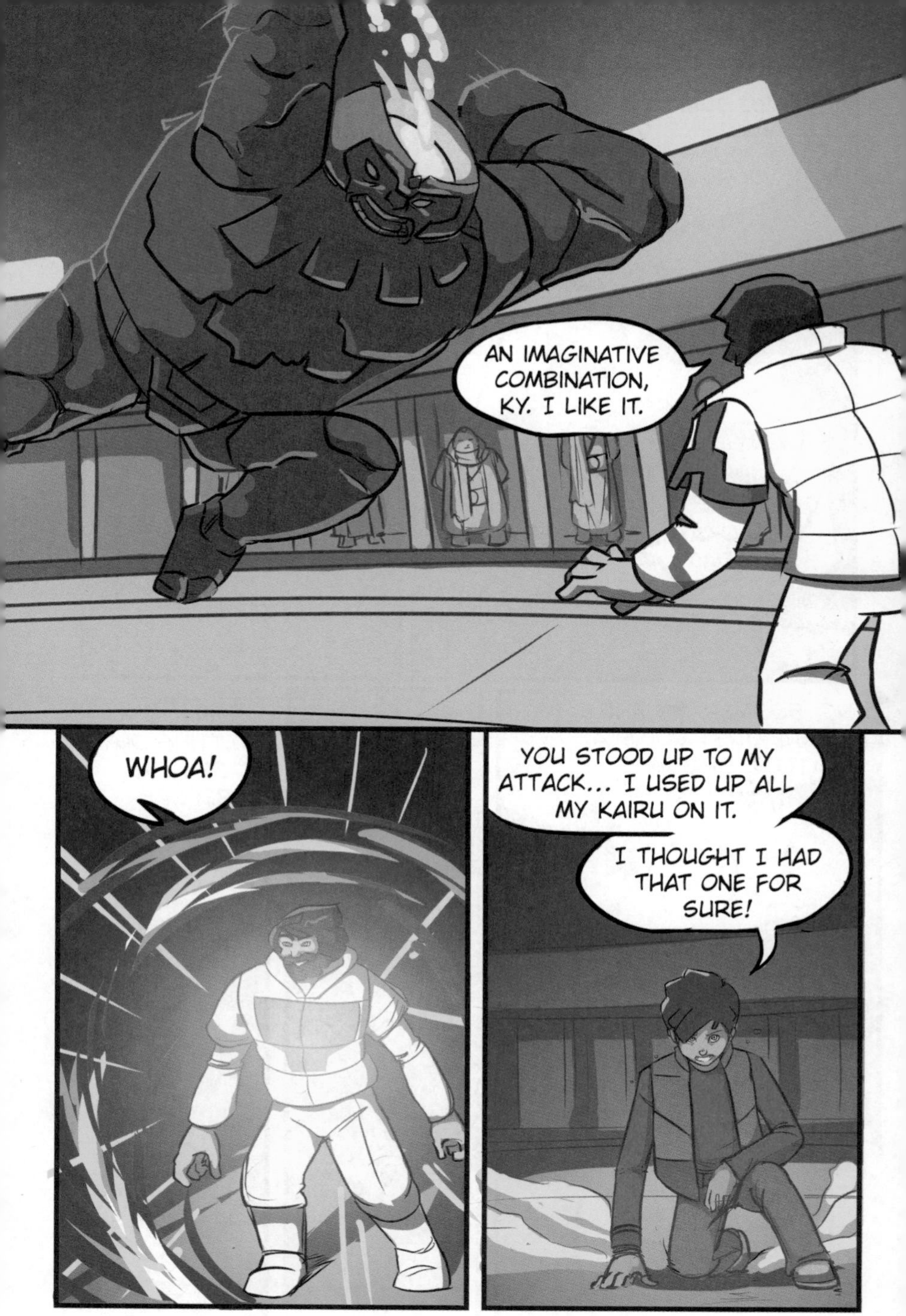
AN IMAGINATIVE COMBINATION, KY. I LIKE IT.
WHOA!
YOU STOOD UP TO MY ATTACK... I USED UP ALL MY KAIRU ON IT.
I THOUGHT I HAD THAT ONE FOR SURE!

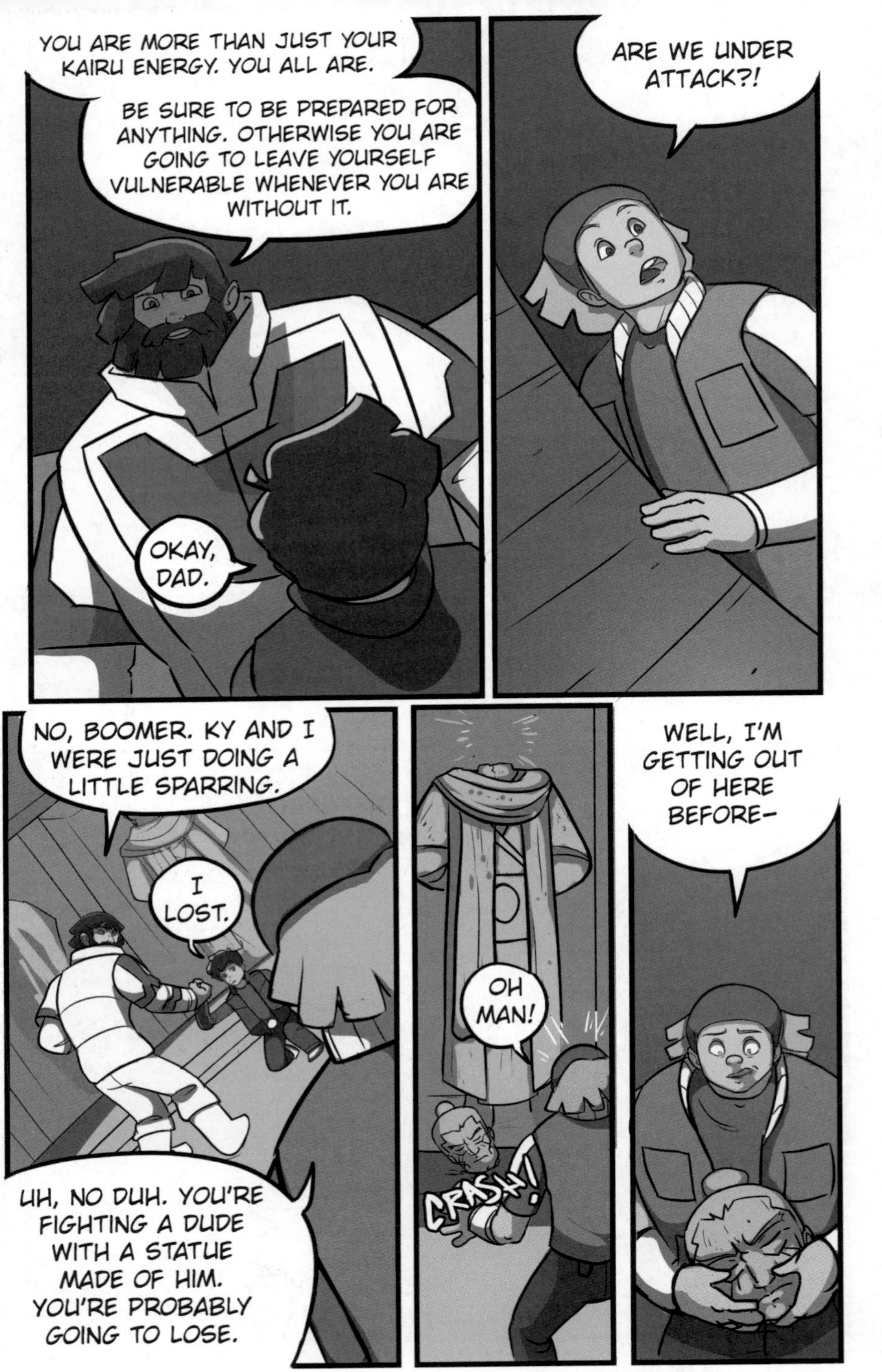
YOU ARE MORE THAN JUST YOUR KAIRU ENERGY. YOU ALL ARE.
BE SURE TO BE PREPARED FOR ANYTHING. OTHERWISE YOU ARE GOING TO LEAVE YOURSELF VULNERABLE WHENEVER YOU ARE WITHOUT IT.
OKAY, DAD.
ARE WE UNDER ATTACK?!
NO, BOOMER. KY AND I WERE JUST DOING A LITTLE SPARRING.
I LOST.
UH, NO DUH. YOU'RE FIGHTING A DUDE WITH A STATUE MADE OF HIM. YOU'RE PROBABLY GOING TO LOSE.
OH MAN!
CRASH!
WELL, I'M GETTING OUT OF HERE BEFORE-

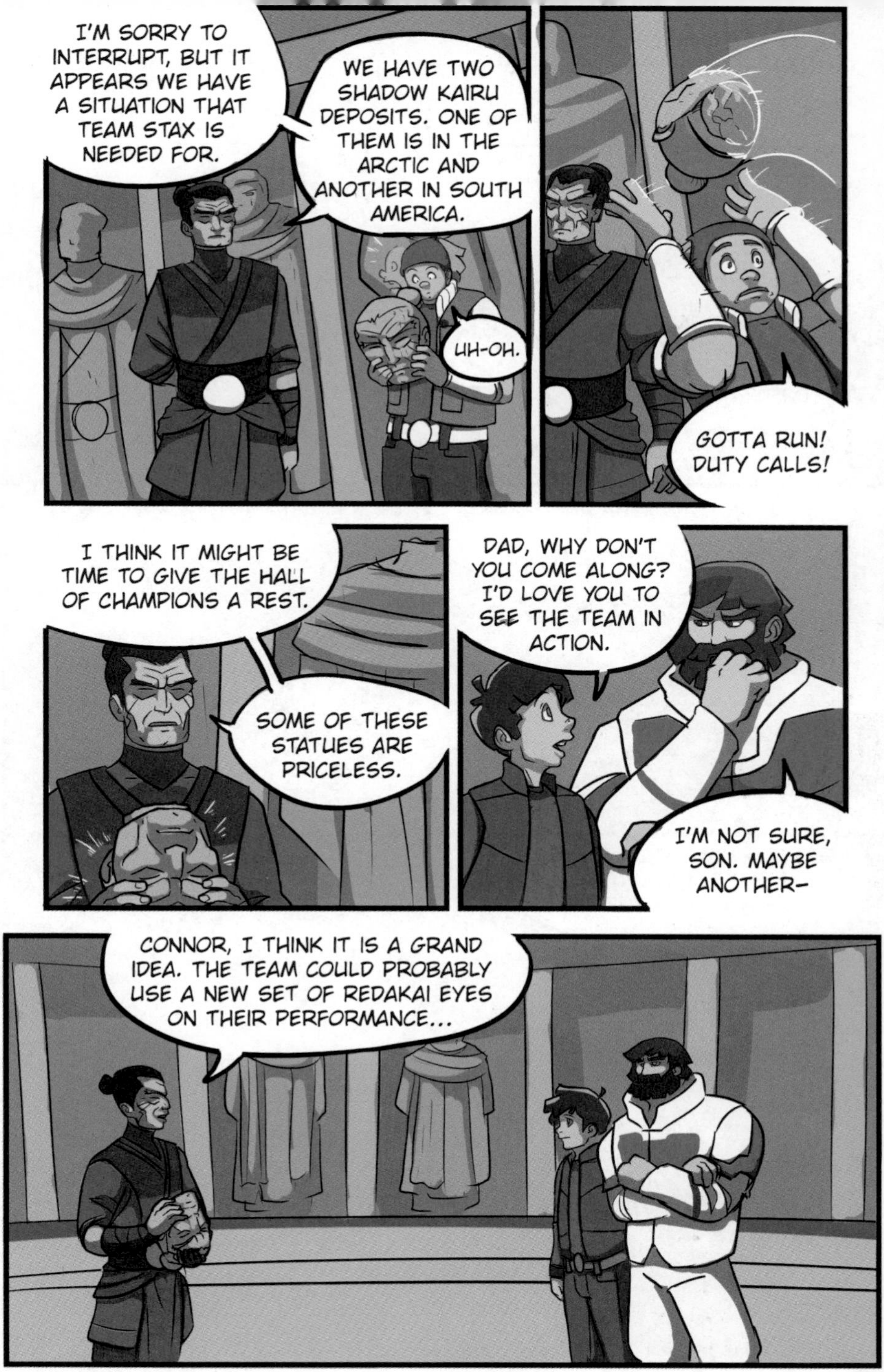
I'M SORRY TO INTERRUPT, BUT IT APPEARS WE HAVE A SITUATION THAT TEAM STAX IS NEEDED FOR.
WE HAVE TWO SHADOW KAIRU DEPOSITS. ONE OF THEM IS IN THE ARCTIC AND ANOTHER IN SOUTH AMERICA.
UH-OH.
GOTTA RUN! DUTY CALLS!
I THINK IT MIGHT BE TIME TO GIVE THE HALL OF CHAMPIONS A REST.
SOME OF THESE STATUES ARE PRICELESS.
DAD, WHY DON'T YOU COME ALONG? I'D LOVE YOU TO SEE THE TEAM IN ACTION.
I'M NOT SURE, SON. MAYBE ANOTHER–
CONNOR, I THINK IT IS A GRAND IDEA. THE TEAM COULD PROBABLY USE A NEW SET OF REDAKAI EYES ON THEIR PERFORMANCE...

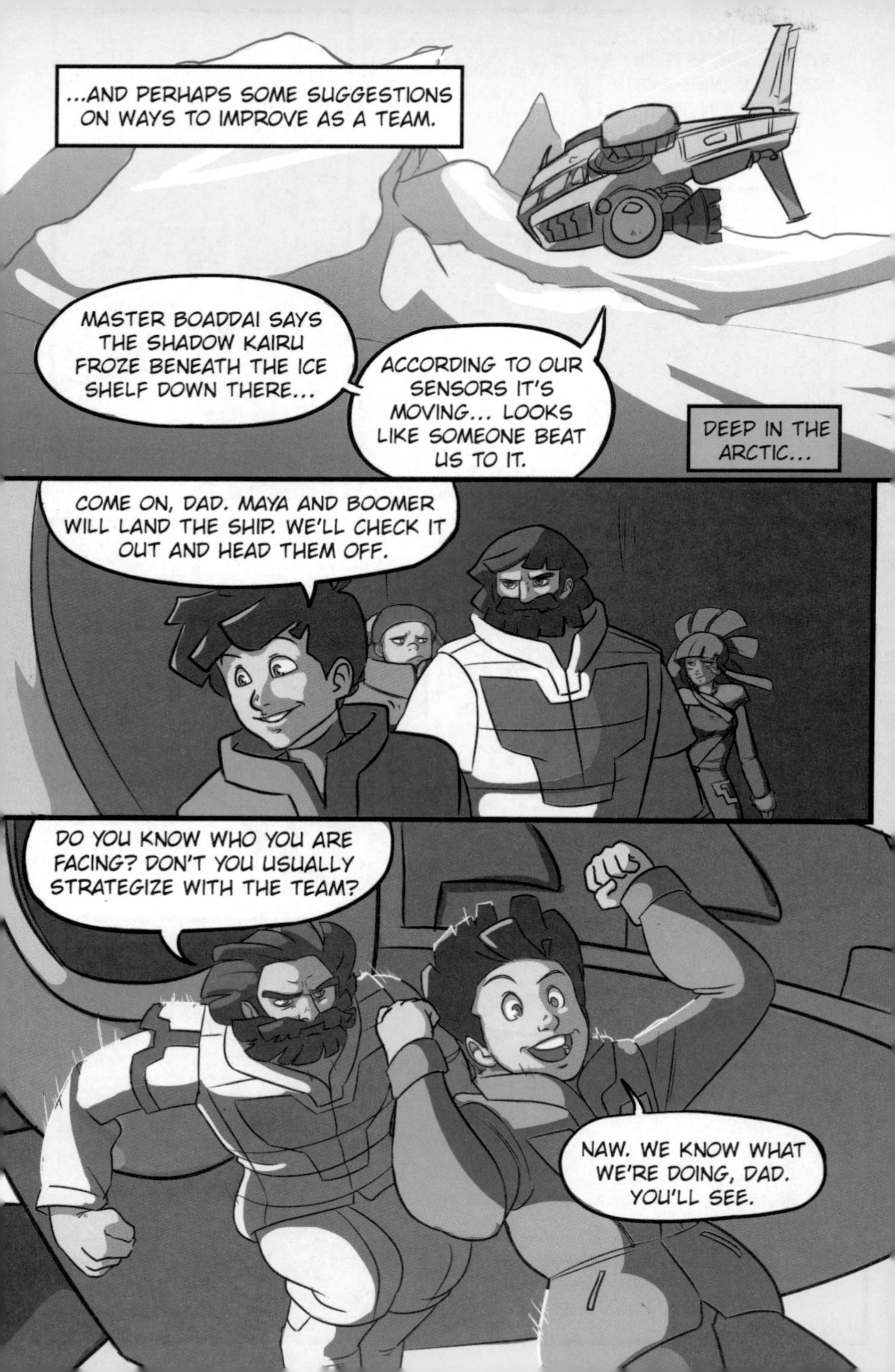
...AND PERHAPS SOME SUGGESTIONS ON WAYS TO IMPROVE AS A TEAM.
DEEP IN THE ARCTIC...
MASTER BOADDAI SAYS THE SHADOW KAIRU FROZE BENEATH THE ICE SHELF DOWN THERE...
ACCORDING TO OUR SENSORS IT'S MOVING... LOOKS LIKE SOMEONE BEAT US TO IT.
COME ON, DAD. MAYA AND BOOMER WILL LAND THE SHIP. WE'LL CHECK IT OUT AND HEAD THEM OFF.
DO YOU KNOW WHO YOU ARE FACING? DON'T YOU USUALLY STRATEGIZE WITH THE TEAM?
NAW. WE KNOW WHAT WE'RE DOING, DAD. YOU'LL SEE.

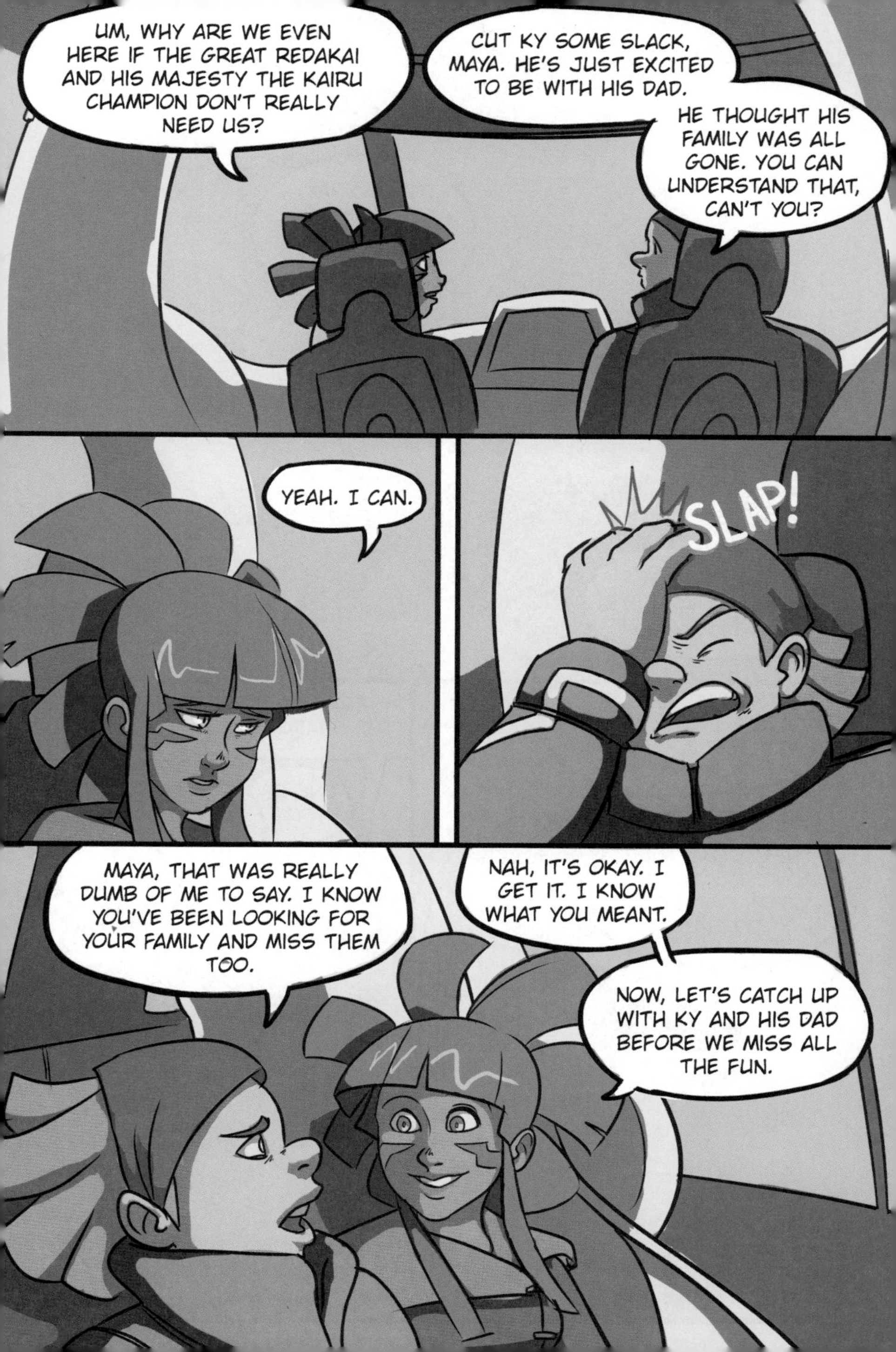
UM, WHY ARE WE EVEN HERE IF THE GREAT REDAKAI AND HIS MAJESTY THE KAIRU CHAMPION DON'T REALLY NEED US?
CUT KY SOME SLACK, MAYA. HE'S JUST EXCITED TO BE WITH HIS DAD.
HE THOUGHT HIS FAMILY WAS ALL GONE. YOU CAN UNDERSTAND THAT, CAN'T YOU?
YEAH. I CAN.
SLAP!
MAYA, THAT WAS REALLY DUMB OF ME TO SAY. I KNOW YOU'VE BEEN LOOKING FOR YOUR FAMILY AND MISS THEM TOO.
NAH, IT'S OKAY. I GET IT. I KNOW WHAT YOU MEANT.
NOW, LET'S CATCH UP WITH KY AND HIS DAD BEFORE WE MISS ALL THE FUN.

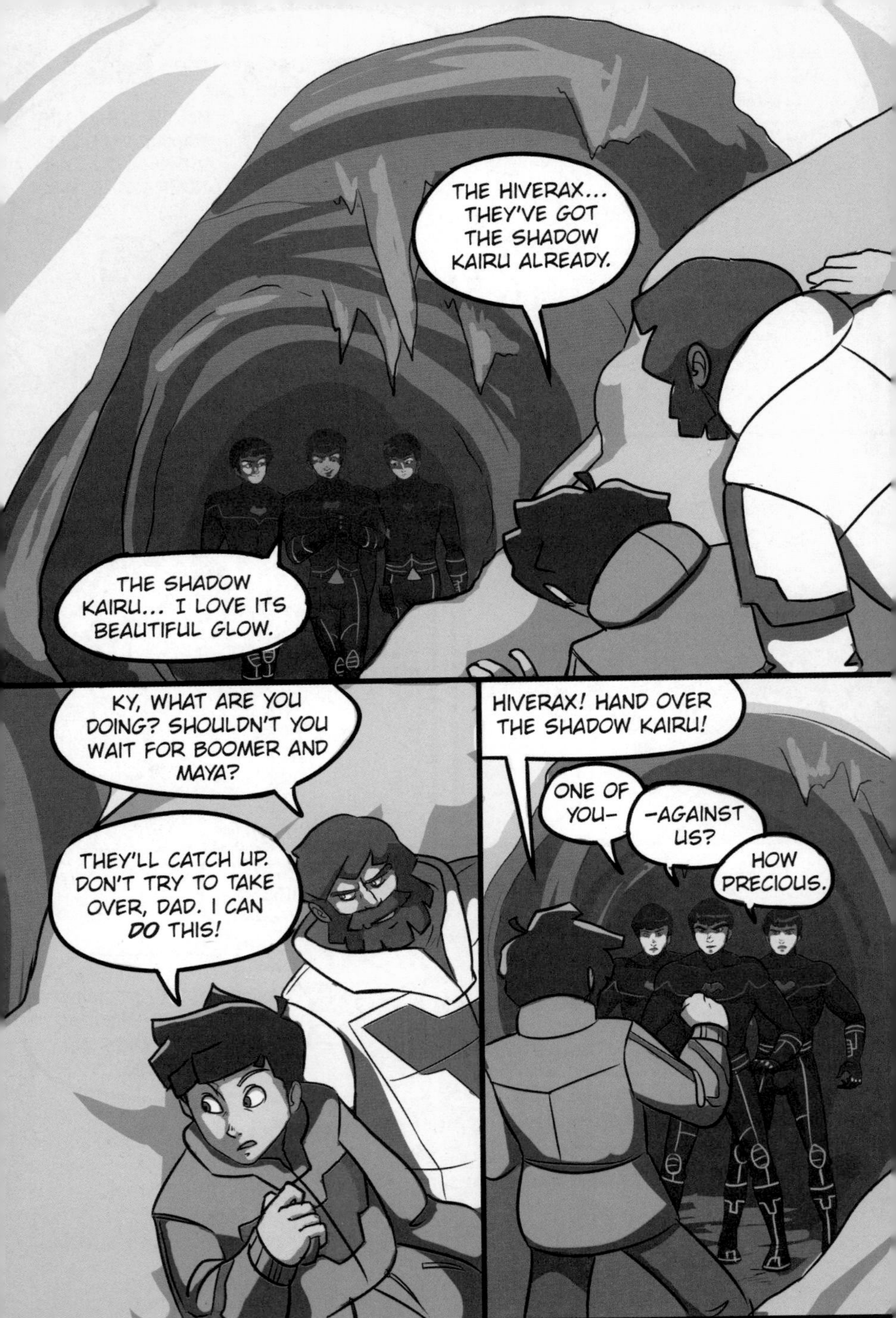
THE HIVERAX... THEY'VE GOT THE SHADOW KAIRU ALREADY.
THE SHADOW KAIRU... I LOVE ITS BEAUTIFUL GLOW.
KY, WHAT ARE YOU DOING? SHOULDN'T YOU WAIT FOR BOOMER AND MAYA?
THEY'LL CATCH UP. DON'T TRY TO TAKE OVER, DAD. I CAN *DO* THIS!
HIVERAX! HAND OVER THE SHADOW KAIRU!
ONE OF YOU-
-AGAINST US?
HOW PRECIOUS.

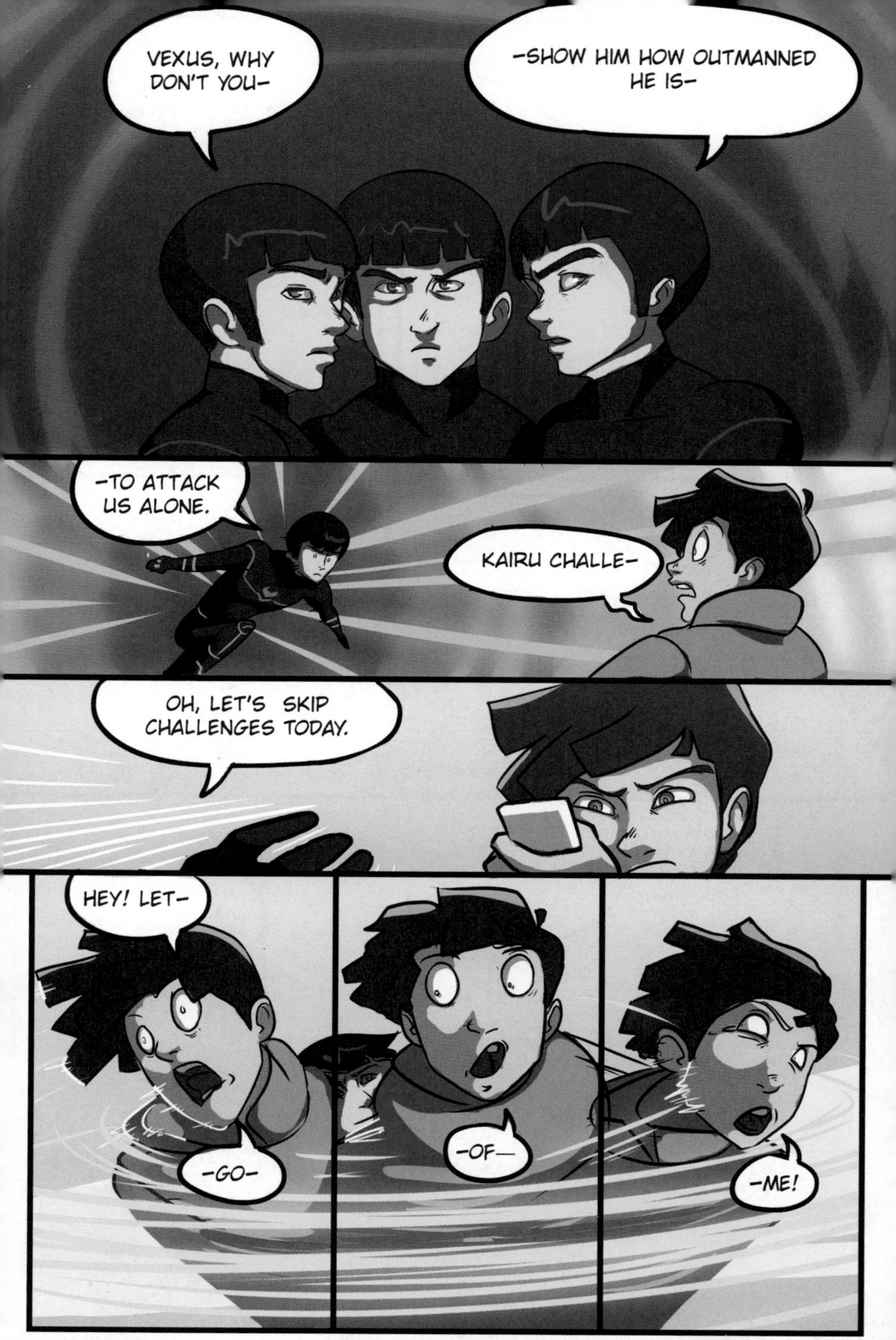
VEXUS, WHY DON'T YOU-
-SHOW HIM HOW OUTMANNED HE IS-
-TO ATTACK US ALONE.
KAIRU CHALLE-
OH, LET'S SKIP CHALLENGES TODAY.
HEY! LET-
-GO-
-OF-
-ME!

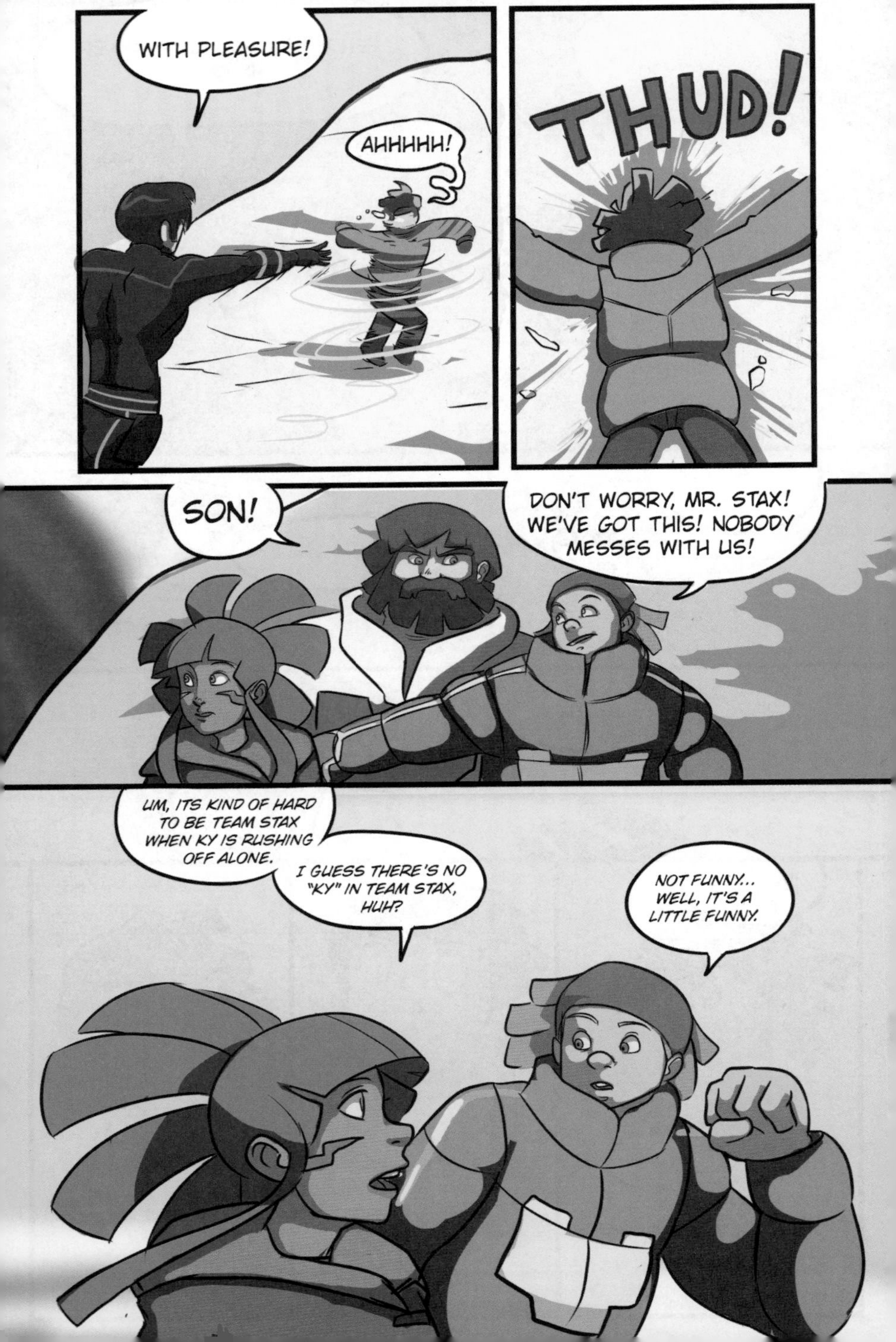

WITH PLEASURE!
AHHHHH!
THUD!
SON!
DON'T WORRY, MR. STAX! WE'VE GOT THIS! NOBODY MESSES WITH US!
UM, ITS KIND OF HARD TO BE TEAM STAX WHEN KY IS RUSHING OFF ALONE.
I GUESS THERE'S NO "KY" IN TEAM STAX, HUH?
NOT FUNNY... WELL, IT'S A LITTLE FUNNY.

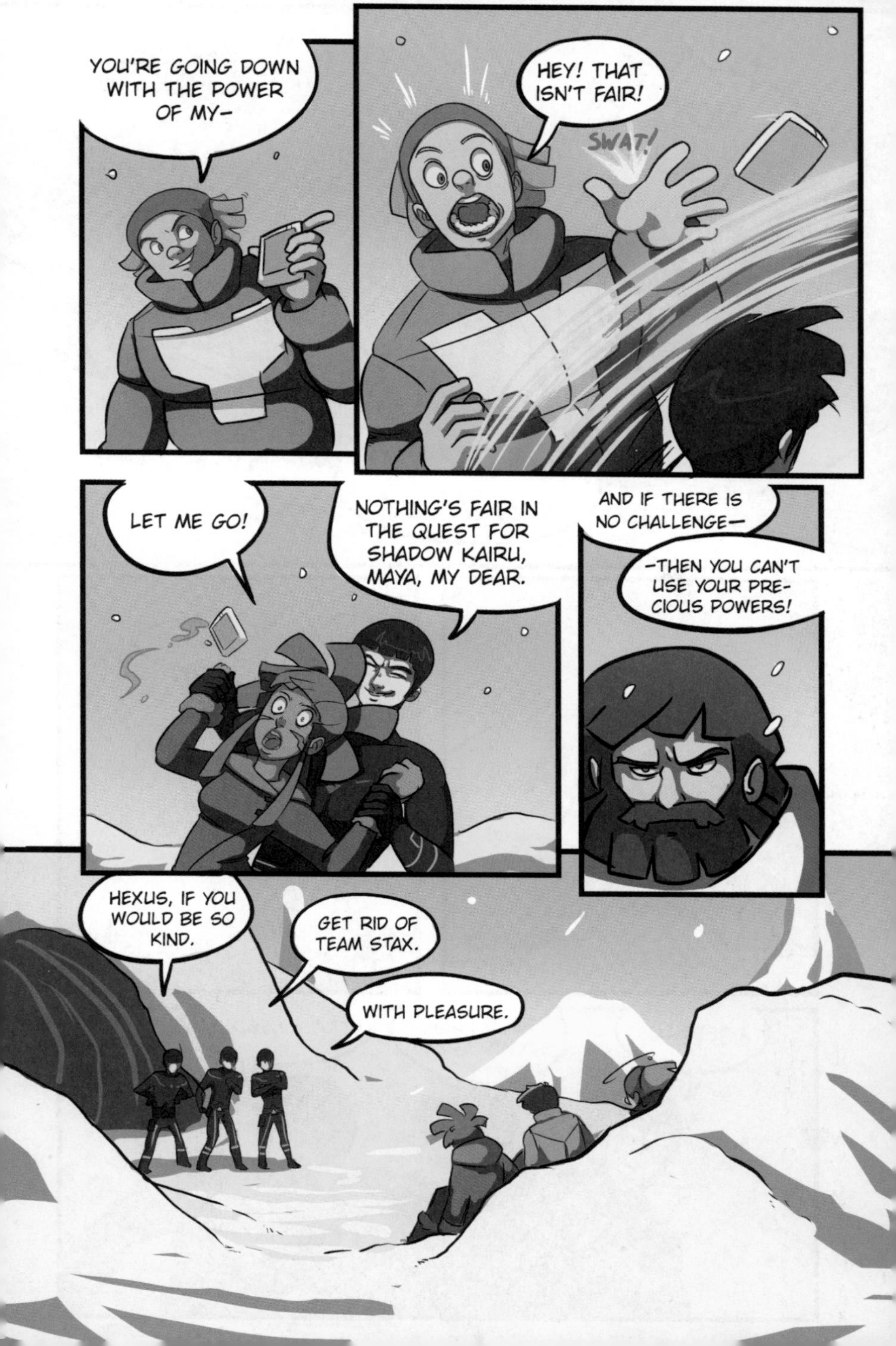
YOU'RE GOING DOWN WITH THE POWER OF MY–
HEY! THAT ISN'T FAIR!
SWAT!
LET ME GO!
NOTHING'S FAIR IN THE QUEST FOR SHADOW KAIRU, MAYA, MY DEAR.
AND IF THERE IS NO CHALLENGE—
–THEN YOU CAN'T USE YOUR PRE-CIOUS POWERS!
HEXUS, IF YOU WOULD BE SO KIND.
GET RID OF TEAM STAX.
WITH PLEASURE.

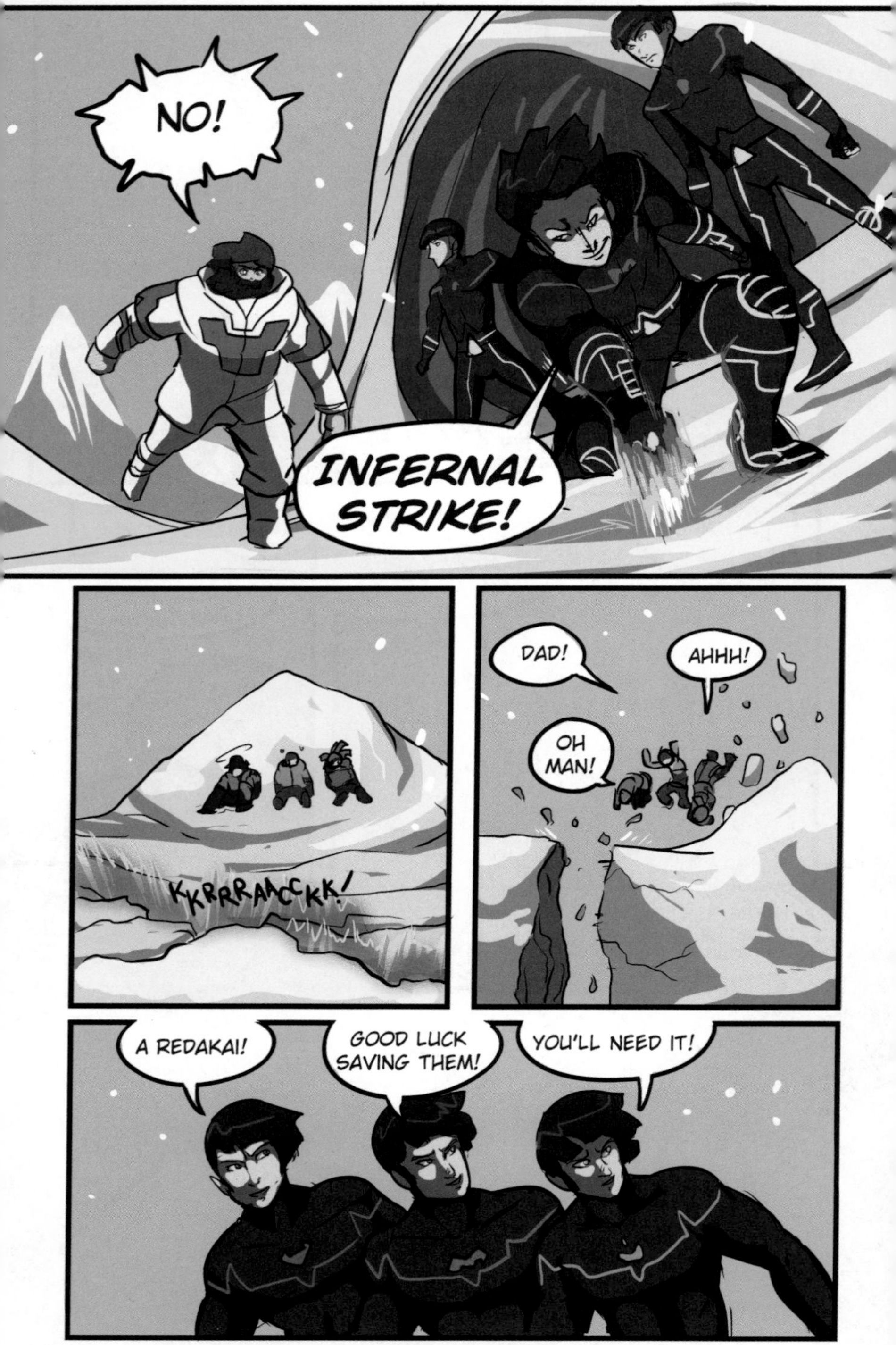
NO!
INFERNAL STRIKE!
KKRRRAACCKK!
DAD!
AHHH!
OH MAN!
A REDAKAI!
GOOD LUCK SAVING THEM!
YOU'LL NEED IT!

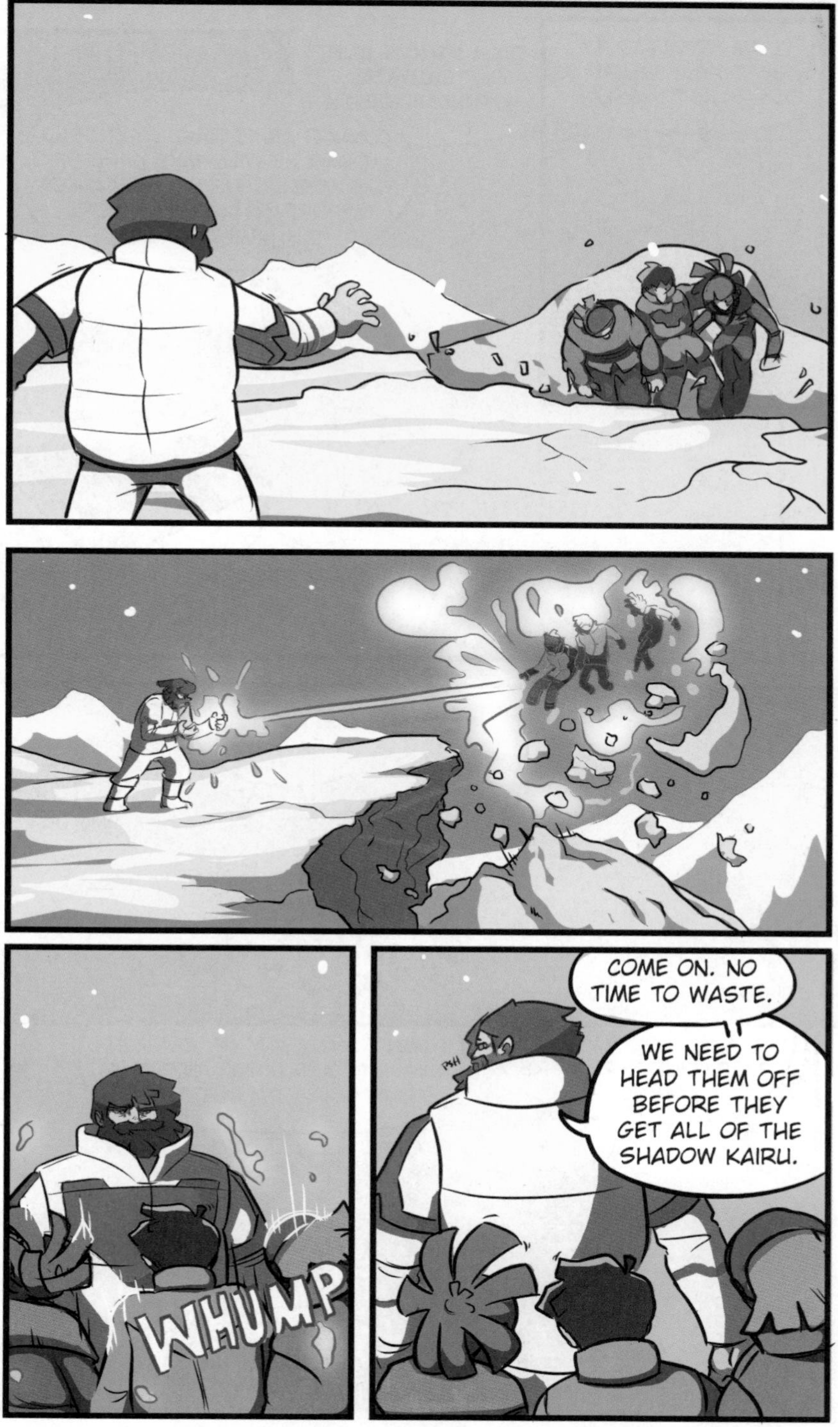
WHUMP
COME ON. NO TIME TO WASTE.
WE NEED TO HEAD THEM OFF BEFORE THEY GET ALL OF THE SHADOW KAIRU.

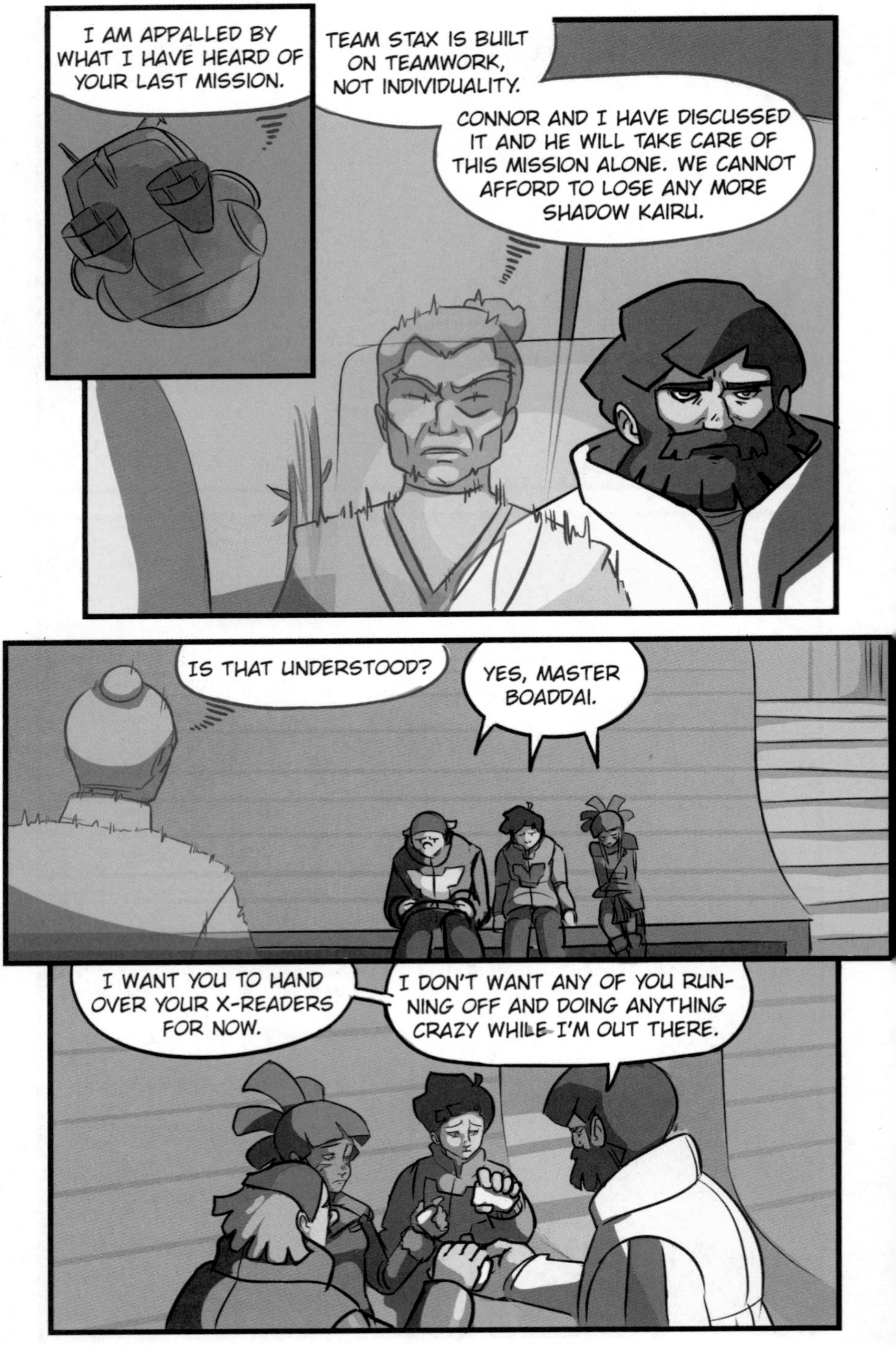
I AM APPALLED BY WHAT I HAVE HEARD OF YOUR LAST MISSION.
TEAM STAX IS BUILT ON TEAMWORK, NOT INDIVIDUALITY.
CONNOR AND I HAVE DISCUSSED IT AND HE WILL TAKE CARE OF THIS MISSION ALONE. WE CANNOT AFFORD TO LOSE ANY MORE SHADOW KAIRU.
IS THAT UNDERSTOOD?
YES, MASTER BOADDAI.
I WANT YOU TO HAND OVER YOUR X-READERS FOR NOW.
I DON'T WANT ANY OF YOU RUN-NING OFF AND DOING ANYTHING CRAZY WHILE I'M OUT THERE.

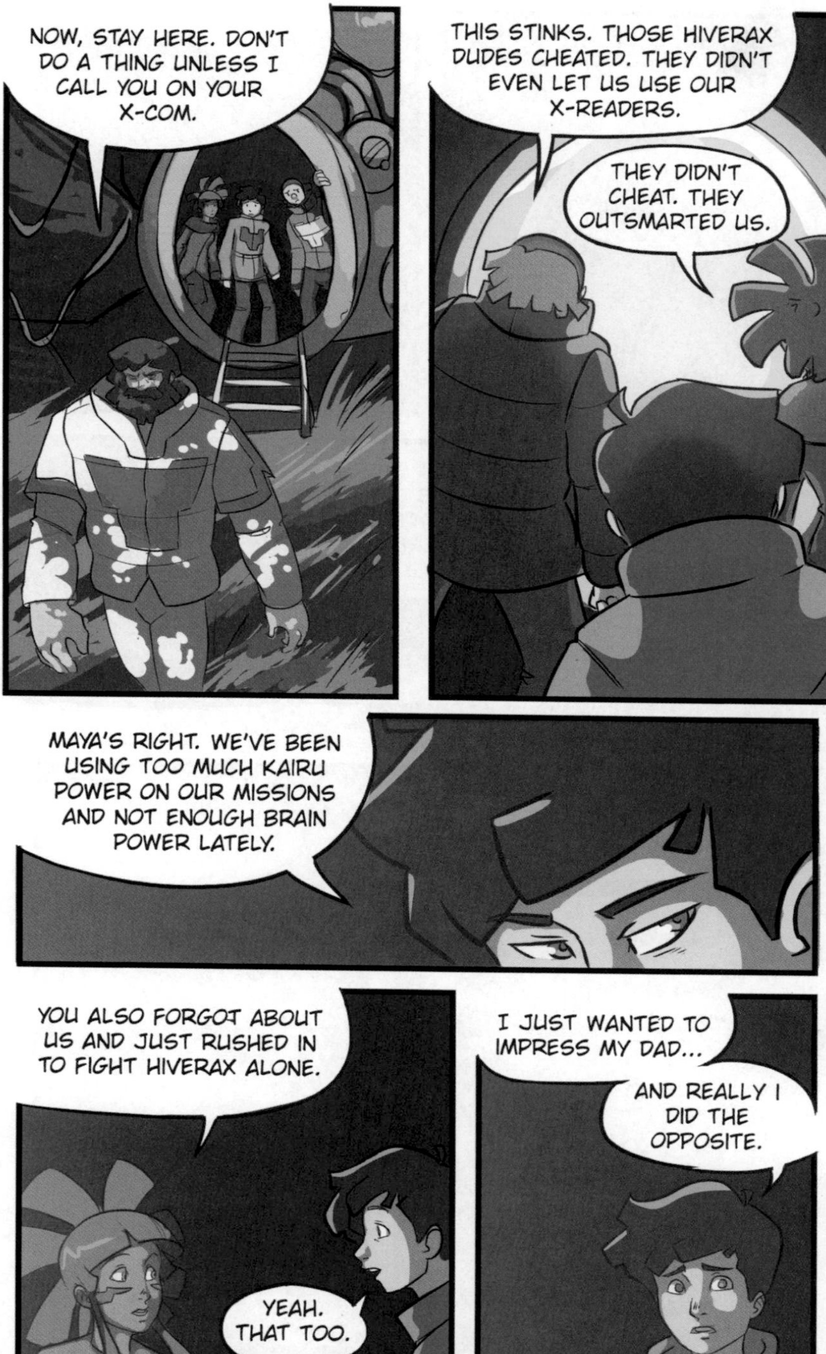
NOW, STAY HERE. DON'T DO A THING UNLESS I CALL YOU ON YOUR X-COM.
THIS STINKS. THOSE HIVERAX DUDES CHEATED. THEY DIDN'T EVEN LET US USE OUR X-READERS.
THEY DIDN'T CHEAT. THEY OUTSMARTED US.
MAYA'S RIGHT. WE'VE BEEN USING TOO MUCH KAIRU POWER ON OUR MISSIONS AND NOT ENOUGH BRAIN POWER LATELY.
YOU ALSO FORGOT ABOUT US AND JUST RUSHED IN TO FIGHT HIVERAX ALONE.
YEAH. THAT TOO.
I JUST WANTED TO IMPRESS MY DAD...
AND REALLY I DID THE OPPOSITE.

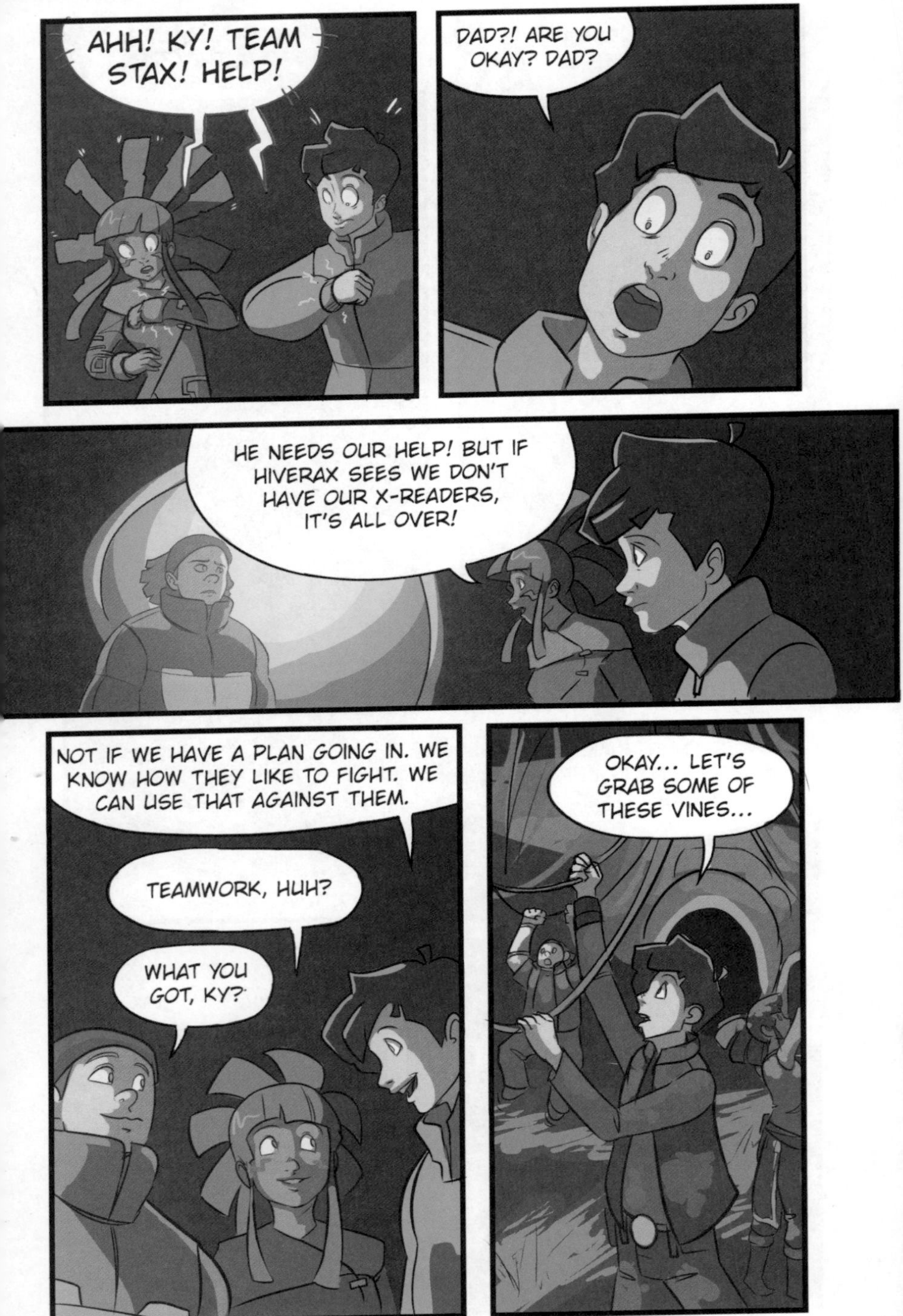
AHH! KY! TEAM STAX! HELP!
DAD?! ARE YOU OKAY? DAD?
HE NEEDS OUR HELP! BUT IF HIVERAX SEES WE DON'T HAVE OUR X-READERS, IT'S ALL OVER!
NOT IF WE HAVE A PLAN GOING IN. WE KNOW HOW THEY LIKE TO FIGHT. WE CAN USE THAT AGAINST THEM.
TEAMWORK, HUH?
WHAT YOU GOT, KY?
OKAY... LET'S GRAB SOME OF THESE VINES...

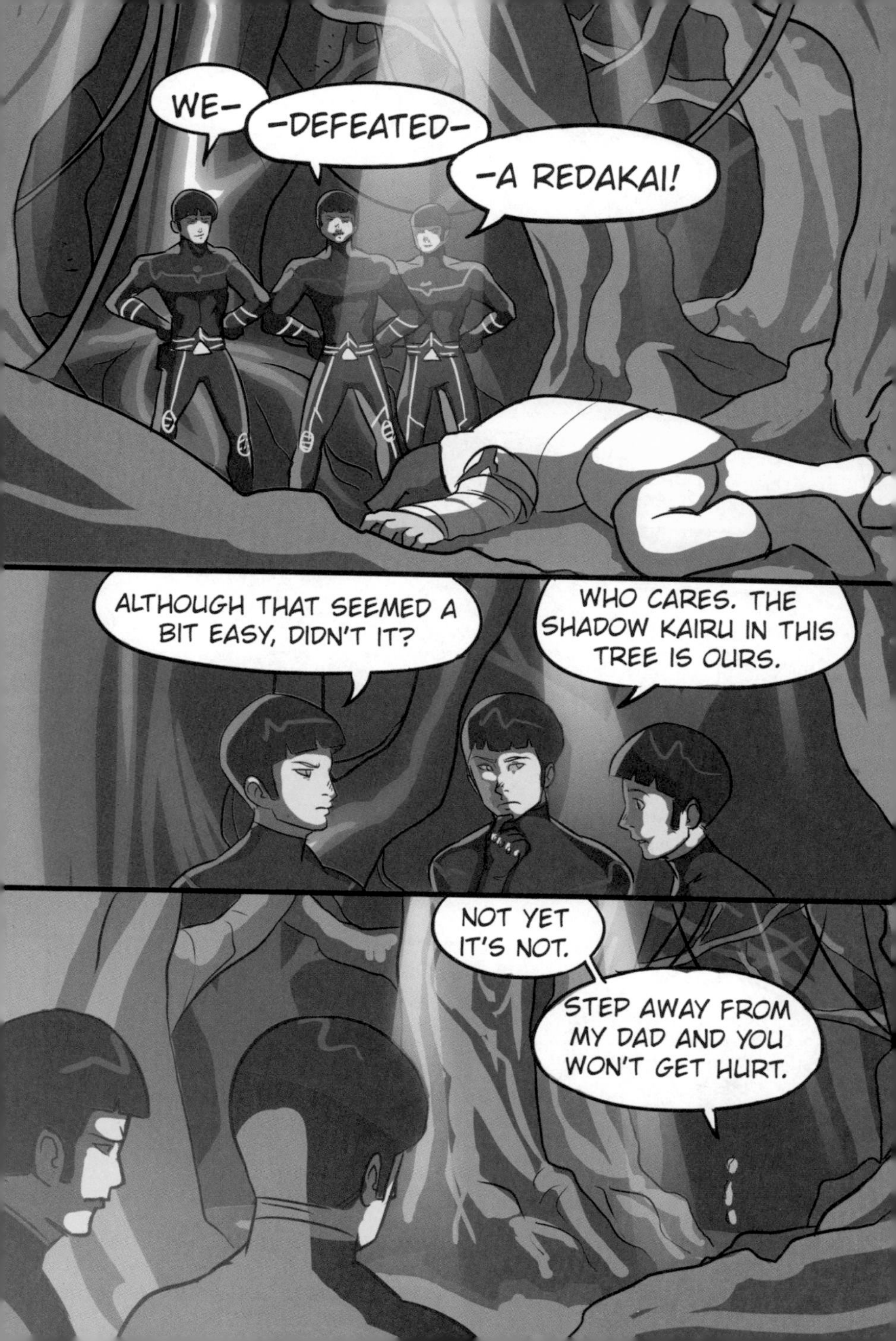
WE—
—DEFEATED—
—A REDAKAI!
ALTHOUGH THAT SEEMED A BIT EASY, DIDN'T IT?
WHO CARES. THE SHADOW KAIRU IN THIS TREE IS OURS.
NOT YET IT'S NOT.
STEP AWAY FROM MY DAD AND YOU WON'T GET HURT.

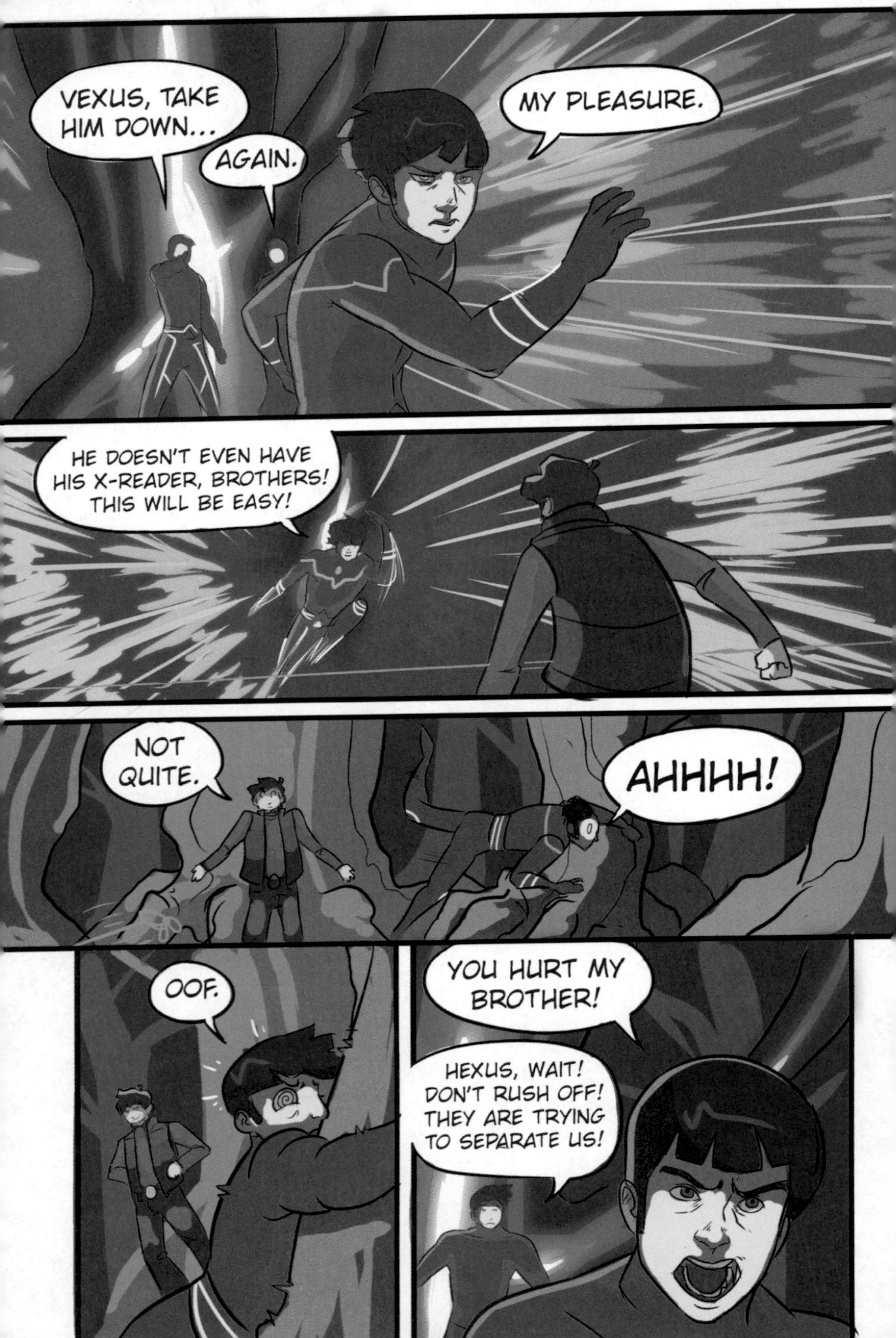
VEXUS, TAKE HIM DOWN...
AGAIN.
MY PLEASURE.
HE DOESN'T EVEN HAVE HIS X-READER, BROTHERS! THIS WILL BE EASY!
NOT QUITE.
AHHHH!
OOF.
YOU HURT MY BROTHER!
HEXUS, WAIT! DON'T RUSH OFF! THEY ARE TRYING TO SEPARATE US!

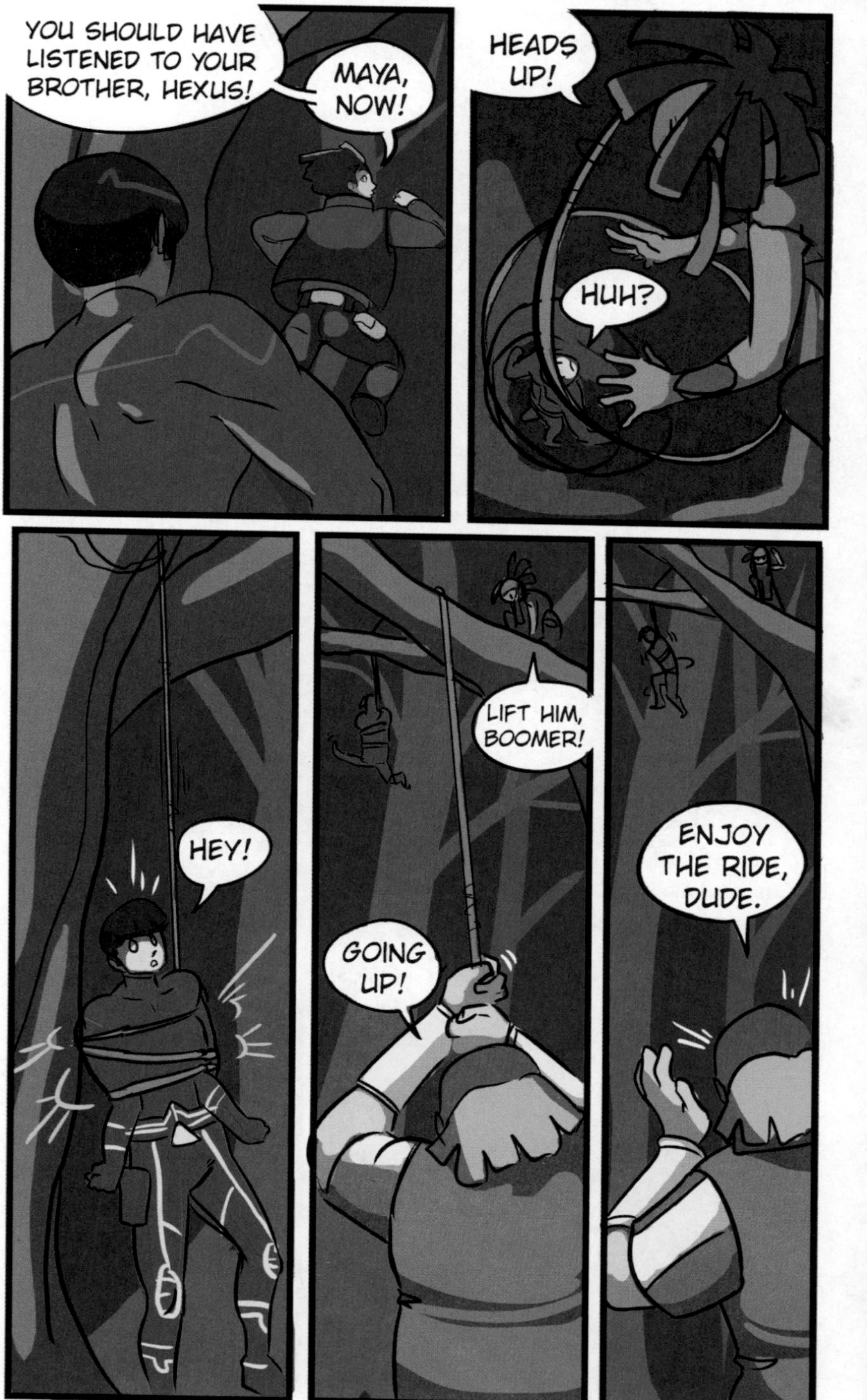
YOU SHOULD HAVE LISTENED TO YOUR BROTHER, HEXUS!
MAYA, NOW!
HEADS UP!
HUH?
HEY!
LIFT HIM, BOOMER!
GOING UP!
ENJOY THE RIDE, DUDE.

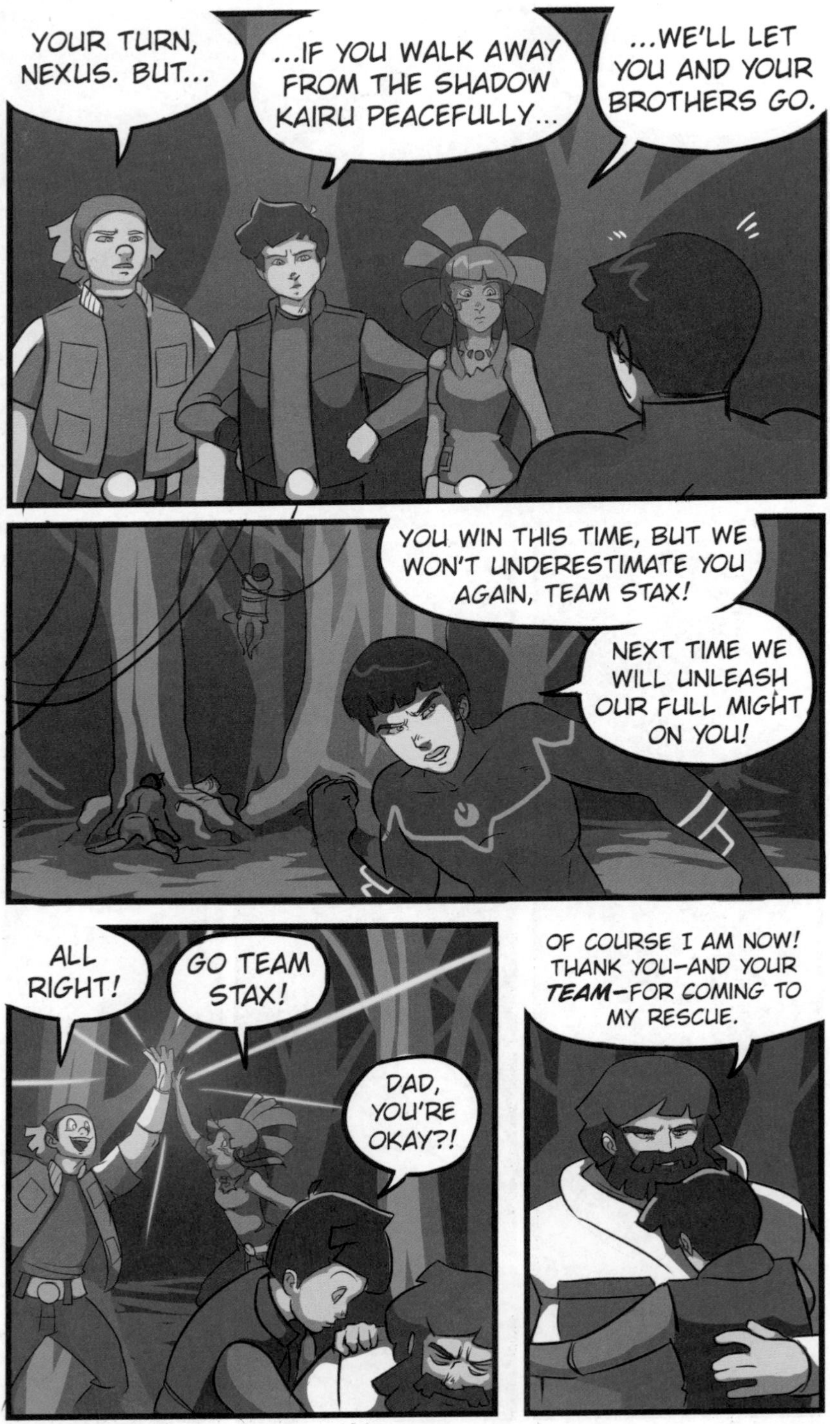
YOUR TURN, NEXUS. BUT...
...IF YOU WALK AWAY FROM THE SHADOW KAIRU PEACEFULLY...
...WE'LL LET YOU AND YOUR BROTHERS GO.
YOU WIN THIS TIME, BUT WE WON'T UNDERESTIMATE YOU AGAIN, TEAM STAX!
NEXT TIME WE WILL UNLEASH OUR FULL MIGHT ON YOU!
ALL RIGHT!
GO TEAM STAX!
DAD, YOU'RE OKAY?!
OF COURSE I AM NOW! THANK YOU—AND YOUR *TEAM*—FOR COMING TO MY RESCUE.

I ASSUME BY YOUR MOOD, THE MISSION WENT WELL.

YOU BET.

NEVER BETTER.

WE WERE A REAL TEAM.

I AM PLEASED TO HEAR THAT.

YOU'VE TRAINED THEM WELL, MASTER BOADDAI. THE POWER OF THE KAIRU CAN HUMBLE THE WISEST OF MEN. THESE CHILDREN ARE ON THE RIGHT PATH.

I HOPE YOUR PRIDE WAS NOT TOO DAMAGED BY FEIGNING DISTRESS. IT CANNOT BE EASY TO APPEAR TO FAIL IN FRONT OF YOUR SON.

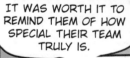

IT WAS WORTH IT TO REMIND THEM OF HOW SPECIAL THEIR TEAM TRULY IS.

KY WAS ONLY TRYING TO IMPRESS HIS FATHER THE FIRST TIME OUT. TEAM STAX WORKED TOGETHER TO SAVE ME...

AND IN THE END I WAS VERY IMPRESSED. ESPECIALLY WITH MY SON. HE IS A GOOD LEADER.

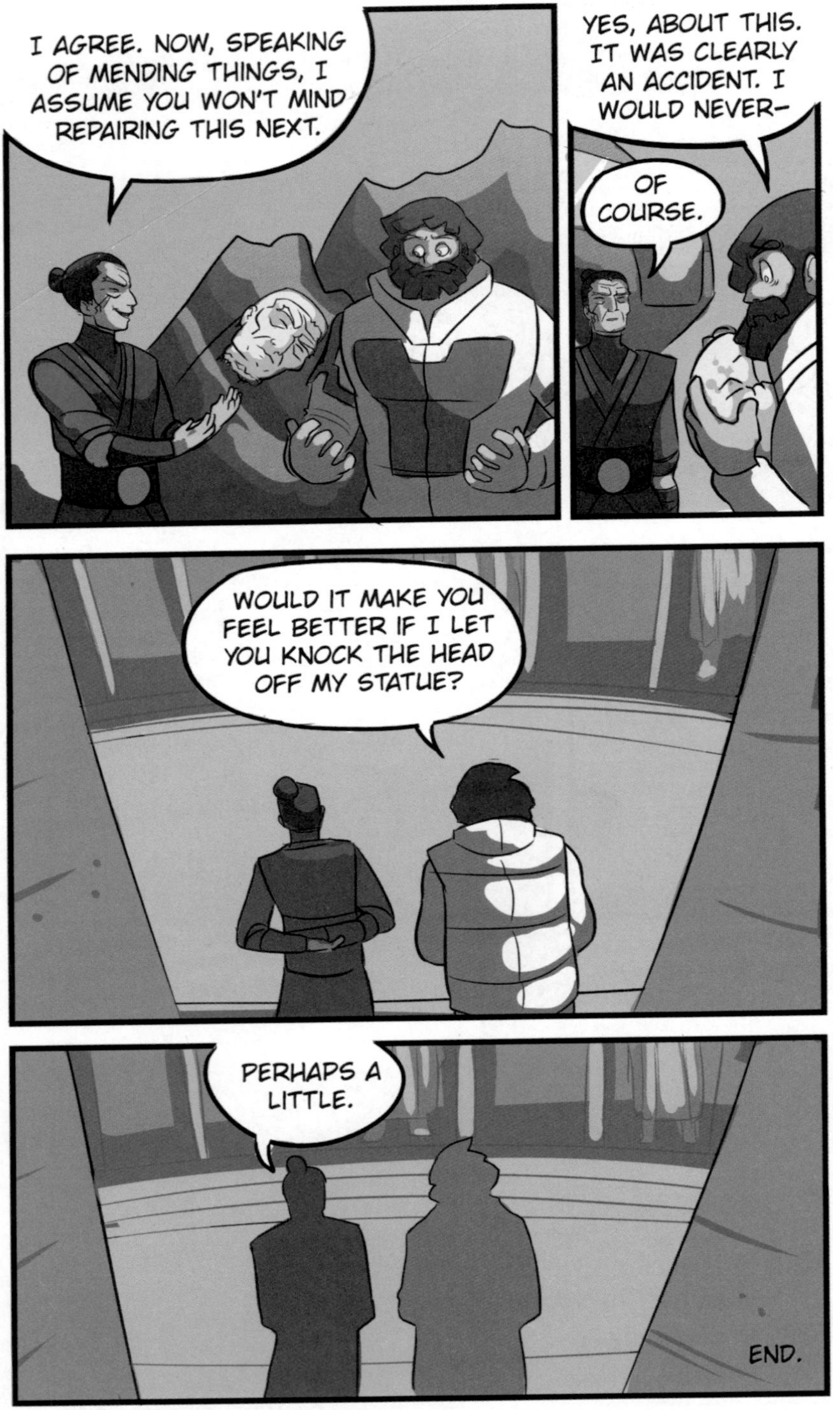
I AGREE. NOW, SPEAKING OF MENDING THINGS, I ASSUME YOU WON'T MIND REPAIRING THIS NEXT.
YES, ABOUT THIS. IT WAS CLEARLY AN ACCIDENT. I WOULD NEVER–
OF COURSE.
WOULD IT MAKE YOU FEEL BETTER IF I LET YOU KNOCK THE HEAD OFF MY STATUE?
PERHAPS A LITTLE.
END.

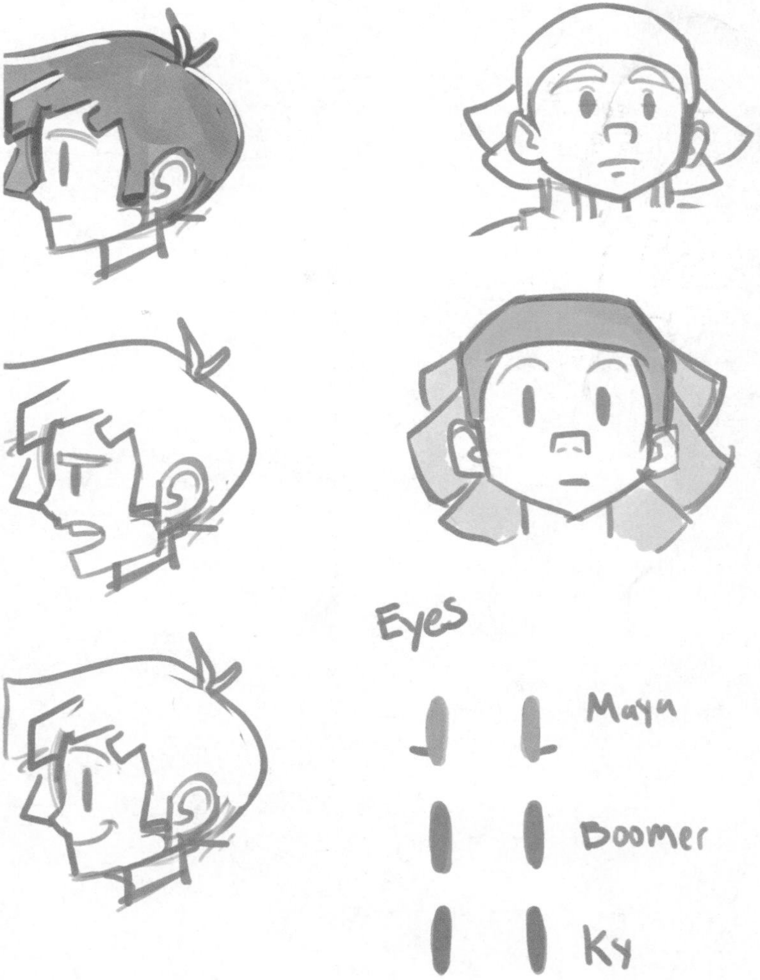
Eyes
Mayu
Boomer
Ky

⚜ WRITERS

TERRANCE GRIEP is a journalist, actor, professional wrestler and writer who has written many comic book series for Image and DC Comics including *Scooby-Doo*, *Superman*, *Batman*, *The Riddler*, *Green Lantern* and *Captain Comet*.

MIKE RAICHT is co-writer and co-creator of the *New York Times* best-selling graphic novel *The Stuff of Legend*. He worked as an editor at Marvel Comics on the *X-Men* line for four years. He's written both *Batman* and *Superman* for DC Comics, *Spider-Man* and *The Hulk* for Marvel and *GI Joe* and *Godzilla* for IDW.

⚜ ARTISTS

WRITE HEIGHT MEDIA is a creative team that includes Ray-Anthony Height who has penciled for *Spider-Man* and *Spider-Girl* at Marvel and *Teenage Mutant Ninja Turtles* for Mirage Studios; artist Nate Lovett who has worked with Hasbro on *GI Joe*, *Star Wars* and *Mr. Potato Head*; Dwayne Biddix on inks; and Mickey Clausen who has done colors for *Toy Story* for Pixar & Boom.

ZACK TURNER is a freelance artist working in comics and illustration. He has worked on several independent books as well as his own projects. He started out in the comics industry as a colorist on *Unimaginable* for Arcana and several projects for Bluewater and more recently has been working on full art duties.